THE
KILLER'S
FAMILY

BOOKS BY MIRANDA SMITH

THE
KILLER'S
FAMILY

MIRANDA SMITH

bookouture

Published by Bookouture in 2022

An imprint of Storyfire Ltd.
Carmelite House
50 Victoria Embankment
London EC4Y 0DZ

www.bookouture.com

ISBN: 978-1-80314-187-9
eBook ISBN: 978-1-80314-188-6

For Dad. If more people were like you, the world would be a better place. I love you.

PART I

ONE

When news broke that Henry Martin had died, everyone pitied the Martin girls, for they'd buried their mother only six months before.

They weren't girls, not anymore, but when someone grows up in a town like Whitehill, they never stop talking about the *girls* and *boys* of their peers. The Martins were a well-known family in Whitehill. Henry had been a beloved history teacher at the high school; Margaret Grace, his wife, had orchestrated the high school choir before she abruptly left her position, due to cancer.

Not even three months later, she was dead.

The entire town had mourned the loss of Margaret Grace. And they showed up again for Henry's funeral. People sat in pews, waiting for the ceremony to start. The girls—women, now —walked down the aisle as though they should be headed to the altar, not grieving the last of their parents.

Cara Martin entered first, although no longer a Martin by name. She was Cara Gibson now, and Tate, her husband, walked a few steps behind her, his hand resting protectively on her shoulder. Cara was the oldest and the shortest of the trio,

with auburn hair that fell down her back in untamed rivulets.
She wore a sleeveless dress and flats—both black.

Rachel Martin walked behind her brother-in-law, her
sunglasses on, a bright red nose peeking out from underneath.
She was the tallest of the three, with straight dark hair that
dangled to just above where her black maxi skirt began. She
walked with purpose, her shoulders back, the fabric swaying
with each step she took. She appeared, some thought, as an
angel of death, a Grim Reaperess. Katelyn, her girlfriend,
waited for her in a pew at the front. Rachel sat, embracing
Katelyn as though her very life depended on it.

Bringing up the rear was the youngest, Molly Martin. She
was wearing black slacks and a burgundy sweater in honor of
her father's favorite color. Her blonde hair was parted to the left
and cut just below her chin in the exact same way it had been
since middle school. Her eyes bounced around the room as
though searching for someone. As she approached the front, she
stared at the floor, careful not to look at her sisters or their partners, least of all the casket. She sat beside Rachel, and began
fiddling with a tissue.

As the last notes of "How Great Thou Art" poured from the
organ, the mourners stared ahead, not at their fallen brother, but
at the three daughters he'd left behind. How tragic for them to
lose both their parents in under a year. Adult orphans. An
entire future of possibilities ripped away. There would be no
one to help them sift through motherhood when the time came,
and Rachel and Molly would never experience their father
walking them down the aisle. The sisters only had each other
now, something that brought comfort and sadness all at once.

In order to bypass their despair, everyone who attended
clung to the past, gripping at memories with white knuckles.
Neighbors stood at the pulpit and spoke about how Henry
Martin had touched their lives. Former students attested to his
wisdom and wit. Close friends detailed his loyalty. Fellow

churchgoers recalled his strong faith. This was what such events were about. Honoring a life well lived, carefully avoiding how unfairly that life had ended.

The Martin girls sat there listening, looking proud. Their father was gone now, just like their mother, but his imprint on the world remained, and it was a good one.

The Martin girls didn't know it then, in the midst of saying goodbye, but a new story was unfolding. One that would challenge everything they thought they knew about their father.

TWO

MOLLY

Molly Martin's cheeks hurt from all the smiling. She was accustomed to this forced cheeriness at the Whitehill Hotel, where she worked as a front-desk clerk. She wasn't, however, used to being polite when her heart was on the verge of breaking.

She'd managed to hold it together during the funeral, then at the burial that followed. Afterwards, neighbors and friends followed them back to the Martin home, bringing food and drinks and more stories that had been too intimate to share during the service. Molly had shaken the hands of countless people, nodded along to their sympathetic words, struggled to hold back tears.

When the last of the visitors left the house, she was relieved, but also overwhelmed. She looked around her childhood home, once the place of many happy memories. She saw collections of artifacts—books, trinkets and artwork—that told stories about the people who turned this house into a home. Henry Martin, the charming academic, and Margaret Grace, his free-spirited wife. It felt empty and endless now, like a reverberating echo that wouldn't stop.

"Is that everyone?" Rachel stood beside her, a drink in her hand. They were eager for the day to end, for it to be nothing but immediate family.

"I think only Elias is left." She nodded toward the living room, where Cara was trapped in the middle of a conversation with their father's oldest friend.

Rachel and Molly smiled conspiratorially.

"Should we rescue her?" Rachel asked.

Elias was jovial and kind-hearted, the type of person who drags you into a conversation and refuses to quit. He'd talk all night if they let him, and he probably preferred to sit around talking, rather than acknowledge the death of his friend.

Elias and Cara were standing in front of the fireplace. Parts of the conversation floated near: *book* and *crime* and *sales*. Cara was a journalist turned true crime writer. She'd published three books in the past seven years. Elias was likely grilling her about her latest release. When Cara caught sight of her sisters, she had Help Me eyes.

Elias stopped talking when he saw them approach, and cleared his throat.

"I was just telling Cara it was a beautiful service." He wiped his eyes with the back of his hand. "It captured the very essence of Henry."

"You were a great friend to him," Cara said.

"He wanted to make sure you girls were okay. He told me that, you know," he said. "When I used to give him a hard time about having so many kids, he'd say, *Margaret wanted three so that when we kick the bucket, at least the girls would have each other.*"

Elias laughed. Molly didn't find it funny at all. She wanted to cry. None of them could have predicted that both their parents would be gone so soon, taken within six months of each other. That the previous Christmas would be their final one as a family.

"Thanks for your help today," Rachel said, pushing the visit closer to its conclusion, but she wrapped an arm around Elias' shoulders, so that it wasn't obvious.

He looked around the room. "I'll get out of your hair, so you can be with family." Then he stood still, like he was hoping one of them would invite him to stay. *Come on, Elias. You're as good as family*, he wanted to hear. But none of them said it. "You'll let me know if you need help with things around the house? Or the cabin upstate?"

"We haven't even discussed the cabin yet," Rachel said. "It'll take the rest of the week to sort stuff here. Hopefully we can get the house on the market soon."

To anyone listening, it might sound like Rachel was greedy, but Molly knew her sister. The sooner Rachel could break free from the memories of this place, the sooner she could start healing.

"It won't feel the same driving by this house with some other family living in it," Elias said. A sadness fell over his face, but he shook it off, winking at Cara. "Let me know when the next best seller comes out."

"Will do." Cara turned quickly, joining Tate in the kitchen.

Molly followed Elias to the front door, holding it open. She had a softer spot for him than her sisters did. Sure, he could be annoying, but there was no denying he had been a loyal friend to their father.

"Take care of yourself," she said.

Elias looked back into the house and smiled. "Take care of each other."

He turned, walking down the cement steps to the sidewalk. She watched him disappear into the night before returning to the living room. Everyone was gathered around the fireplace.

"Finally, you girls can relax," Tate said. "I thought we'd have people here all night."

"It's been nice to see how many people cared about him.

And Mom," Cara said. "Poor Elias. His whole world revolved around Dad. No family of his own. I worry about what he'll do without him."

And there it was again. The casual remembrance that their father was gone. Grief wasn't constant. It was cyclical, like a dangerous tide rising throughout the day, dragging Molly under.

"Might be time for another drink," Molly said, excusing herself. She felt another cry coming, and didn't want her sisters to see. For the moment, they seemed strong, and she wanted them to hold tight to that strength.

She was only a few steps away when she heard Rachel's voice.

"Is she seriously going to ignore the fact Ben skipped the funeral?"

"Not now," Katelyn shushed her.

"If this isn't reason for her to cut him out of her life, I don't know what is."

"She knows that. We all do," Cara whispered. "But let's keep the focus on Dad."

"Right," Rachel scoffed. "One tragedy at a time." Rachel often became opinionated and loud when she was drinking.

Molly clenched her eyes tight and exhaled. Katelyn and Cara were right; she didn't need any reminders about how shitty her boyfriend was. Ex-boyfriend, now. Technically, he wasn't obliged to attend her father's funeral, but if he'd cared about her, or the three years they'd spent together, he would have been there.

From her corner in the kitchen, Molly watched the others. Tate was stoking the fire with a poker. Cara walked up behind him, putting her arms around his waist. He placed his hands over hers, just as she whispered something only he could hear. Tate and Cara had always been one of those couples who were destined to be together; Molly had known since the first time she met him, and even before then, when her usually anti-romance sister was swooning over the handsome cop she'd met. Tate had mellowed her in more ways than one, and Molly was pleased to know Cara wouldn't be alone in her grief.

Only a few feet away, Rachel and Katelyn sat on the sofa. Molly approved of this relationship, too. Having Katelyn around was like being gifted an extra sister, one with the same taming qualities as Tate. She was funny and kind, but most importantly, she'd been there for Rachel when she needed her most. Rachel had taken their mother's death the hardest, and here they were six months later, going through the whole sickening process again.

At least they had had some warning when their mother died. Cancer. There were appointments and chemo, then a hospice soon after. Their father's death was sudden. He went to sleep one night having taken too much medication, and never woke up. Thinking of it now made Molly shudder. She'd been the closest to him, and now he was gone, as though he'd slipped through her fingers into oblivion.

Molly tried not to think about the funeral or her sisters or Ben. Instead, she summoned a happy memory of her father. She pictured the last time they went fishing together at the family's cabin. The summer sun beating on her shoulders, the cool water tickling her shins. Henry had sat beside her on the dock, patient, even though the fish didn't want to bite. A smile crept across her face.

She opened her eyes, and saw her father's portrait staring back at her. It was the large one they'd placed at the entrance of the funeral home. She raised her glass to the picture and drank, wishing the ache inside her would go away.

THREE

RACHEL

Rachel was laughing so hard she thought her guts might burst.

Maybe she had the six whiskeys to thank, but she also owed Katelyn for this brief glimpse of happiness. Being with her made the world a little less bleak, even a world without parents.

When Rachel lost her mother, it felt like stepping off a cliff, falling without anywhere to land. Grief swallowed her whole. The creativity and humor they'd had in common couldn't be matched by anyone else. That same bond didn't exist with her father, not for any particular reason; Rachel simply felt a deeper connection to her mother.

In the weeks following her mother's death, she viewed the tragedy as an opportunity to get to know her father better. After over thirty years of marriage, Henry Martin was hurting as much as Rachel was. She could be there for him. He needed her.

Now that opportunity was gone, and Rachel didn't know what to do with herself.

At least she had Katelyn. And she had a cold drink in her hand. And she had her sisters beside her, telling familiar stories.

"And then what happened?" Katelyn asked, her own voice wobbly from laughter.

"I said good luck finding someone to fix your typos and change the coffee filter for seven bucks an hour," Cara said. "Then I stormed out."

Cara was on the tail end of explaining how she'd quit her job at the *Whitehill Tribune* seven years ago. It was a risky move at the time, and they'd all worried she'd lost her mind, but it ended up being the best decision she ever made. Not long after, Cara started writing her first book, and soon after that, she met Tate. It was one of those impulsive decisions turned comical after a bit of time.

"What ended up happening?" asked Katelyn. Rachel found it hard to believe she was just now hearing the story for the first time.

"Exactly as I thought," Cara said. "My boss spent the rest of the year working the crime beat alone because no one else wanted the job."

"I wish I had the guts to do something like that," Katelyn said, although Rachel knew Katelyn actually enjoyed her job as a real estate agent. "I guess sticking it to the man works after all."

"My boss was a woman," Cara said. "But the same sentiment."

"The story gets better," Molly said. She was sitting in the corner of the room, and Rachel realized she was also laughing, a rare sight these days. "Tell her what Beverley did."

"After she saw the success of Cara's first book, she wrote her own," Tate added, stretching an arm over Cara's shoulders. "In the exact same genre."

"You're kidding," Katelyn said.

"True crime and everything," he said. "I guess she figured if she couldn't beat Cara, she'd join her."

"Well, our topics are slightly different. My books are based on facts, crimes that have already been solved." Cara arched her eyebrows. "Beverley Quinn's book was highly speculative."

"She wrote a book about Gemini," Tate explained. When Katelyn still appeared confused, he continued. "He was this Whitehill serial killer back in the nineties and noughties. He's never been caught."

"Seriously?" Katelyn wasn't from Whitehill, wasn't familiar with the local lore. She looked at Rachel and smacked her arm. "How've you never told me about this?"

"You know I'm not into all that murder nonsense. That's Cara's thing." Rachel nodded to Tate. "Besides, what makes you say *he*? No one knows who it is. It could be a woman."

"My apologies." He held up his hands. "It's *probably* a him, but no one knows for sure."

"Exactly," Cara said. "Especially Beverley Quinn. She basically built a career off making inferences."

"People prefer stories where they can add their own spin. They want to solve the mystery themselves," Tate said. "I mean, half the reason I got into law enforcement was because I wanted to catch guys like Gemini."

"So, what? If he didn't get caught, did he just stop killing?" Molly asked. She knew even less about this area than Rachel did.

"Doubt it," Tate said. "He could be dead. In prison for another crime. In this day and age, I think it's too hard to stay hidden. But he's only human. Some cousin with a guilty conscience will probably end up spilling the beans one day."

"Let's just hope I get the scoop before Beverley Quinn," Cara said, sipping the last of her drink.

"I'm heading to bed," Tate said, kissing her on the forehead.

"I think I'll join you." Cara stood. "Are we still planning on going through the house tomorrow?"

All of a sudden, Rachel remembered why they were all

together. In the midst of the storytelling and the drinking and the laughter, she'd forgotten.

"I'm off the rest of the week," Molly said.

"I don't have classes either," Rachel said. She was on the last leg of earning her graduate degree in film studies. Given the circumstances, her professors had been understanding.

"I can stay," Katelyn offered. "It's really not a big deal for me to call out of work."

"I wouldn't want you to do that," Rachel said. "You put in enough effort tonight. Besides, it would be good for the three of us to do this together. It feels like..."

It feels like a proper goodbye, she wanted to say, but instead let the words linger. Truthfully, Rachel was looking forward to having a few days with only her sisters. She loved Katelyn and Tate, but it felt like going through their parents' belongings was a burden they needed to shoulder together. A *we started this, let's finish it* sort of thing. Their family was forever fractured, and only the three of them could figure out how to regroup.

"You all really were so lucky." Katelyn stood, her jacket draped over her arms. "I swear, when I first met your parents, I didn't know families like yours existed. I figured the world was too woke. That every family had some type of pent-up trauma they had to take out on those around them, mine included. You guys were different. You really loved each other."

A memory floated into Rachel's mind. The first time she'd taken Katelyn to their family's cabin. Having grown up in the city, Katelyn wasn't used to the rugged accommodations, although she appreciated the raw beauty of the place. Both her parents had been wonderful hosts, especially their father. He took careful time to show Katelyn how to fish, shared helpful advice about the woods and its secrets. In some ways, he'd been more attentive to Katelyn on that trip than he had ever been to Rachel, but she wasn't bitter about it. She was happy her family brought Katelyn into the fold so effortlessly.

Then Rachel remembered that visit was the last time she'd been at the cabin when both her parents were still alive. A cry was on the verge of escaping, but she locked eyes with Katelyn instead, and smiled. She was the exact kind of stability Rachel needed. The Bacall to her Bogie, their mother might have said.

Outside on the patio, Katelyn asked, "Are you sure you don't want me to stay the night?"

"I'll be fine."

Katelyn nodded at the glass in her hand. "You won't be if you don't slow it down."

"I'm switching to water."

"Good." She smiled. "Call me in the morning?"

They kissed, and Rachel stood in the doorway, watching Katelyn's car disappear down the street, wishing she'd left with her. Maybe it was the talk of serial killers that had spooked her. Maybe it was the realization that her life moving forward would never be the same.

Whatever it was, Rachel didn't want to go back inside that house.

FOUR

CARA

Cara couldn't sleep. She kept going over everything in her mind. The service. The burial. Her whole life, it seemed. Tate was out as soon as he hit the mattress. He'd trained himself over the years, after working endless shifts at crime scenes. If he had the chance to sleep, he needed to take it; there was no telling when the next opportunity might arise.

Cara crept out of bed and went downstairs, taking in the dark living room for what felt like the first time, through the eyes of an adult who no longer had the safety of parents. Mom's piano, Dad's books. She touched random items, wondering if she could somehow feel closer to them.

Pictures of her family covered the walls. Graduations and birthdays and vacations. Her wedding with Tate. The biggest picture, in the center, had been taken at their family cabin. Both her parents looked happy to have their girls so close, still under their wings. A lump formed in her throat and she had to hold her breath to keep herself from coming undone.

She wandered into the kitchen and looked out the window behind the breakfast nook. During the day, there was a spectacular view, but now all she could see were the small lights that lined the walkway leading to their dad's shed. That had been his true happy place, surrounded by wood and metal and other materials. Even now, staring at the lonely building in the dark, Cara felt warm, as though she'd wake up in the morning and find her father working out there.

Screw it, she thought, putting on her coat, preparing to brave the cool night. Normally, she wouldn't go outside this late, but the sudden tragedy had altered the metronome of her life. It was like being on some type of holiday, but much, much sadder.

The lights were already on inside the shed. In one corner, sifting through a cardboard box, stood Molly. She was wearing a bathrobe and slippers. She smiled when she realized Cara had joined her.

"Can't sleep either?"

"Not a wink." Cara sat on a dusty bench by the door. She watched her sister with sad eyes. It was no secret Rachel had been closest to their mother, and Molly to their dad. Cara, at times, felt pulled in all directions, preoccupied with caring for the whole lot. "How are you holding up?"

"It's not hit me. I don't want it to ever hit me, really." Molly shrugged, placing the box she'd been holding on the ground. "It feels different than it did with Mom, doesn't it? We got to prepare. With Dad... it just feels like he's supposed to still be here. *He* thought he would still be here. We'd made plans to go to the cabin next month."

Margaret Grace Martin's death was sudden, and it wasn't. She'd been diagnosed with stage four breast cancer and told she'd have at least two or three years if she responded to the treatment. Three months later, she was gone, leaving Henry and the Martin girls in shambles.

"I wasn't prepared to let Mom go," Cara said. "And it's no easier with Dad."

Henry's death came out of nowhere, and Cara couldn't help but blame herself. They all knew their father was slipping after losing their mother, but Cara believed, being the oldest, she had more responsibility than the others to look after him. She should have visited more often. Maybe she would have seen that he was overusing his pain medication, and when he fell asleep last Thursday, he would have woken up the next morning as usual, instead of fading into a forever sleep.

"It's going to take ages to sort through their things."

"There's not a deadline or anything. The house is paid off. We can sit on it as long as we want before we sell. And I'm sure Katelyn will get us a good deal."

"You're right." Molly looked down. "We should wait until we're ready."

I'll never be ready, Cara thought. She wasn't a stranger to death. In fact, her career revolved around it. She wrote about crime for a living: awful stuff, people murdering strangers, or killing those closest to them, and yet this overdose was more painful because it had happened to her family. It wasn't spectacular from anyone else's standpoint; no one would write a book about it. But, to her, the loss was overwhelming. Maybe her career had helped her cope with the logistics of death, but it hadn't prepared her for the grief.

There was a sound outside, and they both jumped. The door creaked open, and Rachel stepped inside. When she saw her sisters, she laughed.

"I'm guessing we all had the same idea?"

"Dad was always happiest here. It's the first time we've all stayed in the house since..." Molly's words drifted. "I guess it just felt right being here with his things."

Cara turned, her sadness making it difficult to look at her sisters. Instead, she glanced at the various items in their father's shed. He'd spend early Saturday mornings and late weekday evenings here, only rarely asking his daughters to join him. Cara never felt rejected, rather she thought it was his way of teaching his daughters boundaries. *Strong fences make good neighbors*, he used to say, misquoting Robert Frost. The shed was his fence, his symbol that he was a full person aside from his more traditional roles—husband, father, teacher.

"It looks different, doesn't it?" asked Rachel.

Cara agreed. She couldn't quite decide what it was, but something seemed off. A table rearranged; a collection misplaced. Perhaps it had been too long since they'd been inside.

"When's the last time you were in here?" Molly asked.

"I can't even remember," Cara said. *Back when both my parents were still alive*, she wanted to say.

"It's been a while for me, too. I thought coming out here would make me feel closer to him somehow," Molly said. "Last time we talked, he said he was redecorating the place, making it a man cave. I guess that's why it looks different."

"Could be." Cara ran her hand along an oak bureau, opening one of the drawers. Inside were smaller tools and miscellaneous screws. The bureau was familiar, and yet it looked as though it didn't belong in this spot, under this lighting. She smiled as she repeated, "A man cave."

Rachel laughed. "Yeah, can you imagine? Like he needed a place to watch football and drink beer when he had the whole house to himself."

Cara closed the drawer, a little too hard, because one of the flimsier shelves at the bottom fell.

"Oh, shit." Rachel jumped back.

Molly walked over. "Jesus, Cara. Don't go breaking his things."

"It's not like I did it on purpose." Cara bent down to help clean the mess. The hazy light made it difficult to see what had fallen. She felt around the dusty floor. Her hand reached beneath the bureau, and her skin snagged on something. When she raised her hand, there was a small cut on her thumb.

"Shit." She instinctively drew her thumb to her lips, sucking on the wound until her mouth tasted of iron.

"What did you do now?" Rachel asked. "Prick yourself on a nail?"

"No," she said, before quickly bringing her finger back to her mouth. "It wasn't anything *on* the floor. It was something in it. Like a crack or something."

"A crack in the concrete?" Molly dropped to her knees and pulled out her cell phone to get a better look. "Wait a minute. I think I see what you're saying."

"Told you."

"But it's not a crack. It's part of the floor." Molly looked at her. "Don't tell me I've lived here the majority of my life without knowing we had a storm shelter."

"We definitely don't have a storm shelter," Cara said.

"Look for yourself." She handed over the phone and waited for her sister to join her on the floor.

Molly was right. There was a clear indent running from just beneath the front end of the bureau, and when she moved the light, Cara could see it extended to the far wall. An identical line ran about four feet in the opposite direction.

"What the hell is that?" She stood, returning the phone and sticking her thumb back into her mouth.

"Maybe it's part of the plumbing or electrical." Molly was almost flat on the ground now, shining the light as far back as it would go. "Wait, I think I see a handle."

"A handle?" Rachel asked. "Like for a crawl space or something?"

"Get up before you get a spider bite," Cara said.

Molly stood, but she ignored her sister's demands to back away. Instead, she started pushing the bureau.

"What the hell are you doing?" Cara said.

Molly looked over her shoulder, her eyes glistening. "I'm curious now."

The wood must have been cheaper than it looked. In two quick shoves, Molly pushed the bureau against the far wall, revealing a rectangular door underneath. It did look like the entryway to a crawl space, but that couldn't be what it was. After an entire lifetime in this house, they would know about it.

"Do you think Mom and Dad knew this was here?" Molly asked.

"Dad was in here all the time," Rachel said. "He had to know."

"What do you think is in it?"

"I don't kn—"

But before Cara could finish the sentence, Molly was back on her knees, pulling on the handle with both hands.

The door raised, and Molly reached inside the hole.

"What is it?" Rachel asked.

"A bunch of stuff," said Molly. "Boxes."

She pulled one out, and Cara could see the indentation in the dirt beneath where it had sat. She caught a whiff of dank earth.

Molly lifted the lid and peered inside, shuffling through a stack of papers. She leaned in closer, then pulled back and dropped it. "Gross."

"What?" Rachel asked.

"What is it?" Cara echoed, pushing past Molly to get a better look.

There weren't papers, but pictures. Cara stared at them, tuning out her sisters' voices. Her mind was trying to make sense of something, find a reasonable explanation for what they had found. *Think, think, think.* A sickness started forming in her gut, clenching her insides and squeezing tight.

She knew what the pictures were.

FIVE

MOLLY

Molly stared at Cara, wondering why the color had drained from her skin so suddenly. She looked gray beneath the weakened can light hanging from the ceiling, and droplets of sweat had started to form along her hairline.

When Molly found the pictures, catching a quick sight of a female in an alley with her legs spread, she'd reacted out of disgust. But Cara didn't seem grossed out. She seemed disturbed. And unlike her, Cara couldn't stop staring at the pictures.

"What is wrong with you two?" Rachel said, grabbing the photos out of Cara's hands. Cara let go without a fight. A mixture of confusion and repulsion seemed to fall over Rachel. "What the hell is this?"

"I don't know," Molly said, stammering. "Do you think it's some kind of porn?"

"This isn't porn," Rachel said, squinting to get a better look, flipping one picture behind the next. "No one is naked. These are pictures of women. They look like they're sleeping."

"They're not sleeping." Cara grabbed the pictures and shuffled through them with renewed urgency, like she was looking for something specific. "They're dead."

"Dead?" Molly stepped back, feeling as though the word had assaulted her. "They can't be dead."

"How do you know that?" Rachel asked, an equal dose of disbelief in her voice. "Have you seen these before?"

"No. Yes." Cara rubbed the back of her neck. "I've seen them before, but not here."

Molly took a breath, trying to dissipate the confusion. "Cara, tell us what you're saying."

Cara pulled the pictures close to her face, inspecting each one. There was a tremor of terror, then she'd move on to the next picture. When she'd finished sorting through the stack, she exhaled slowly and looked away.

"What I'm trying to say is I recognize these women from crime scene photos. That's how I know they're dead."

"Why would Dad have these?" Rachel asked.

"I... I don't know."

"Are they copies from a newspaper?" Molly asked. "A book or something?"

"No, it doesn't look that way. See for yourself. These are Polaroids."

If Molly was thinking with her right mind, she would have recognized that herself. But she hadn't. She was too hung up on the word *dead*. And now other details were coming into focus. In some of the photos, splotches of red on their clothing and arms. In others, sliced skin across their necks. She gagged, as though about to be sick.

Rachel, as she often did when pieces didn't line up, became frustrated. "But why would Dad have them? It doesn't make sense. Maybe you're wrong."

"I'm not wrong," Cara said firmly.

Rachel grabbed Cara's arm, as though she needed a physical jolt in order to think straight. "Then what are you saying?"

"These... these pictures." She looked down at them, then dropped them, each one scattering to different parts of the floor. "They're pictures of the Gemini victims."

"The what?" Molly asked.

"That serial killer from when we were kids," Rachel said. "The one we were talking about earlier tonight."

"Yes." Cara's voice was clipped, like she was being strangled. "They're pictures of the victims."

Rachel walked to the other side of the shed, as if to get as far away from the pictures as possible. Molly crept closer, bending down to get a better look.

"I recognized this one first," Cara said, tapping her foot against a photo of a woman in an alleyway. She was wearing a turquoise dress. A ring of dark liquid covered her neck and chest. "And there were others I recognized, too. I can't say I've seen all of them before, but some of them are definitely the Gemini victims. And they look like they were taken after the murders took place, before the police arrived."

"How could you know that?" Molly was holding the picture of the woman in turquoise up, examining it closer. She found it difficult analyzing the image of the murdered woman. All she could see was pain and loss, nothing relating to her father. Why was it here? She had to look away.

Cara danced her fingers around the edge of the photograph. "There's no one on the scene. No police tape. It's like the only two people present are the woman in the photo and the person taking it."

"Are you saying that Dad took the picture?" It was Rachel again, her voice angrier than before.

"I... I don't know. But the police didn't," Cara said. "I can tell you that."

It sounded like Cara was doing much more than accusing their father of taking pictures. She seemed to be saying he was responsible for something much worse. Murdering these women? The pure thought of it made Molly want to laugh or punch something, she wasn't sure which. How could Cara—his own daughter—even think such a thing?

Molly dropped the picture, moving closer to the bureau and the hole in the floor.

"What are you doing?" Cara asked.

"I'm seeing what else is in here," she said, and started digging. She'd only grabbed the first handful of photos on top— six or seven pictures at most. There were three plastic boxes, the lids on all ajar. She lifted the first one out and dumped the contents on the floor. Something had to explain why her father had these images.

In the narrow confines of the shed, they were surrounded. By pictures upon pictures of sleeping women. Bleeding women. Dead women. And something else clattered against the floor. A wad of tangled jewelry. Necklaces and rings and bracelets wound together, forming a metallic knot. Cara fell to her knees and started examining them. Molly closed her eyes just as Rachel began to scream.

SIX
RACHEL

Rachel wished she hadn't stepped closer. The images she saw, however brief, scarred her mind, and even when she closed her eyes, she could still see those women with the blood across their necks. And now there was a pile of jewelry.

"What the hell are you doing?" she wailed, turning her back on her sisters. "Put it away."

"We're trying to see what all is here," Cara said.

"There's got to be at least fifty pictures," Molly said, ignoring her. "What's with the jewelry?"

"Gemini was known for taking a piece of jewelry from each victim," Cara said.

First, the pictures. Now, the jewelry. Two links between their father's shed and a number of unsolved crimes. Thoughts were whirling through Rachel's mind so quickly, she felt dizzy. She headed for the door.

"This is crazy," she said. "I have to get out of here."

Normally, she wasn't one to seek confrontation, although she wouldn't shy away when one was presented. She'd rather pretend tonight never happened than keep digging.

"Lower your voice. Tate is still asleep. We don't need him

coming out here," Cara said. She was standing now, walking toward Rachel. "Aren't you curious why Dad had these hidden in the floor of his shed?"

Any answer wouldn't be a good one. It wasn't normal for a person to keep images like that, let alone hide them. Or random pieces of jewelry. Her father wouldn't have kept anything valuable beneath the floor of his shed. Rachel thought of their mother. The flamboyant choir teacher who had nightmares after watching Hitchcock movies. If she saw these images—if she could hear what Cara was saying this very moment—she'd be horrified.

"Keep looking," she said, reluctantly. "Maybe there's something else in the boxes to explain why he had them."

Molly went back to the boxes while Cara continued examining the jewelry. Rachel sat on the bench by the door, her arms crossed. She stared at the floor, careful not to let her gaze wander too close to the pictures.

"They're all women," Molly said. Then, as if to reassure Rachel, she added, "Dad isn't in any of them."

"Well, that's comforting," Rachel said, sardonically. "At least we don't have *proof* Dad was there."

"Look at these," Molly said. "These are random pictures of women taken at different places. The grocery store. The mall. On the street."

Rachel got up and came closer, peering over her shoulder. She was right. These images weren't disturbing; they were perfectly boring. No blood and gore. These women were alive, walking around without a care in the world.

"Wait a minute." Cara paused, her eyes moving between the photos. "These are the same women. He took these when they were alive. Almost like he was watching them beforehand."

"Great," Rachel said, moving back to the wall, her hopes deflated.

"You're saying he was hunting them," Molly said, followed by an awkward silence.

"If he hurt these women," Cara said, "he would have spent time watching them beforehand."

"*If* Dad hurt these women!" Rachel shouted. "Are you listening to yourself? Do you really think—"

"Of course, I don't think Dad would hurt them!" Molly shouted. "I'm trying to make sense of this, just like you are." She looked at Cara. "There has to be an explanation for this, right?"

"This is proof Dad, or whoever took these pictures, watched the women for a while before they died," Cara said. She gasped, staring at one in particular. "Look at this one. See what she has around her neck."

Rachel moved closer. The woman seemed to be photographed in a grocery store parking lot. The image was hazy, but the shot was close enough to see the silver necklace resting atop her turtleneck. The pendant at the center was in the shape of a bird.

Cara nudged her. In her hand, she held the exact same necklace. Rachel blinked, trying to wipe the image away, and yet it remained.

"Tell us everything you know about Gemini," Rachel said, reluctantly, hoping Cara would catch herself, stumble upon something that would disprove what they'd found.

"Off the top of my head, I know the killings started in the nineties. All the victims were women. They were stabbed multiple times and their throats were slit." Cara rattled off the details like most people would run through a shopping list. Rachel felt her body tense with each new detail, while Molly stared ahead, blankly. "All the bodies were left in a public place, and there was always a piece of jewelry taken from the victims. Not all of it, like a robbery gone wrong. Only one piece. There were a few instances where the killer sent messages to the police."

"What kind of messages?" Molly asked.

"It was like he was taunting them. He never threatened to kill again, but he wanted to let them know he was smarter than them."

"Sounds just like Dad," Rachel said under her breath, but it was too loud. She shuddered with shame. Was she actually starting to believe her father could be responsible? Seeing the necklace in Cara's hand—the same one the woman was wearing in the photo—made it seem possible.

"Don't say that!" Molly marched toward Rachel, as though she could read her mind, but Cara stepped in the way.

"We're not going to resolve anything if we start fighting with each other. We need to stay focused."

Cara moved to the next box. Rachel watched, her teeth gritted.

"Be careful," Molly said, pointing into the box. "There's glass."

"It's broken pieces," Cara said, lifting what appeared to be the various parts of a shattered Polaroid camera.

"Do you think it's the same one used to take the pictures?" Rachel asked, just as Cara reached back into the box.

But Cara wasn't listening. She was holding a piece of paper, silently reading. After a few charged seconds, she covered her mouth. "My God." The words were muffled as they tried to escape.

Rachel dared to step closer. Fear climbed her spine, sending her nerves ablaze. She didn't want to acknowledge the significance of anything they'd found, but with each reveal, it was getting harder to ignore. "What is it?" she asked.

When Cara spoke, her voice sounded broken, much like the camera beside her, as though the emotions she'd been stifling finally found their release. "It's a letter."

Now, Rachel was close enough that she could see. She

recognized her father's handwriting instantly. "What does it say?"

"It's a confession."

SEVEN

MOLLY

As soon as the words left Cara's lips, Molly stepped forward, jerking the paper out of her hands.

"You're wrong," she said. "That can't be what this is."

"Read it yourself," Cara said, still unwilling to look her in the face.

Rachel stepped forward, peering over Molly's shoulder, waiting.

Molly looked back at the paper, and began to read.

My name is Henry Martin, and I am the Gemini killer. I've killed seventeen women. Whoever finds this must already be on a quest for answers, so I won't insult you by denying my actions. I wish I could explain my motive, but I can't, not even to myself.

If the truth comes out about what I've done, I hope you'll share the news gently with my daughters. And if one of them is reading this, I hope you'll have it within yourself to forgive me.

Henry M. Martin

The letter was short. The handwriting, which looked like their father's, climbed the page in a wobbly fashion, as though it had been written in a hurry. Again, Molly couldn't deny what she had read, but she couldn't accept it as truth either. She blinked, and warm tears settled in her eyes. She knew her face must be flushed with frustration and anger, and beneath all that, disbelief. She couldn't deny what was in front of her, how incriminating what they'd found appeared to be, but she was also reluctant to admit that their father, the person she loved more than anyone in the world, was responsible for these crimes. Her father wasn't a killer.

"This doesn't prove anything."

"Of course, it does!" Rachel shouted. "It's a confession."

"But it doesn't make any sense! Why would he write it?"

"For exactly the reason he said. If anyone came digging, he wanted to leave an explanation."

"But why? Serial killers don't do that, do they?" Molly looked at Cara now, expecting her to have all the answers. "I can't imagine a person murdering people and then caring about what others think of that."

"Most serial killers don't have families," she said, dryly. "At least the ones that get caught."

Molly looked back at the letter, reading it over again, looking for any discrepancy. Then she looked back at the box filled with pictures of the crimes detailed in the letter. The jewelry belonging to victims. The proof was right in front of her. Cara and Rachel were already believing it, but she couldn't. She kept thinking of her father. The man she admired. The man who taught her everything she knew about life.

"What if someone made him write it?"

"What do you mean?" Cara asked.

"What if the real killer planted all this stuff here, and forced Dad to write this letter?"

Rachel sighed in frustration. "Listen to yourself, Molly.

Why would anyone do that? Gemini hasn't been active in over ten years. Why would he pick a random house, force Dad to write a letter, then plant all the evidence in his shed?"

"I don't know." She snapped her eyes closed and pinched the bridge of her nose. "It doesn't make sense, but anything is more plausible than Dad being a serial killer."

"It's his handwriting," Cara said.

"But it's not *him*," Molly shouted. "He wouldn't do something like this."

"Maybe it's not a confession," Rachel said, her arms crossed over her body, as though bracing herself for what was next. "Maybe it was a suicide letter."

"What?" Molly was outraged, as though she'd just been struck in the face. "Dad didn't take his own life."

"He killed seventeen women! I don't believe any of us are capable of knowing what he would and wouldn't do."

"It was an overdose," Cara said. "Rachel could be right. Maybe he felt guilty, wrote the letter, then took his own life."

"After all these years?" Molly asked. "You said it yourself. Whoever killed these women isn't going to randomly start feeling bad about it now."

"He changed after Mom died. We all did," Rachel said. "Maybe her death forced him to admit the things he'd done, and he decided he couldn't live with himself anymore."

"It's like we're not even talking about the same person. Our father wouldn't do this."

"Look at all the jewelry. The pictures. The letter." Rachel waved her hands around the shed. "Your idea about someone planting everything here doesn't hold up."

"Of course, you'd say that. You always had issues with him."

"That's not true—"

"It is. You weren't close to him like you were Mom. If someone was framing her for murder, you'd be more vocal about preventing it."

"We can't start tearing each other apart," Cara said, and it was difficult to tell which, if either, side she was on.

There was a sound outside, and the motion detecting lights flashed on. The girls went silent, each holding their breath. Then, a voice.

"Cara? Are you out here?"

It was Tate. Cara looked at her sisters, then quickly slid out of the shed.

Left alone, Molly and Rachel didn't say anything for several minutes. Molly wished her father would walk in and clear everything up. Provide an explanation for this situation, as he had every other obstacle in her life. Rachel and Cara wouldn't dare make such allegations to his face. If only he could wrap his arms around her this very minute, and tell her everything would be okay.

"I just don't understand how this is so easy for you," Molly said, at last.

"Nothing about this is easy."

Cara came back in, closing the door behind her.

"Tate heard yelling and came down to investigate."

"Did you tell him—"

"I didn't tell him anything." She exhaled slowly. "But we aren't going to figure this out tonight. We're tired and emotional and confused. Tate will leave for work in the morning. We can talk about this then."

"Yeah," Rachel said, her arms still crossed. "Maybe we just need sleep."

"Right," Molly echoed. "Maybe in the morning we'll all feel..."

But she never finished her sentence. If she had, she knew they wouldn't have listened. They were together, and yet each alone, in their own minds, thinking about what they had found.

EIGHT

RACHEL

Once inside, Rachel settled on the living room sofa.

The house always looked scarier at night; she'd thought that since she was a child. Downstairs, there were two family rooms and an office branching off from the kitchen. The Martin family home had a Victorian feel to it. Maybe it was Margaret's traditional furniture choices, or the dark molding framing the walls and doors. Maybe it was her father's antiques, each globe and spyglass carrying with it its own story. Growing up, Rachel's friends described the house as charming, like something out of a storybook. But there'd always been a chill to this place she couldn't quite describe, and it was only growing colder.

Maybe, Rachel thought, she'd stumbled upon the reason why she'd always felt on edge in this home. Molly was trying to deny the significance of what they'd found, but the answer was there: their father had those pictures and accessories hidden in his shed because he was a murderer. A notorious one, at that. She burrowed deeper into the sofa, trying to banish the nausea rising.

And yet, she had to keep a clear head and think. Rachel

wasn't lying when she said she knew little about the case. She pulled out her phone, and started researching Gemini.

At first, she held out hope it was a misunderstanding because their father's birthday was in November. He was a Scorpio. Of course, an unmasked killer has little influence on the name given to him. The name didn't relate to the victims either, although some of the women shared the same sign. It didn't take long for her to uncover that the name Gemini stemmed from the time when the victims were killed: late May into mid June.

Something about those dates felt familiar, but she couldn't figure out what. Cara's birthday was in May, but that wasn't it. She thought back to her childhood, finally realizing that was the time of year her family chose to visit the cabin upstate. Another flare of hope surged through her, but it was soon extinguished. Her mother would usually take the girls to the cabin when the school year was over, at the end of May. They'd stay well into June, but their father wouldn't join them until halfway through the month. He was usually busy teaching summer school and tying up loose ends at home. Or so he said.

A sickening realization. It was the only time of year he had an extended period of time to himself. If he had a hobby of killing women—and that was a huge, unbelievable *if*—it would make sense that he would wait until his family was out of the house to commit the crimes. *Hunt*, as Molly had said. Rachel's stomach dropped further.

She thought again of her mother. Like most people, she had always noted how different her parents were from each other, but assumed that was what held them together. Where her father was solid and dark, her mother was soft and light. Her father was thought-provoking prose, and her mother a happy song. Margaret Grace Martin couldn't have known what her husband was really like, and for the first time, Rachel was grateful she hadn't lived to find out.

But there was something else about that time of year that bothered her, and she couldn't place it. She tossed and turned, her drunken brain fighting against adrenaline, trying to remember. When it hit her, she sat up on the couch, looking around the dark room as though someone else might be there.

Memorial Day weekend. It had always been a difficult time for their father, and part of the reason her mother always tried to get them out of the house. The holiday held a somber significance for her father because that was when his young sister had died.

Aunt Rosemary, he called her, although she died years before any of the girls were born. Henry was only eighteen himself. Rosemary Martin was two years older than her brother, a sophomore in college at the time of her death. She'd been killed in a drunk driving accident on Memorial Day weekend. The driver of the vehicle had survived with only a few cuts and spent the next decade in prison.

Their father talked about her often. Mainly because he wanted to honor his sister's memory—the two had been close— but also because her death was a cautionary tale. Rosemary hadn't done anything wrong that weekend, but her life was still cut short because of the demons of others. Because of reckless drinking and careless driving. It was a story he told often over the years, and even now, Rachel could recall the dark look in his eyes when he told it. As though a sadness had taken over him, transforming him into a different person altogether. A colder person.

As Rachel finally began to doze, her mind kept revisiting that dark look in her father's eyes when he'd talk about their aunt Rosemary. And then she'd think back to those pictures of the women in the shed.

NINE

CARA

Cara never slept. She couldn't. Like Rachel, she spent the majority of the night searching the internet for known facts about Gemini, scanning crime scene photos to make sure the images in her mind and the ones in the shed were the same. Without question, they were.

And she looked up other details, mainly ones that could disprove the theory her father was Gemini. If one of the crimes was committed during an impossible moment, perhaps, but as she'd already pieced together, the crimes happened when Margaret and the girls were out of town, at the family's cabin. Convenient. Deliberate? On years where she knew her father couldn't have committed a crime—in 2001 when he had back surgery, in 2007 when they vacationed in Europe—there were no Gemini victims reported.

When her head began to ache from the phone screen's glare, she tried to sleep, but was left to sift through her own memories instead. She dissected years and years worth of moments, events, conversations, still hunting for anything that could disprove this bizarre theory.

Once. She'd only heard her father discuss Gemini once, and

the memory, which until this moment had been forgotten, was now seared into her mind.

Until her parents' deaths, the months after she left the newspaper had been the darkest of her life. Cara, who had held a job since the age of fifteen, had quit in a rage without giving a two-week notice. Without thinking of her bills or the astronomical rent in her downtown apartment. She'd not reacted logically, only with emotion. Looking back, this would be a turning point for her. The darkness before the dawn of her new career. But in the moment, it was full dark, and she couldn't see her way out. So, she did what most twenty-something millennials did in a time of crisis: she moved back home.

She got to know her parents better in those months, with both Rachel and Molly living at their respective dorms. She enjoyed the late movie nights on weekends and early breakfasts before work. She always thought Margaret Grace treasured those extra months together, too. It was a second chance for her to parent one of her fast-growing girls.

It was during one of those breakfasts, after many weeks of lounging around the house with little to do, that she told them her idea for a book. She'd stumbled upon a case in California. A woman was accused of murdering three of her husbands. She'd poisoned them all over the span of eighteen years, cashing in on more than half a million in life insurance policies. It wasn't until the third victim's family started asking questions that an investigation started, and the woman was arrested. The case had been popular in the media, and Cara had the idea, given her background in journalism, to write a book about it.

Still, at the time, it was a big leap, going from a stable job to abruptly quitting and then writing a book. It seemed both possible and ridiculous. The type of plan she couldn't jump into without running it by her parents.

As expected, her mother found the idea vulgar. Not writing

a book, per se. She had faith in her to do that, but she didn't like the subject matter.

"Why can't you write a romance novel?" she had asked, half-joking. Cara could still remember the three of them sitting around the breakfast table. Margaret Grace was placing strips of bacon on their plates.

"I don't know anything about writing fiction. My background is in journalism. I don't want to step too far out of my comfort zone."

"I think the idea has great potential," Henry had said, flapping the newspaper in his hands. "Interesting subject matter."

"Does it have to be about murder?" Margaret continued. "You could write about the old railway station in Whitehill or the history of Broadway."

"Mom, no one wants to read a book about the Whitehill railway station, and I'd be bored to death writing about musicals," she had said. "No offense."

"I guess you did develop a thick skin working the crime beat." Her mother paused, then raised her finger like she'd stumbled upon a brilliant idea. "I know. If you're going to write about crime, why don't you write a book about Gemini?"

The name was familiar but distant. "Wasn't that a case from when we were kids?"

Her father, who was chewing his bacon, had almost choked when she said that. Margaret Grace even stood from her chair, patting her husband's back.

"My goodness, Henry. Slow down," she'd said.

"Went down the wrong way." He grabbed his orange juice with shaky hands and sipped, watching Cara from over the glass.

"That case hasn't been solved," Cara said. "I'd rather write about hard facts. That's what I do best."

"It was only a suggestion," Margaret said. "If you're going to write about murder, I'd prefer to read something that could shine a light on who did it. I've always wondered. You know, it really used to worry me back in the day. I'd always look over my shoulder around that time of year. And make sure the doors were locked."

"I think Cara is trying to say the topic is too salacious. She's a journalist, not a gossip columnist," Henry had said, his voice calm and stern. "I think the California story sounds interesting, and if anyone can breathe life into it, it's you."

He'd put his hand over hers and squeezed. But looking back, she remembered thinking he looked pale. His palm felt sweaty. She thought something more was bothering him. He didn't believe in her, perhaps. After all, it was a big jump in her career, and Henry was used to taking calculated, practical steps. That must have been what was worrying him, right?

As Cara stared at her parents' ceiling, made gray by the shadows of the surrounding night, she wasn't sure. Maybe his stunted reaction was because it was the only time anyone had ever mentioned Gemini in his presence. He wasn't worried about Cara embarking on a new career, but concerned she might uncover his crimes, find a connection no one else had. Until now. Maybe he'd never really cared about Cara, only himself.

How had she forgotten that moment? The entire conversation, all the details. It was one of thousands of shared discussions over the years. It meant nothing.

But now? It meant everything.

TEN

MOLLY

Unlike her sisters, Molly fell asleep with ease. Disturbing thoughts still plagued her mind, but her body took over, much like when she had a fever forcing her into rest. When she woke, the sun was shining into her childhood bedroom, the only one her parents hadn't converted into something else in the years since they moved out.

Her phone buzzed with a text message from Ben.

Let me explain. I need you to understand...

She stopped reading, uninterested in whatever excuses he might present. Yesterday, she'd been so angry with him for missing her father's funeral. Now, that problem seemed miniscule, overpowered by the feelings swelling inside her chest. Every problem she'd ever had was instantly minimized when stacked against what they had found in the shed.

There was a sound coming from the front of the house. She assumed it was Tate leaving for work, but the noise persisted. Someone was knocking. She stumbled out of bed and marched down the hallway. Rachel was tossing and turning on the sofa, as though she was still struggling to sleep. Molly looked at the front door, saw a shadow bobbing behind the thin curtains.

On the front stoop, a black beanie covering strands of stringy hair, stood Elias.

"Morning. Hope I'm not stopping by too early."

"Morning, Elias," she said, loud enough for Rachel to hear. "Everything okay?"

"Well, I've been kicking myself since last night. There's something I wanted to give you girls, and I guess I was so overcome yesterday... well, I just forgot." That's when she noticed the box in his hands. It wasn't gift wrapped, but there was an attempt of a bow dressing the lid.

"Now isn't the best time," she started to say, but stopped when she felt a hand on her back. It was Cara.

"We had a bit of a late night," she said. "Come on in."

"Oh, it'll only take a minute. I know you girls are busy. I don't want to take up your time."

They wandered into the living room. Rachel was sitting upright on the sofa, her hair disheveled. She looked like death, but Elias probably assumed she was still grieving the loss of their father. He'd never know something much worse was bothering them.

Elias placed the box on the table and stepped back, pleased.

"Well, go ahead. Open it."

Molly was the only one to move. She untied the shoddy bow and removed the lid. Inside, was a framed photo of her father taken outside Fenway Park. Henry looked to be in his early thirties. He was wearing a chunky sweater, a Red Sox cap, his hands stuffed into the front pockets of his jeans.

"This picture was taken on one of our favorite trips. You know, we used to drive up there whenever we could when we were younger. Your father loved baseball. I think the only thing he loved more was you three."

Rachel and Cara were standing behind her now, peering

down at the picture. She hadn't heard them move, and yet here they were, staring at this idyllic image.

"It's beautiful, Elias," Molly said. "Thank you."

"This is how I'll always remember him," he said. "Young. Full of life. Happy. I thought you girls should remember him like this too."

At that Rachel turned quickly, stomping out of the room. Before she turned the corner, Molly caught sight of her shoulders shaking. And they could hear the muffled sobs she failed to suppress.

Elias looked between them, a bewildered look on his face. "I... I'm sorry. Maybe I should have known better. It's too soon. I was just trying—"

"It's a lovely picture," Cara said, placing it back on the table. "We really appreciate it. But our emotions are still a bit raw."

"I know, I know. I'm going through it, too." His gaze went blank then, as though he were looking into the past searching for memories, or looking toward the future and coming up empty. "Anyway, I just wanted to do something nice for you girls. Your dad always did so much for me over the years."

"Thank you," Molly said again, then added, "Thank you for being his friend."

Elias nodded, and Molly gently escorted him to the front door. She watched him leave, then returned to the living room. Both Rachel and Cara were gone. Molly looked down, her eyes landing on the portrait of her father. A mix of pride and shame filled her, and she felt the familiar pressure of tears building in the corners of her eyes.

ELEVEN

RACHEL

Rachel had never had a panic attack before, but that's what it felt like was happening. Her lungs were closing in, her face warm as though she'd spent hours in the sun. Her skin felt electric, her nerves standing at attention.

She went outside to the backyard and leaned against the large oak tree at the landscape's center. An old swing dangled from the largest branch, a symbol of the happy childhood they'd had. Her initials, along with her sisters', were carved into the tree's trunk. To her left, was a perfect view of her father's shed, that awful place with the horrifying secrets it kept.

Don't think about it, she told herself. She inhaled through her nose, exhaled through her mouth. That was the calming breathing Katelyn did during yoga. Maybe it would work for her, but at the back of her mind was the terror that nothing would work ever again. That she'd be stuck in this cycle of horror and sadness and panic for the rest of her life.

There was a hand on her shoulder, and she jumped.

"Are you okay?" Cara asked. Her voice was slow and cautious, as though talking to a small child.

"I'm never going to be okay. How could you even ask?"

When she spoke, she lost control of her breathing again, and was gearing up to hyperventilate.

"Just keep breathing. We can get through this."

"I can't go the rest of my life pretending Dad was this decent person. A loving father and loyal Red Sox fan. Some normal fucking guy. He was a serial killer!" She was shouting now. "He murdered all those women and never even got punished."

"We don't know that," said Molly. She had joined them outside, and was leaning against the same tree, facing a different direction.

"Gemini had seventeen victims," Rachel said.

"I know," Cara said.

"I guess because it happened so long ago, it never felt real. You hear the phrase *serial killer*, your brain doesn't stop to think that seventeen women earned him that title. Seventeen lives gone. Seventeen families ruined."

"Did you stay up all night googling Gemini?" Molly asked.

"Didn't you?" Rachel asked.

"I tried to sleep," Molly said, standing upright. "Why are you so quick to accept the idea Dad was a killer? What we found was damning, but what if there's another explanation?"

"What other explanation could there be?" Cara asked.

"Anything would be more believable than our father being a notorious serial killer," Molly said.

"It's hard to ignore the stolen jewelry," Cara said, unwillingly. "And the letter."

"Someone could have planted the jewelry," Molly said. "We don't know he wrote the letter either. Sure, the handwriting looks like his, but what if it's not? The more I think about it, the more I'm convinced it looks different. What if someone is framing him?"

"That's just you coming up with excuses," Rachel said.

"No, I'm trying to think about this logically. Did you ever

know Dad to write letters? Have journals? It's not like him to write down his biggest secret. There's something off about that note."

"If the writing looks different," Rachel said, "it's probably because he was having a manic episode right before he swallowed a bottle of pills."

No one spoke after that. Only the birds twittering above broke the silence.

"I can't believe you said that," Molly said. "He didn't kill himself."

"We can't keep attacking each other," Cara said. "There's too much we don't know, and arguing won't bring us any closer to answers."

"Haven't either of you thought about why he killed when he did?" Rachel asked.

"The kills took place every year when we were at the cabin." Cara nodded along, like she was already several steps ahead. Rachel didn't need to ask whether Cara had stayed up all night googling. She already knew the answer.

"I'm not talking about that. Some of those women were killed before we were even born, long before we were going on vacation. I'm talking about the *timing* of the murders." She waited, neither of them seeing. "Memorial Day weekend."

Cara's eyes widened. Molly's jaw slackened. They hadn't made this connection.

"Every year, Dad was sad that time of year. I remember Mom worrying about leaving him alone a couple of times. She didn't want to be gone because she knew Dad wasn't in his right mind. He was too upset because—"

"That's when Aunt Rosemary died," Cara finished. She wrapped her arms around her waist and turned. Whatever evidence she'd been racking in her mind against their father, this seemed to be the missing piece.

"Exactly," Rachel said.

"But it still doesn't make sense," Molly said, her voice weak. "Dad's sister died in a car accident. It happened that weekend, but it doesn't mean anything."

"It could be his trigger," Cara said, her voice determined.

"What does that mean?" Molly asked.

"If Dad had these... impulses, these issues, it would have been difficult for him to suppress them. Difficult, but not impossible. Rachel's right. Every year around Memorial Day, he acted different. We all assumed it's because it brought back memories of Aunt Rosemary, but what if we were wrong? Maybe his grief made it impossible for him to hold back anymore."

"It makes sense," Rachel said, looking at Molly for a reaction. "None of us want to admit he did this. But we can't deny what is right in front of us."

"This can't be real." Molly looked away, her chin beginning to tremble. Within a few minutes, she was full on crying, the reality of the conversation finally sinking in.

Rachel gave her a few minutes to compose herself before she continued. "If we really think this, that Dad had something to do with these deaths, we need to do something about it."

"What can we do?" Cara said. "Dad is dead. Those women are dead. We can't change any of that."

"No, but we can provide answers. We can show the police what we found."

"You aren't serious," Molly said.

Cara crossed her arms. "Naming Gemini now, after all these years, will do nothing but cause pain for us."

"But it's the right thing to do," Rachel said. "There are people out there whose lives were destroyed by our father. We have to give them answers."

"Answers won't bring back their loved ones," Cara said. "Trust me, no good will come from telling people about this."

"I don't expect good to happen," Rachel said. "But it's the right thing to do."

"I know the alternative. I know how people target the killer's family. Do you really want media following you on campus? Showing up at Katelyn's work asking for a comment?" Cara looked at Molly. "And think about your job. The hotel won't stand by you if you bring bad press. We have to think about this stuff. Our friendships. Our relationships. We risk losing everything if this comes out."

Rachel clenched her jaw. Cara seemed to know she'd touched a nerve then, so she pressed further. "Do you really want to tell Katelyn what we found in that shed? Aren't you worried it will change things?"

"Nothing will change her feelings for me," Rachel said. She was confident and sure. There had never been any secrets between them, but then again, this was an enormous issue to confront. She imagined the look on Katelyn's face as she told her she was related to a serial killer. She wanted to believe Katelyn would stand by her, but what if she was too disturbed? Her voice turned quiet. "But no, I don't want to tell her."

"It would be different if Dad was still alive," Cara continued. "If he could be arrested. Go to trial. Receive a punishment. But he's dead, and we would be the ones punished."

"Are you going to tell Tate?" Rachel asked.

Cara thought for a moment. "No. I think it would change how he feels about me. He wouldn't want it to, but I don't think he could help himself. He was a cop before he met me."

"What if we're wrong?" Molly asked. "It's not fair to smear Dad's name when he's not here to defend himself."

"Maybe you're right. Maybe Dad didn't do this and there's someone else out there. The police will be able to figure that out. They can clear Dad's name and find the real killer." Rachel didn't believe that for one minute; in her mind, the evidence they'd found in the shed was irrefutable, but she had to convince her sisters that turning in the evidence they'd found was the right decision.

"I agree with Molly," Cara said. "We don't need to get the police involved yet."

Rachel threw her hands in the air and exhaled. "There's no reasoning with the two of you."

She started walking toward the backyard gate, which led to the sidewalk.

"Where are you going?" Cara asked.

"I need some time to think."

"Let one of us go with—"

"No. I need to be alone."

The only person she could trust to do the right thing was herself.

TWELVE

MOLLY

Molly retreated to the same place she did when she was a child: the swing hanging from the large oak tree. The seat was drier now and the ropes frayed, but it didn't give when she sat. She started to swing back and forth, hanging her head back, the sunlight warming her skin. She was dangling between earth and sky, much like her thoughts were hovering between denial and acceptance.

"She's worrying me," Cara said, her eyes still watching Rachel across the street.

"She's never been good at handling her emotions."

"Can you blame her? I'm not coping well either."

Molly wasn't naïve. She couldn't deny the significance of what they'd found. People didn't keep photos of dead women hidden inside their homes without reason. And she didn't need Cara's background to know they weren't pulled from a crime scene. She'd seen them. Whoever had taken those photos had done so intimately.

She thought of her sisters, how each of them had handled the discovery. When Rachel was upset, she turned mean and unpredictable. When Cara was upset, she became pretentious, acting as though she was above the drama, forgetting she made a career from it. Other people's drama, never her own.

But unlike both of them, Molly was holding onto the memory of who her father was. He was her protector, her leader. That same person couldn't have been responsible for killing seventeen women and hiding the secret all these years. Seventeen! It seemed like an outrageous number. Henry Martin couldn't be at the center of it all.

"Are you absolutely sure he did this?" Molly asked. "You don't think there's another explanation."

"If an innocent person had access to those pictures, they would have turned it over to the police. *Should* have turned it over. And finding the letter alongside them..." Cara's words drifted. She seemed eager to talk through it with someone, but she obviously didn't want to push Molly further away. "The timelines fit. Even what Rachel said about Aunt Rosemary makes sense. Plus, the pictures." She paused, letting Molly digest each morsel of evidence. "I don't think we can deny what Dad... was. There's too much stacked against him."

"Why did he just stop killing?" Molly asked. She knew very little about serial killers or crime in general, but most television series made it seem like the compulsion to kill was one that couldn't be sated.

"He wouldn't be the first person to kind of grow out of it." Cara shook her head, dissatisfied with her own lame excuse, and continued. "The more accurate answer is that killing, like most other hobbies and careers, can't be carried on forever. Gemini's last case generated more forensic evidence than all his other cases combined. Dad was smart enough to know when he was getting sloppy and made a choice. Stopping was better than getting caught."

"Why keep the pictures? Something that could easily get him caught?"

Cara bit her lip, as though reluctant to continue. "He probably kept them to relive his kills. It might have kept him from acting out."

"Acting out," Molly said, her mind chewing over the words. "What do you mean by that?"

"Dad is the last person anyone would expect to be guilty of something like this. Everything in his life must have been to hide who he really was, keep him in line. Those pictures allowed him to act out without actually killing. If that's who he was, then everything else was his attempt at hiding it."

This image Cara was presenting of her father didn't fit. It belonged to some convicted felon with a rap sheet a mile long. Or an evil nemesis in a thriller. Henry Martin was calm, reliable. She'd never known her father to be violent, and every decision he'd made in his adult life had been logical, made for the betterment of his family.

His early years hadn't been the easiest. Molly's paternal grandparents weren't involved in Henry's life. They had their own issues, mainly substance abuse and financial problems. Her father didn't enjoy talking about them. But he was close with his sister, Rosemary. He often praised her successes, her work ethic and achievement as the first person in their family to enroll in college, before her life was taken at the hands of a drunk driver.

Still, her father didn't let his rocky beginnings deter him from what he wanted to accomplish. He worked his way through school. Earned a degree. Married their mother and planted roots in the Whitehill community. For over forty years, he worked at the high school, mainly because he hoped to touch the lives of unfortunate youths like himself, guide them in a better direction. Was Cara suggesting that was all an act? A character created to hide who he really was? Molly wasn't convinced.

"If Rachel wants to go to the police, she's going to do it," Molly said. "She always acts impulsively."

"We have to try and talk her down," Cara said. "I know her

heart is in the right place, but she has no idea how destructive coming forward with something like this could be."

Molly tried to imagine how she would feel if the roles were reversed, if she'd lost her mother or her friend or one of her sisters to a serial killer. She'd want to know who did it, and she wouldn't care how much time had passed. But she wasn't on that side of the argument; she was still trying to defend the father she loved against an awful accusation. And seeing how easily Cara had used his defining traits against him—turning his predictability into methodology, his devotion to family into a means of protection—worried her what outsiders would do with the same information.

She stepped off the swing, her balance recalibrating with the earth beneath her feet. "I think I know what we should do."

"What?" Cara looked skeptical, but at the same time, desperate, grateful for any idea that might bring healing or hope.

Molly told her.

THIRTEEN

RACHEL

Rachel's cheeks were stiff from dried tears.

She hurried away from the house, following the familiar paths and trails she'd taken her entire life. As children, she and her sisters joined forces with the other neighborhood kids, exploring the small suburb on their bikes. The community had a never-changing charm she admired.

There was a small park in the neighborhood's center, with little more than an outdated charcoal grill, a swing set and a rusty slide. She couldn't remember the last time she'd seen a child play there. The Martin sisters had gone there from time to time, and when she was older, Rachel would sneak out of her house to meet friends there to smoke joints.

Her father had found her once. It was nearing ten o'clock on a summer night. The Martin girls had a strict curfew of eleven. Before going home, she'd hid behind the pavilion with a few other teenage ne'er-do-wells and passed the joint around. Her father happened to drive by, although she always thought he was purposely out searching for her that night. Why, she didn't know, but it was too hard to believe that routine-oriented Henry had just stumbled upon his daughter while she was doing something wrong.

She hurried into his car, aware that he'd already figured out what she was doing, and she wasn't going to insult either one of them by lying about it. Henry Martin drank, but nothing else. He often complained about the ignorance of smoking cigarettes, let alone anything stronger. And Margaret Grace, despite her flair for the creative, was as strait-laced as they come. Some parents might turn a blind eye to such behavior, but the Martins weren't like them. For several blocks, she sat in silence, waiting for the inevitable lecture.

As they pulled into the driveway, Henry turned to her. "That wasn't very smart, was it?"

She shook her head, still too frightened to speak. Since they were children, Rachel was the most likely to get in trouble—for breaking things, daydreaming at school, back talking—so she was used to receiving punishment, but she was never used to the ache of knowing she'd disappointed her parents.

"I'm sorry."

"When you make poor decisions, Rachel, it doesn't just impact you. It's a reflection of my parenting. Of your mother's parenting. It affects your sisters, too."

Rachel didn't know what to say. Molly would never think about touching drugs, and if Cara had, she'd be too stubborn to admit it.

"I won't do it again—"

"Don't tell me that. It's a lie and I know it." There was a long, sickening pause. "Just remember the ones you're hurting when you act however you want."

She swallowed her shame that night, and every time she'd messed up since. Rachel wasn't a bad person, she knew that, but sometimes when she thought of the way her father had looked at her that night, and other nights to come, she'd believe she was. It added to her anger—and shock and confusion—that the same man who had ridiculed her for age-appropriate behavior was responsible for murdering women. Talk about shame. Maybe those moments of cruelty and judgment were his dark side finding a small release.

Her phone started ringing. Katelyn.

Was it selfish Rachel had barely thought of her since last night? Her mind had been elsewhere, pulled and pushed through time, forced to confront a dozen horrible truths.

Still, the idea of Katelyn's voice, seeing a glimpse of her face on the screen, gave her hope.

"Good, you're awake," Katelyn said. "I was afraid I'd call too early."

"Yeah, we wanted an early start."

"What's wrong?" She sensed it immediately, that something was off. More than just the fact that the funeral had been the day before. "Did you get any sleep last night?"

"Some." Rachel didn't know what to tell her. She wanted the thrill of confessing what was on her mind, but not the responsibility of upsetting the person she cared about most. "It's just been a long week, you know."

"I can leave the office at lunch."

"No, I don't need you to do that."

"I don't know why I didn't do it earlier. You obviously—"

"I'm fine." Her voice was more urgent this time. "I'm going through things with my sisters. Emotions are running high. But I don't need you to come over."

"If you're sure." Katelyn exhaled, and it was difficult to tell whether she sounded relieved or sad. "I just hate this for all of you."

Images popped into Rachel's mind; she was helpless at keeping them out. The sleeping women. Their bloody necks. That hastily written confession.

"Katelyn, I really have to go," she said, hanging up before there was a chance for a response.

Already, she could feel the course of her life changing. A wall was building, brick by brick, closing her off from those around her, closing her off from herself.

But it didn't have to be this way. She'd already gone through the worst—admitting to herself that her father was a serial killer, that he alone was responsible for the pain of so many others. Coming forward with the evidence they'd found would present new challenges, but it wouldn't be harder than what she'd already experienced. It was the right thing to do, and maybe providing answers to his victims was what she needed to start moving forward.

She turned, making the trek back to her house. The clouds were no longer banding together, revealing patches of blue sky. Across the street, she waved at a neighbor whose face was familiar but whose name she'd forgotten. What would this person think once the news broke? There would be no more waving, no more friendly chatter. And like Cara said, there would be some people hostile to them. They'd blame them because Henry was gone.

But most sensible people would understand the Martin girls had nothing to do with their father's crimes. They would even admire them for coming forward. It would take time, years and years, but in the future, they would find peace with what their father had done. They would counteract their father's evil by doing what was right.

And she knew Katelyn would be one of the sensible ones to stand by her side. It would be shocking, sickening, but Rachel knew Katelyn wouldn't blame her. And she needed Katelyn's guidance to get through this. In that moment, she realized telling her the truth about her father would be more bearable than keeping such a colossal secret. It was always secrets that tore people apart, never the truth.

The truth about her father had been a lone exception.

Rachel was less than a block away when she caught a whiff

of something in the air. The smell of fresh-cut grass and morning dew had been replaced with something heavier. After a few more steps, the back of her throat began to itch.

She was smelling smoke.

She picked up her pace, sprinting the last few meters to her childhood home. She thought of Cara and Molly, alarmed.

When she saw them, they were standing beside a metal bin, bright orange flames spewing from the top of the can.

"What are you doing?" Rachel asked.

Cara and Molly looked at each other, then Molly spoke.

"We're getting rid of it."

That's when Rachel realized that all the evidence she would have brought to the police—the pictures and the jewelry and the letter—was burning right before her eyes.

FOURTEEN
CARA

Cara clenched her fists inside her jacket pocket, her eyes darting between Rachel and the burning bin. Molly's idea to burn the evidence had bothered her at first, grated against the writer inside, her role as preserver of facts. But she knew Rachel was hard to control. If she wanted to ensure Rachel wouldn't accuse their father of being Gemini, she had to take away what little ammunition she had.

"You didn't even give me a chance!" Rachel cried, running close, then stopping when she felt the flames' heat. She had a manic look in her eyes, and Cara wondered if she was still buzzed from last night's booze, or if she was fueled by anger and confusion. The wit and vitality and beauty that defined her sister was gone. She was a broken woman.

"If we go to the police, we'll live the rest of our lives with this hanging over us." Cara looked back at the flames. "This is the first step in moving on."

Cara couldn't stand watching Rachel cry, but she couldn't offer much in the form of comfort. Part of her agreed with her sister, the same part that longed for justice. After all, she wasn't solely writing about crimes to sell books; she believed she was shining a light on victims and their stories.

At the same time, she'd seen what that spotlight could bring. No one wants their loved ones to be the victim of a violent crime, and it's a shadow that follows the living the rest of their lives. And the family members of offenders? That shadow turns into a black hole, destroying their very existence. Cara knew what would happen to them if word got out Henry Martin was Gemini. They were all too invested in Whitehill to move away, but even if they did, their father's sins would follow them. His legacy would precede every detail of their lives. Every job interview, every date, every party invitation for their future children.

Sure, people would say they could separate the Martin girls from their father's actions, but the truth was, people were afraid of getting too close to darkness, lest it rub off on them. It was better to stay away, isolate. And that's just the good-hearted people. Some wouldn't even try to separate the two, and because Henry Martin was no longer around to pay for his crimes, they'd go after other targets. His daughters.

"What we found inside the shed was horrible," Cara said. "And I know we'll be dealing with this for a long time, but it needs to stay between us. Involving others will only make it harder to move on."

"There is no moving on!" Rachel shouted. "You think burning the evidence is going to stop me? The jewelry might be damaged, but it won't disappear. I can still go to the police. I can still tell them everything we found, and blame you two for covering it up."

"Go ahead," Molly said, defiantly. "Tell them Henry Martin is the Gemini killer. Their old history teacher. Their hunting buddy. The deacon at the fucking church! You can tell them whatever you want about Dad, but now there is nothing proving what you say."

"Enough!" Cara shouted, her voice trying to drown out both her sisters. "We can't let this tear us apart."

Rachel opened her mouth to speak then closed it. She started pacing the backyard, moving between the fire and the tree. Then she let out a roar. "I'm so angry with both of you. I'm angry with him and the whole world."

"We're angry, too. But if we bring others into this, we'll regret it."

"So, that's the pact then?" Molly asked. "We keep it between us. Only us three."

"Yes," Cara said.

Molly nodded. Cara feared her youngest sister still didn't want to admit the truth. Whether or not she believed Henry was guilty no longer mattered; ignoring what they had found was a consolation she could accept.

She could read the hesitancy on Rachel's face. "Looks like you didn't leave me a choice."

Cara knew all three of them would grapple with this in the years to come, but she believed she was making the right decision in keeping Gemini's identity a secret. It would be better for them this way. Their father was a monster, but she couldn't let him destroy their lives.

"It's like any other type of grief," Cara added, trying to make them feel better. "We can't bring him back. We can't bring back his victims. We just have to move forward from this. It's over now."

Most of what Cara believed had been tested in the wake of her father's death, but one thing she knew, with certainty, was that even monsters couldn't come back from the grave.

PART II
ONE YEAR LATER

FIFTEEN

Water splashes against the splintered wood on the old dock. A man ties a rope connecting the boat to the post, triple-checking his work. He takes off his brown cap and wipes his brow. He's the last one here, the sun beginning to edge closer to the still waters beyond.

He nods his head as he passes me, a gesture of respect not recognition. It's been a long day on the water, and now the only person left along the shore is inside the rental place, waiting to call it a day.

I walk inside and see her behind the counter. She's wearing a flannel shirt and leggings, her hair cut to just above her shoulders. She smiles when she sees me, but I can see beyond her kindness. Her eyes are tired. It's closing time, and she's ready to go home.

She has a nice home. I've driven by it a dozen times. It's a mile or so away from here, the lake taking the place of her backyard. She has her own little dock where she likes to sit in the evenings. It's covered, which makes it a nice place to watch the storm roll in or steal shade during the heat. She shares the home with her husband. No kids. Usually, he closes up the shop with her, but he's out of town now, which is why I've waited until tonight.

One of the reasons I waited for tonight.

She doesn't know it now, as she's looking at me with those calm eyes, but she'll never see that home again. Or her husband.

"I was just about to close up," she says, the smile falling slightly. "We won't work full hours until after this weekend. Maybe I can set you up with something next week."

"That's right! This is Memorial Day weekend, isn't it?"

"It's when the lake season officially begins."

I tell her I only wanted to check prices, that I'll return later. She tells me there are a couple of spots available to rent, that she can show me the bays on her way out, if I'm willing to wait.

Wait I do, watching to make sure no other cars enter the parking lot. This place is practically deserted, what with all the holiday specials at restaurants and pubs downtown. She's right; the weekend will mark the official opening of business at the lake, but she'll be long gone by then.

When she walks outside, a tote hanging from her shoulder and keys in her hand, I allow her to lead the way. We walk toward the water, the old planks moaning with each step.

"Right here," she says, stopping by an empty bay. "This one's the cheapest because it's so small, but depending on your—"

I cover her mouth with the cloth, feeling her body jolt in surprise and fear. I wrap my arm around her, holding her tight so we don't go over the edge, into the water. She kicks for a few seconds, then her body goes still. Her mind, too. When she awakes, she'll barely remember her life as she knows it now.

She'll be in too much pain.

She'll be desperate for it all to end.

If I'm being honest, she doesn't deserve this, but it's a necessary part of the plan.

I drag her behind the boat rental building, a spot I'd scoped out weeks before. This corner is hidden from the water, the road, the parking lot. No one will be able to hear her screams. It's as though we're the only two people left in the world, like we've been brought together by something bigger than ourselves.

For now, there is quiet, only my labored breathing and the sound of water breaking against the shore.

SIXTEEN

CARA

Cara and Tate moved into the Martin family home not long after the funeral. The sisters had talked about selling the place, but that was before.

Before the shed.

Before the pictures.

Before they'd made their pact.

Cara had no desire to tell the truth about her father's identity; that was easy enough. But she did feel a need to learn everything about him that she didn't already know. A compulsion, really. Like she might approach one of her books, she aimed to understand her father's life, and his crimes. Had the father she'd known and loved ever existed? Or, had Henry Martin only pretended to be that person in order to mask his true identity as a serial murderer?

Moving into the house was supposed to help her find answers. Even though she'd lived there her entire childhood, she viewed the beaten wood as new terrain that needed to be explored. Foraged. There were secrets hidden in these walls, she convinced herself. Figuratively. Unlike the very literal secrets that had been hiding beneath the floors in her father's shed. If she wanted to get inside her father's mind, she had to walk in his shoes, see the world as he saw it, take in the same sights and smells.

It had been months since they moved in, and she was no closer to understanding Henry Martin. She'd not found further evidence in the house—and she'd certainly looked. She'd upended the attic, the basement, each and every closet. She'd even spent a weekend at the family's cabin upstate, curious if Henry left anything incriminating there, but she came up blank. There were no more confessional diaries or letters, no hidden jewelry. Henry Martin knew it was best to keep all evidence that could be used against him in one place, but that hadn't deterred Cara from hunting, as Molly might say.

At times, she could still feel her father's presence in the house. As though his spirit lingered, watching as she struggled and searched, refusing to interfere. In at least one regard, she'd followed in his footsteps. She was keeping secrets. Tate didn't know about what she'd found in the shed. He didn't know about her manic research into her father's past and Gemini's crimes. Or the real reason why they'd moved. Inheriting a furnished house in an historic neighborhood? It sounded like a sweet deal to him, and she let him believe it.

There was only one person she felt she could really turn to for comfort anymore. It wasn't either of her sisters. And it wasn't Tate.

Her phone pinged with a text from James.

Checking out of the hotel at noon. Meet me at the bar?

She smiled. It wouldn't be a long visit, but it would be enough.

"Looks like I'm going to have to cancel lunch," Tate said, leaning against the wall. He was dressed in a dark suit, his hair combed to the side.

Cara stood in the kitchen, sipping the last of her morning tea. She put her phone away. "Lunch?"

"Last week, we said we'd swing by McGuire's for turkey clubs." He looked back at his phone. "They found a body down by the docks last night. Looks like I'll be working the scene most of the day."

Cara hadn't heard anything about a body, but she tried to avoid the news. She didn't need more reminders of how ugly the world could be. A rumble of shame burrowed into her belly. She'd been so eager to meet with James, she'd forgotten about the lunch plans with her husband.

"The closer we get to summer, the more calls we get. Sadly." He put away his phone. "Maybe we can plan something for next week."

"It's a date," she said, followed by an artificial smile. "I'm slammed with work, anyway."

He watched her for a few minutes, and she didn't like the feeling of his eyes on her. In the past, his gaze had admired her. Now, his stare asked too many questions. He could probably tell she was lying about something. It wouldn't be the first time in the past year she'd blamed her busy schedule on work. Or lied. She had to quit using work as an excuse; sooner or later he'd expect to see a finished product, and there wasn't one.

Cara turned in the direction of her study, but Tate stopped her, pulling her back to him. He kissed the top of her head.

"I love you."

It was obvious Tate was missing her, needing reassurance about their relationship. Cara wanted to apologize for being such a shitty wife, for not taking the time to consider his needs or wants.

"Be safe," she said instead.

Their relationship hadn't always been this way. She knew Tate believed she'd withdrawn so much in the past year because of her grief. He didn't know the real reason. She wasn't mourning her father's death, but the life she never knew he had.

Not even two minutes later, a fist pounded against the front door. She assumed Tate had forgotten his keys, giving her a chance to tell him she was sorry for her behavior, but her hopes plummeted when she opened the front door and saw Tate's car was gone. Elias stood on their front porch.

"Morning, Cara," he said, his gums visible when he smiled. He ran a hand through his hair.

Cara held the door tighter, disappointed Tate was gone and Elias was in his place. "How've you been, Elias?"

"Good, good." He looked up and down the street. "I was in the neighborhood and thought I'd pop in. Haven't seen you girls for a while."

"We're fine," she said, keeping a firm hold on the door.

She could tell he wanted an invitation inside, but Cara wasn't up for a visit, even though she pitied him. Her father had been his only friend, and the past year had likely been difficult on him too, although for different reasons.

"Looks like you've done well looking after the place," he said, eyeing the flower bushes skirting the front windows, the mowed lawn. All credit was due to the gardening service she'd hired, not herself.

"Thanks. You know, it would be nice to catch up, but I have work—"

He raised his hands before she could finish. "I understand. I don't want to bother you. I was just in the neighborhood."

Cara didn't think that was true. Elias lived on the outskirts of town, closer to the woods. And she doubted he knew anyone else in this area. He was probably lonely, which made her pity him more. He started to walk down the porch steps, then turned back.

"Say, I did want to ask you. Have you and the girls decided what you're going to do about the cabin?"

"What do you mean?"

"I got a phone call about renting the place. I didn't even know the listing was still online. Henry used to handle the technical stuff. When your father was alive..." He stopped and winced. "Henry trusted me to look after the place and arrange renters throughout the year. We could start renting out again. I'd take care of everything."

"We've still not decided what to do with it." It was the truth. It was one of those lingering responsibilities that fell to the wayside in the wake of her father's death, following the revelation that he was a serial killer.

"Just let me know. You girls might like the extra money the place brings in." He paused. "Henry would want me to keep an eye on you girls. And I could use the work."

Was he desperate for a job or more time with them? It was hard to tell. Either way, Cara felt sorry for him. She ended the conversation as gently as possible, letting out a sigh of relief when he was gone.

Cara was alone again. The silence in the house was almost accusatory, daring her to think about topics she'd rather ignore. Tate. James. Elias. Her sisters.

Dad.

It was all too much to think about, and she longed for a distraction.

SEVENTEEN

CARA

A half hour later, Cara had put on makeup for the first time all week. She wore a black dress covered in small white flowers. The fabric pulled with the wind as she crossed the street in front of the Railway Hotel.

It was one of the nicer establishments on the far end of town. That's why Cara suggested James stayed there. He was based in Boston. They'd met, like most people do these days, online. He came to Whitehill for the occasional conference, and, of course, to meet Cara. They'd spent weeks chatting online before meeting in person, and even though it was yet another secret she had to keep, she did. James had been her only ray of light in the dark, dark year.

James was sitting in a booth at the back of the hotel bar. He stood when he saw her walk in, and the two hugged, clinging to each other as though the embrace could somehow counteract the time they'd spent apart.

"Have time for another drink?" She fiddled with her fingers. James still made her nervous after all this time.

"Sure. My car will be here within the hour." He flagged over a waitress and ordered two glasses of red wine, their usual.

"Nervous about the flight?"

"Nah, I'm getting used to it now." He blushed. "I guess I'm just bummed about going our separate ways."

Cara smiled. "I know what you mean. Sometimes there's not much to return to in the real world." That's how her meetups with James felt. Like an intermission from reality.

The waitress returned, first putting down two cardboard coasters, then their glasses of wine. As Cara reached for her drink, her gaze stretched across the room. She spotted a woman hovering by the entrance to the dining hall. She was in her forties with short hair and a purple pantsuit. There was a week-ender bag hanging from her shoulder as she spoke with the hostess.

Cara recognized her instantly.

"Shit." She moved so that her face wouldn't be visible.

"What is it?" James asked.

"I know that woman standing by the hostess stand."

James looked over her shoulder, trying to glimpse the woman. "Know her how?"

"She's my old boss." Cara cut her eyes across the restaurant, looking for possible exits. "Do you think we can move this to the patio?"

"Sure," James said, grabbing his drink, but Cara had already left the table. She was marching ahead of him, pushing through the double glass doors leading outside.

"Is everything okay?" James asked, once he'd caught up to her.

"Yeah. I wasn't expecting to see anyone I know. Looks like she's back in town." She looked back into the restaurant. The woman was out of sight, and Cara sighed in relief. "Beverley was my old editor at the newspaper, and she wasn't a very good one. She's the reason I ended up leaving, actually. She left me and the rest of the team to do all the hard work, while she took all the credit."

"And then she moved away?" He sat down at one of the wrought-iron tables, and she joined him.

"Well, she copied me first." Cara scoffed, but when James still looked confused, she explained. "She saw that my first book did relatively well, and like I said, she wasn't making many friends down at the paper. She ended up leaving and writing her own true crime book. About Gemini."

She was so busy explaining her history with Beverley that she didn't realize she had uttered the word she vowed to never speak in James' presence. He looked at her quizzically, and she knew she had no chance of bypassing the topic.

"He's like a local legend around here. You've never heard of him?" When he shook his head, she continued. "Gemini is a Whitehill serial killer from the nineties and noughties who was never caught. He's been inactive for years, so his name isn't as known as it once was."

She tried to convey the information without betraying her emotions. Beneath the table, she pinched her forearm to remain focused, fearful the truth would find a way out of her. *Gemini, that monster, is my father.*

James could never know. No one could.

"That's wild." James said it in a way you would expect anyone to react to a random piece of trivia. There was some interest, but not a true investment. He was still looking through the doors leading to the restaurant, as though Beverley might reappear.

"Was her book any good?"

"I guess. *Written in the Stars.*" Cara rolled her eyes. "It's not half bad, except she, like the rest of the world, doesn't know who Gemini actually is."

For a brief moment, Cara relished the fact she held the answers Beverley so desperately sought, but it passed quickly, and she was filled again with shame. "Do you think we could talk about something else?"

"I'd prefer to, actually. Talking about this stuff gives me the creeps."

"That's how my mom was, too. She'd rather get lost in a musical or comedy than anything scary." Cara laughed, taking another sip of her drink, letting the alcohol ease her nerves. She noticed James still appeared on edge. "What's wrong?"

He didn't answer right away. "The way you acted when you saw that woman... you couldn't wait to run off. Like you were embarrassed of me, or something."

"I'm not embarrassed," she said, knowing, even as the words left her lips, they sounded false. "Beverley knows I'm married. It wouldn't look right."

He nodded, mockingly. "That it wouldn't."

"I'm sorry I overreacted—"

"It's fine, really. I guess I should be used to it by now."

"Look, this hasn't been easy on me either. But this is a small town. People talk. I don't want something getting back to Tate or my sisters without me telling them first."

"*If* you tell them." He looked away, apparently regretting the words he'd let slip.

"I'm going to tell them, okay? Now isn't the right time."

"It's just hard being on the other side. I don't like feeling like I'm your secret."

"You won't be for much longer, okay? I promise."

He reached across the table, placing his hand over hers. "This isn't how I wanted to end our time together. I shouldn't have brought it up."

But the fact that he did spoke to how he truly felt. James was tired of being some guy she met at a hotel twice a month. He wanted to be part of her life. When she smiled back at him, it only hurt a little. The truth about James would come out eventually.

All secrets do.

EIGHTEEN

RACHEL

Rachel's head hurt before she even opened her eyes. Memories from last night were blurry, but she knew she had passed out in between episodes of *Friends*. She tasted a hint of whiskey on her gums, which made her nauseous and hungry at the same time.

There was a knock on the door, followed by a voice.

"You alive?" It was Ryan, her roommate.

"Barely." She pulled the pillow over her head, blocking out the intruding sun.

"The fridge calendar says your shift starts in an hour."

Fuck. She'd forgotten about that in the middle of last night's bender. It's not like it would have really mattered. She was used to going into work hungover.

"Yeah, yeah. I'll be out in a sec."

She rolled into the center of the bed and stared at the ceiling, allowing her memories to come back. What Chandler and Joey were up to. What she and Ryan had laughed about last night. Then, further back. The hurt on Katelyn's face during the breakup. The punch to the gut that was knowing her father was a serial killer.

She entered the shower, allowing the water to wake her and erase her at the same time. That's all she did these days, it seemed. Find new ways to forget. New drugs and old drinks and constant stimulation. She relied on the sensations of the present to remove the pain of the past.

She'd tried to act normal in the months that followed her father's death, and Katelyn tried her best to support Rachel through her grief. But then there were those quiet moments. Late nights and early mornings. Afternoons when Katelyn would be at work and Rachel wouldn't and all those dark thoughts would creep into her brain. Memories of the shed and her sisters and the smell of fire. It was too much. It was too *loud*. She had to drown out her thoughts, which is why she'd started drinking more. Smoking more. Relying a little too heavily on prescription medication.

After she tugged on a pair of distressed jeans and a black crew neck speckled with lint, she joined Ryan in the kitchen. He was sitting at the breakfast bar staring at his phone, his square-framed glasses balancing on the bridge of his nose. He had a soda in one hand, and another on the counter beside him.

"That one mine?" she asked, her damp hair drenching her shirt.

"Yep."

"You're too good to me."

"For what you charge me to stay here, it's the least I can do." He smiled. "There's a sandwich on the counter, too."

She ripped open the wrapper and took a bite. She hadn't realized how hungry she was until she tasted the flaky goodness in her mouth. For a brief moment, she was thankful Katelyn was gone and a conscientious Ryan had taken her place. Of course, it wasn't just the two of them living there. There was also—

"Who used all the hot water?"

The shriek came from their third roommate, Cindy. Ryan

was right; Rachel cut him way too good a deal on rent and she had leased the third bedroom to make up the difference. It was a decision she regretted almost immediately, and she was now counting the days until their initial agreement was up and she could tell Cindy to move out.

Rachel and Ryan locked eyes, laughing at the sound of Cindy's approaching stomps. When she joined them in the kitchen, she had a pink towel wrapped around her petite frame. Her blonde hair was piled atop her head, held in place with a large green clip.

"I should have guessed." Cindy crossed her arms over her body, nodding at Rachel's damp hair.

"I took a shower," Rachel said. "Big deal."

"I take a quick, normal shower. Not one of those marathons you take just to wake up after last night's bender."

Rachel rolled her eyes and took another bite of the sandwich.

"Hey, let's not overreact—" Ryan tried to intervene, but Cindy continued talking.

"I mean, there are three of us sharing one shower. Is it that hard to be considerate of others?"

"I'd just like to add," Ryan said, raising a finger, "I don't have a problem with how long either of you take in the shower."

"That's because you're a guy," Cindy said. "You don't have to worry about being late because your hair isn't dry."

"You sit behind a desk all day," he said. "I highly doubt you need a shower before meeting up with your friends at the bar."

"Stop making excuses for her." She waved a hand toward Rachel. "That's called *enabling*, Ryan. And it's not healthy for her."

"Don't talk about me like I'm not standing right here!" Rachel said. "I'm letting you live in my apartment. I think that's considerate enough."

"It's not charity, Rachel. It's a rental *agreement*." When

Rachel didn't bite, Cindy huffed, pulled her towel tighter and marched toward her bedroom. "Forget it. Thank God for dry shampoo."

Rachel pressed her palms together in mock prayer and looked upward. "Yes, thank God."

Ryan took another sip of his drink, trying not to choke with laughter.

"Here's an idea," he said. "When her lease is up, can I sit in on the next roommate interview?"

"You think I should conduct interviews?" She tilted her head, playfully.

"It might save us headaches in the long run. You can't expect to find a sane person on Craigslist."

"That's where I found you."

"I'm the exception to the rule." He looked down the hallway, lowering his voice. "Cindy is a prime example of why you don't find roommates off the internet."

"Got it." She tapped her temple with a finger. "Thanks for the sandwich, but I gotta run."

"Your hair is still wet."

"It'll dry soon. My standards aren't as high as Cindy's."

"You do know you're a bit of a hot mess, don't you?" he asked, lovingly. Ryan was honest, but gentle, unlike Cindy who liked to shove Rachel's every misstep in her face. He knew Rachel was having a hard time, even if he didn't fully understand why. Like everyone, he assumed she was struggling with the breakup; Rachel's father had never been discussed.

"Yeah, yeah. You can say it." She pointed at the closed third bedroom door. "That bitch can't."

NINETEEN

RACHEL

Rachel started the short walk to McGuire's, her full-time job since she dropped out of graduate school. It was the Friday before Memorial Day, and the bar would be packed. She needed calm before the circus fully unleashed, but she accepted it was good for her to be around people. Too much time alone was when she started thinking about the sad story her life had become over the past year.

She thought about her dad, that sick son of a bitch. He'd spent his adult life torturing victims, toying with police. Now, even in death, he'd found new victims, except this time it was his daughters, tortured by the knowledge of what he'd done.

And she thought about her sisters, how they joined forces against her. She'd been close to them her entire life, but every conversation since that day in the backyard had been strained. The three Martin girls were the only ones in the world who knew the truth about Henry Martin. They were the only ones who knew the true identity of the Gemini killer. Keeping that secret had destroyed her relationships.

With her sisters.

With Katelyn.

With herself.

To cope with what they'd uncovered, her behaviors were on an endless loop, predictable and pathetic. When she wasn't working, she was drinking. And if she wasn't wasted, she was sleeping it off, preparing to start the cycle again.

Groundhog Day.

The movie summed up Rachel's current situation. She often thought of her life in terms of movies, and for that she thanked her mom. Cara was always lost in a book, Molly explored the outdoors, but Rachel, like her mother, was entranced by the cinema.

Her mother was the one who introduced her to classic films: *Casablanca* and *Rear Window* and *Breakfast at Tiffany's*. Rachel loved being transported to a different world. Sure, the world back then could be harder on women, especially women like her, but the films didn't hint at the reality of that, only highlighted the best parts, with vibrant technicolor and witty dialogue.

Margaret Grace had studied film when she was in college. She spent her freshman year planning a move to California, hoping she could land a job working on sets. By her sophomore year, she had met Henry Martin, and her plans changed. At least, that's how she told the story, without any hint of resentment or regret. She was happy with where she ended up. When Margaret Grace talked with Rachel about her father, she'd call him her Cary Grant or Jimmy Stewart. She'd believed wholeheartedly she'd made the right choice. Her mother got the raw end of that deal, and lived her entire life without knowing it.

The sisters had thrown a surprise party for their parents' thirtieth anniversary. They passed around food and drinks, strings of lights twinkling in the branches of the backyard tree. Friends and family gathered, congratulating the couple on the life they'd built together. Rachel felt inspired by her parents that night, especially when she saw the genuine smile on her mother's face. She was a woman in love and at peace. Now when Rachel thought back to that night, she couldn't stop picturing her father's face. That thin smile. He must have felt clever, knowing he'd fooled everyone, including his wife. Henry had used her, their marriage and their children to thwart suspicion from his brutal crimes. Her mother had deserved better. They all did.

And she knew Katelyn deserved better than her, at least the version of herself she'd been since the funeral. She couldn't be honest with Katelyn anymore. First, about her father. Then, about her relationship with her sisters—the couple often spent evenings and weekends with Cara and Molly. She couldn't distance herself from them without telling more little lies to Katelyn. And then there was the drinking and drug use. Katelyn couldn't understand what happened to the woman she loved, and Rachel was reluctant to fill in the blanks.

The last straw came when Rachel dropped out of school. She didn't tell Katelyn about it at first. It wasn't until she started making plans for a graduation celebration that the truth came out.

"I don't understand why you would drop out when you are this close to getting your master's degree," Katelyn had said, once Rachel finally told her.

"You wouldn't understand." Rachel was standing in the kitchen, her back to Katelyn, a fresh glass of whiskey in her hand. "Both your parents are still alive."

Rachel regretted the words as they left her lips. She didn't know why she was this way, why she had to spout off the cruelest remark just to deflect what she was really feeling. Katelyn, to her credit, never fought fire with fire.

"I don't know what you're going through," she said, calmly. "But I've tried to support you through it. I've tried to give you space while you sort through your grief. But this... dropping out of school will wreck your future. It will wreck our future. And it's not what your father would want."

Rachel spun around then, the liquor in her hands splashing onto the counter. "Don't talk to me about my dad. You don't know anything about him!"

How many fights had they had like this in the past six months? Twenty? A hundred? All Rachel knew, was that this argument felt like the last. Katelyn rounded up her things. She stopped briefly at the front door, before walking out for good.

"You're the one I don't know anymore."

And she left Rachel there alone, the room around her filled with secrets screaming so loudly, she thought her head and heart might burst.

A car horn blared as Rachel stepped off the sidewalk. She'd been so lost in thought she hadn't seen the large SUV speeding in her direction. If it hadn't been for the cautious honking of another car, she could have been hit. Her heart started pumping faster, adrenaline spreading through her body. She had to stop letting her father mess with her life. Mess with her head. She was the one who would end up paying the price.

By the time she reached McGuire's, the patio was full of patrons. It was Memorial Day weekend, which meant all hands on deck. The weather had finally peaked, tempting locals to thaw beneath the sun and along the sidewalks. She checked the time—she was ten minutes late. It was happening more often than it wasn't, and she wasn't looking forward to getting cussed about it.

Ivan was a helluva boss. In his mid-fifties, he was short and squat with a bald head and meaty muscles beneath his shirt. He often wore dive bar shirts and cargo shorts, even in winter, not that you'd notice much; his clothes were covered by a white, floor-length apron that belonged in the kitchen, but he wore it around the front-of-the-house anyway.

When Rachel walked inside, he was making drinks, no

doubt the ones she should have been making. She tried to slink in, bracing herself for a sly remark, but it never came. Ivan and the customers sitting at the bar were watching the television in the top right corner of the room. The local news was playing.

A body was found by the docks early this morning. Police haven't confirmed anything yet, but sources are saying the case resembles characteristics of the...

Rachel, like everyone else, was glued to the screen.

Unlike everyone else, she was stifling the urge to scream.

TWENTY

MOLLY

Molly puckered her lips and exhaled, thankful her shift at the Whitehill Hotel had ended. She'd always liked the idea of working in hospitality, but the day-to-day aspects of the job were beginning to bother her. The complaints seemed endless. Rooms were too small and views were too narrow. The soda machines needed restocking and the ice dispenser on floor three was broken. Why couldn't people simply take the good with the bad and go about their day? Their lives could be much, much worse.

She rummaged through her locker, grabbing her belongings.

"Someone's in a hurry," said Fiona. She was another front-desk clerk who had been there almost as long as her. She had long dark hair and makeup that looked like it took half the morning to apply.

"I've got a shift at Chester House."

"I'm heading there, too," Fiona said, sliding a slick coat over her uniform. "Charlie's shift is about to end."

Molly and Charlie volunteered at the animal shelter together. She'd reluctantly introduced him to Fiona three months ago, and the two had been dating ever since. Molly didn't have many friends, and it surprised her that the two people she spent the most time with, Fiona at the Whitehill Hotel and Charlie at Chester House, had a romantic spark.

"Don't you get worn out?" Fiona asked. "I mean, Charlie is only volunteering at Chester House until he finishes his degree. It's like you go from one job to the other."

"It's actually the best part of my day."

"If you say so." She rolled her eyes. "Wait up. I'll walk with."

"Sure," Molly said, holding open the door that led out onto the sidewalk.

Molly and Fiona didn't have much in common, other than Charlie and their jobs. Fiona's life appeared to be filled with people and experiences and excitement. Every Monday, she came in with a new story about the chaos her weekend had brought, although those stories had died down a little bit since she started dating Charlie.

Molly, on the other hand, spent most of her time alone. She had few people in her life these days, which afforded her the opportunity to work overtime and volunteer. As they walked in the direction of Chester House, Fiona babbling about something uninteresting, Molly watched the people who passed. Some looked to be around retirement age, while others were on the other end of the spectrum, lugging strollers and toddlers. There were several people carrying laptops under their arms, likely able to work wherever they pleased. She thought about Cara, the freedom she had as a writer to create her own schedule.

She missed Cara.

And Rachel.

Just two short years ago, Molly had felt content with her life. She had parents who loved her, two sisters always in her corner. When they received their mother's cancer diagnosis, she thought it would be the darkest point in her life. In all their lives. But nothing had been more destructive than what they found in the shed. She missed her sisters, but at least they had their partners.

Molly was all alone.

Suddenly, in the crowd of happy strangers, she spotted a familiar face. Katelyn. She was standing by the crosswalk with another woman. Likely a client. Molly hated to interrupt if she was working, but then there was that pang again. Loneliness. It had been so long since she'd seen Katelyn or Rachel or Cara.

"Just a sec," she told Fiona, who was mid-sentence.

Katelyn saw Molly approaching her and froze, whispering something to her companion. Molly worried she was going to dismiss her, but instead Katelyn held out her arms, initiating a hug.

"What a surprise," Katelyn said.

"I don't mean to interrupt—"

"You're fine." Katelyn seemed nervous, glancing back to the woman she'd left at the corner. "How've you been?"

"Good. Busy." That's what she told people anyway, even if it wasn't true. She added, "When I'm not working, I've been volunteering at an animal shelter. Chester House. I'm headed there now actually."

"I've heard of that place." Katelyn smiled, genuinely. "That sounds right up your alley."

"How's Rachel? I feel guilty about not checking in more often. Maybe she'd like to join me at Chester House. Or you too. We're always trying to recruit new volunteers."

Katelyn opened and closed her mouth. She looked back over her shoulder at the woman. "Rachel and I... we're not together. We've not been together for months."

Molly wasn't expecting that. She felt her cheeks burning and tittered. "Oh. I guess I really have been out of the loop." Then, more seriously, "What happened?"

Katelyn looked down. "You might want to talk to Rachel."

"I know it's not any of my business, but you two were great together. And you always seemed so happy. And—"

She stopped talking when she sensed her words were causing more harm than good. Katelyn looked like she was trying to hold back tears.

"I guess you two really aren't talking, huh?" Katelyn said eventually.

"Not enough, it seems."

"Rachel has some issues. They were just getting too big for me to handle."

"I didn't realize things were so bad."

"I worry about her, Molly. I know the three of you have been struggling since your parents... gosh, I can't even imagine. But I really worry about her."

Molly knew that losing their parents wasn't what was tearing Rachel up inside. What was destroying all of them was something much, much worse.

"I need to call her."

Katelyn looked back at the woman again, who was clearly more than a business associate. She reached for Molly's hand and gave it a squeeze. "I'm really glad I ran into you. I miss you. And Cara. And—"

She stopped talking.

"Good seeing you too."

Molly stood there, watching as Katelyn walked away. Within seconds, there was a smile on Katelyn's face as she resumed conversation with the blonde.

So, that's what it looked like to move on. To keep living.

"What was that?" Fiona asked. Her voice was casual, but her eyes were wide, her senses recognizing drama was afoot.

"Nothing." Molly wasn't used to having people she could vent to, but maybe that was part of the problem. Maybe if she wanted more people in her life, she needed to learn to open up. "She's my sister's girlfriend. Or ex-girlfriend, I should say."

"Is that a good thing or a bad thing?"

"Bad because I really liked her, and worse because I had no idea they'd broken up. I made a total ass of myself, or my sister. I'm not sure which."

"Give your sister a call. Check in on her."

Fiona was all about clearing the air. And Molly knew she was right. She'd been close with her sisters her entire life. Only the events of the past year had pushed them apart. It was time for them to start rebuilding their relationships with one another.

It's what their parents would have wanted.

TWENTY-ONE

MOLLY

Sure enough, when they arrived outside Chester House, Charlie was there, taking out the trash. Charlie clanged the lid on top and turned to see Molly and Fiona walking his way. He smiled.

"Thank God," he said. "I thought I was going to be stuck with Marsha all night."

Marsha was their supervisor, twice their age with half their manners. She had a good heart, otherwise she wouldn't be there, but her abrasiveness was part of the reason Charlie and Molly had become such close friends.

"And you," he said to Fiona, in a fake authoritative voice, "are you the newest volunteer?"

"Please," she said, leaning in for an embrace. "Like I have time to sit around and play with puppies all day." She looked at Molly. "No offense."

Charlie gave Fiona a kiss on the lips, but she grabbed his head, kissing him harder.

Molly winced in disgust. She didn't want Charlie for herself, but suspected Fiona wasn't really Charlie's type, whatever that was. She also sensed Fiona was insecure, and even though the friendship between Charlie and Molly was strictly platonic, Fiona was marking her territory with saliva and tongue.

When Charlie came up for air, he looked at Molly and blushed. Like her, he was an introvert and likely not used to public displays of affection, especially with someone as beautiful as Fiona.

"You ready to head out?" Fiona asked.

"Actually, I just got here."

"I thought you worked the dayshift?"

"That was yesterday. I'll be here until ten."

"Oh bummer," Fiona said. "I've been missing you."

"Hey, it's a long weekend. We'll have plenty of time together."

"Say, I'm free after my shift ends," Molly said, her tone upbeat. "Maybe we could go out for drinks? I hear the Mexican restaurant down the street is having two for one margaritas."

She'd done more than merely hear it. She'd stalked the Facebook page, trying to work up the nerve to ask someone to go with her. She'd ask Charlie, but he didn't drink.

"Eh, I've been feeling a cold coming on. I'll probably down some NyQuil and get in bed early." She looked back at Charlie, before walking off. "I'll call you later."

Molly waved goodbye, thankful Fiona was so self-involved she hadn't noticed how much the rejection stung. Fiona wasn't really her type either, but it had been a long time since Molly had a true friend.

Charlie, on the other hand, noticed the awkwardness and tried to smooth over the conversation.

"I'm happy you're here," he said. "I wanted to give you a hard time about something."

"Don't tell me. Marsha has a new idea."

"Better. Or worse. Depending on how you look at it." Charlie leaned against the building and folded his arms. He smiled. "You were supposed to be my official tour guide of the area."

"Please, tell me what I've missed."

"You didn't tell me this place had its very own serial killer."

A strange heat started at the back of her neck, spreading its warmth across her ears and cheeks. "What?"

"Gemini? That's all people are talking about today."

Molly could feel her heart beating faster. She inhaled through her nose, trying to steady her breathing. "Who... why would anyone be talking about *that*?"

"Apparently he struck again. The police found a body by the lake," he said, making a point to look over his shoulder. "To think, I've been walking around the neighborhood all alone at night, and you didn't even give me a warning."

He was only kidding with her. He wasn't asking about Gemini because he knew, she realized, although her stumbling reaction probably struck him as odd. He'd been asking because there was a new victim. Another murder committed by Gemini.

But that couldn't be. And only the Martin girls knew it.

TWENTY-TWO

CARA

After leaving the Railway Hotel, Cara returned home. She was ready for another predictable day of staring at a blank document, words refusing to come. She turned on the news, curious to see if there was information about the body found at the docks. And that's when she saw it.

The banner at the bottom of the screen read: *Has Gemini Returned? Body Found at Whitehill Lake.*

She blinked several times, rubbed her forehead, then looked again. The words were still there, and her body felt like it was about to overheat. Gemini couldn't have returned because he was dead, but there were only three people in the entire world who knew it.

She spent the rest of the afternoon gathering information about the latest crime, which wasn't much, and comparing it to what she did know, which was a lot.

The victim was a female in her thirties, whose name hadn't been released. She was found by the docks, left on the sand for an early morning walker to find. Based on the way the body was positioned, and considering the holiday weekend, more than one outlet was claiming the return of Gemini.

Sure, the media loved a story, and a dormant serial killer renewing his killing spree was a good one. Cara had built her career off good stories, but she knew the press wouldn't announce Gemini was the culprit this early in the investigation unless they had overwhelming proof.

Cara padded back to the office, notes in hand. She unlocked the bottom drawer of her desk. Inside were the pictures they'd found in the shed after their father's funeral. It wasn't all of them, of course. Most of them had been thrown into the fire, Molly's way of stopping Rachel from going to the police.

But the journalist inside Cara couldn't stand the idea of watching the only evidence linked to an unidentified serial killer turn into ashes. The jewelry was unsalvageable, but there were dozens of pictures of the victims. When Molly wasn't looking, Cara had taken some of them and hidden them in the shed. Later, after her sisters had gone home, she'd gotten them back out and hidden them in her father's office. For a year, she'd been studying them, trying to make sense of the crimes he had committed.

The night of their father's funeral, she only knew the broad facts about Gemini, but she'd uncovered much more since then. Seventeen victims spanning twenty years. All were women in their late twenties to mid thirties. The women were petite and thin, although not necessarily fit. If you were to see one of them walking down the sidewalk, you'd probably think they were attractive but not capable of fighting back. That's what Gemini must have thought, anyway. Most, but not all, were brunettes.

Millie Rothenberg, found in the mall parking lot, was a blonde. Savannah Christiansen, found on the elementary school grounds where she worked, was a redhead. Everyone says killers have a type, but sometimes that type is the right person at the wrong time.

Victimology didn't connect the women, but their manner of death did. All were stabbed multiple times, the final slash cutting across their necks. This was what first connected them in investigators' minds. Most killings took place at night; all bodies were posed in a public place to be found in the light of day. In most cases, like Savannah Christiansen, they were left in a location that bore some meaning to the victim, which suggested Gemini spent time scoping out his prey. The additional pictures they'd found in the shed confirmed this theory.

And each woman was missing an important piece of jewelry. If they were married, it was usually their wedding ring. If they weren't, it was another significant accessory. Necklaces or bracelets with birthstones, class rings. Janet Lane, found downtown in an alley, had been wearing a necklace with a sparrow pendant. The same one Cara held in her hands the night they raided the shed.

After interviewing the known associates of each victim, it seemed none of the women had reported odd occurrences in the weeks leading up to their death. No stalkers. No strange phone calls. No evidence someone had tampered with their homes. Many of the women were surrounded by people in the moments leading up to their death, but for whatever reason, they ended up alone. Donna Winters had gotten into a fight with her boyfriend and stormed off before she was snatched. Penny Mayweather opted to walk home the night of her death, declining a ride from a friend, because she wanted to enjoy the moon.

All these women, their stories, their desires had been squelched by the same monster.

Gemini.

Henry Martin.

And now there was another woman to add to the list, although it was impossible.

But there had to be a reason the media believed Gemini was back. A letter. That must be it. Someone must have sent a letter claiming to be Gemini. Although the police weren't taunted after every kill, Gemini was known for goading law enforcement. In all the times Cara had wrestled with the fact her father had committed these crimes, never once did she question whether he was capable of sending the letters. It reeked of her father's superiority. Henry Martin always had to be the smartest person in the room.

She heard footsteps on the front porch. The clock on her desk said it was after seven o'clock. She'd spent her entire afternoon sifting through evidence, coming up empty, and now Tate was home.

She only had a few minutes to hide everything. She gathered the pictures of Gemini's victims, the close-ups of each woman's swollen cheeks and open necks, and stuffed them in the bottom drawer of her desk, twisting the lock with a key. She shut down Excel and Word, hiding the timelines she'd made of the victims' deaths and the maps of where their bodies had been found. She slid her corkboard, covered in more evidence and handwritten notes on index cards, behind the large bureau.

By the time Tate entered the study, the only item left on the desk that had any connection to the Gemini case was a picture of Henry Martin with his daughters. It had sat there for many years—moving it now would be suspicious.

As soon as he was within earshot, she asked, "Do they think it's really Gemini?"

Tate leaned against the doorframe. The top buttons of his shirt were undone. "There are a lot of similarities, but we can't say for sure."

"What do you think?"

"I'm on the fence."

Tate knew almost as much as she did about Gemini. Nothing would thrill her husband more than to be the person responsible for nabbing him, and the fact that would never happen had been something she couldn't face telling him. It was one of the biggest unsolved mysteries in the area. *Almost* unsolved.

"The victim was stabbed?"

"Yes." He sighed. "Her throat was slit. And it appears her wedding ring has been stolen."

He paused, his professional reluctance getting in the way. Most husbands on the force talked as little as possible about their cases to their wives. Legally, they weren't supposed to say anything at all. But Cara and Tate's relationship always existed, even originated, in a gray area. He talked to her, only withholding information that could hinder an ongoing investigation. If the media had already caught wind of something, it was fair game.

"Her body was left in an area that was special to her," he added.

"The docks?"

"She and her husband owned a boat rental company. Spent most of their time on the water."

"Is anyone looking at the husband?"

"Of course. It's unlikely he's involved, though. He was out of town when the murder took place. All anyone seems to be talking about is Gemini." He said it like he wasn't quite convinced. Tate was a good detective, and even though Cara couldn't tell him he was right, she admired him for not taking the bait as easily as everyone else. Most people wanted the glory of solving a high-profile case, but Tate wanted to get it right.

"Was there a note?"

A small smile crept across his face. He clearly admired her background knowledge. He didn't have to waste much time filling her in.

"It wasn't like one of the old ones, which makes me skeptical. He didn't send it to the police station. He tacked it to the body."

"The body?"

"Left it pinned to her coat. It said, 'He's back from the grave.'"

Cara stopped breathing, or rather, the air seemed to have been sucked from her lungs. When she did speak, her words were weak. "It said what?"

"He's back." Tate paused, waving his hands to signify he was moving on to the next part of the sentence. "From, the grave. That was the sign-off. It's like the vic was telling us 'He's back.'"

Cara's pulse slowed, but only slightly. That full sentence, *He's back from the grave*, startled her. How could anyone else know that? But if it was written a different way, *He's back—from, the grave*, it took on a different meaning.

"Gemini didn't talk like that in his letters."

"I know, which is why I'm skeptical. If the *He's back* is some kind of threat, I guess we'll have to wait and see what his next move is."

Cara pressed her lips together and looked away. *He's back from the grave.* Was it a different kind of message? One meant for her? She felt an uncontrollable rage at the fact there was nothing anyone could do but sit back and wait for this guy to make another move.

"Are you thinking copycat?" she asked.

"Could be. There are enough inconsistencies already to suggest that, but who knows? Maybe the real guy decided to change things up. Make a dramatic reappearance."

"Maybe." Cara knew it wasn't true. The real Gemini, Henry Martin, was dead. All that remained of him was the blood pumping through his daughters' veins.

"The victim," she said. "What was her name?"

"Margaret Grace Fulton." Tate looked alarmed when Cara stood abruptly. "What is it?"

"Margaret Grace." She repeated the words back to him.

"Yeah. Did you know her?"

"No, but that's Mom." She looked away, her breaths growing more ragged. "I mean, it's Mom's name. Margaret Grace Martin."

"Oh yeah." He settled down, still taken aback by his wife's sudden reaction. "I guess I didn't catch that."

His phone beeped, and Cara quickly looked away.

"This is the boss," Tate said under his breath, walking into the other room.

She hadn't meant to react so suddenly, but hearing her mother's name associated with this case was something she wasn't expecting. She needed to be careful. Between the note left on the body—*He's back from the grave*—and the victim's name—Margaret Grace—Cara feared this was more than a random murder.

Gemini wasn't killing people, but the person who was might be sending a message.

To them.

Cara grabbed her phone and sent out a text to her sisters. She seemed to scroll for ages before finding their group chat. It had been that long since they all talked.

Have you seen the news?

TWENTY-THREE

RACHEL

Rachel sensed something falling over her head, but it didn't alarm her. The startle came seconds later, when she felt a hand smacking against her cheek.

"Wake up. It's past noon."

Groundhog Day.

But she didn't have to work today; this was supposed to be her chance to sleep in. And she wasn't getting a wake-up call from her roommates. Rachel would know that uppity voice anywhere. Cara.

"How did you get into my apartment?"

"Your roommate let us in," Molly said. "One of them, anyway. She told us you have a guy living here, too. Since when do you have roommates?"

"Where's Katelyn?" Cara asked.

"They broke up," Molly said.

"Since when?"

"Can you guys stop asking so many damn questions?" Rachel sat up in the bed, giving the room a tired once-over. It looked so strange seeing her sisters here, in this dark, dingy place. "Since when do you two just show up?"

"Since you stopped returning our calls," Cara said.

"I've not talked to either of you in weeks—"

"Have you seen the news?" Cara cut her off.

A beat of silence. All the sisters looked at each other, daring not to breathe.

"Yes, I've seen the news," Rachel said, pulling the covers off her legs. She stood, slowly walking across the room, her limbs struggling to reach wakefulness.

"Then why didn't you respond to our messages?" Molly asked.

"I didn't get off until late. Then, I don't know." The thing was, she really didn't. She remembered coming home, hanging out with Ryan. She poured another drink and everything blurred together.

"We need to talk about Gemini."

Cara had no trouble saying the word. Molly flinched. Rachel marched toward the door, making sure it was shut properly.

"Can you keep it down? As you said, I have roommates now."

"Who are they?" asked Molly.

"I found them off Craigslist."

Cara scoffed. "Really? Dump Katelyn for some strangers you found online. You're really on a roll with the decision making."

"You don't know what you're talking about—"

"I know your whole room smells like booze and weed." She waved her hand over the cluttered desk in the corner of the room. "You've got enough pill bottles to start a pop-up pharmacy."

"I have prescriptions for that—"

"All of it?"

She didn't have to respond. They both knew the answer.

"Between Katelyn leaving and Dad *dying*, I'm going through a rough time right now. Okay?"

"We're not here to fight," Molly said. As usual, she adopted the role of peacemaker whenever the older two started bickering. "We're here to talk about Dad."

It was interesting how each of them chose to look at the same situation. Cara wanted to talk about *Gemini*. Molly wanted to talk about *Dad*; she seemed to be the only one who still thought of their father fondly. Rachel didn't want to talk about any of it.

"I saw the television reports, but I tried to avoid it, really." Rachel sighed, sitting on the corner of the mattress. "Gemini was a name I was hoping I'd never have to hear again."

"As of this morning, every local news station is reporting the Gemini killer is back. Even a few national stations, too," Cara said, her tone taking on that of a reporter in a newsroom. "I'm still hoping it's a fluke, but the press wouldn't claim Gemini was back without having solid proof. I even saw Beverley Quinn yesterday."

"Really?" Molly asked. "Where?"

"Just out in town." Cara averted her eyes.

"What proof could they have?" Rachel asked. "The Gemini killer is dead."

"We know that," Cara said. "No one else does. And there's more. I talked to Tate last night..."

Rachel and Molly listened as Cara told them about the missing wedding ring and the note found on the body. *He's back from the grave.* And her concern that the victim had the same name as their mother.

"What are you saying?" Rachel asked. "That you think this person is trying to get our attention?"

"Don't you?"

A year ago, Cara had been the one most determined to drop the subject. Now, she was being the most vocal about discussing what the re-emergence of Gemini meant. Rachel didn't want to think about another murdered woman or her father. She wanted to get back to the life she'd been living, as pathetic as it was.

"If we'd gone to the police about what we found in the shed, none of this would be happening." She waited for Cara to respond, but all Cara did was clench her jaw and look away. Rachel continued, "I don't think we're being targeted. You're reading into this because of what we already know. It's a trick of the mind. Some psycho fan is trying to copy Gemini. That's all."

"You could be right," Cara said, but her voice was unconvincing. "The case was big enough for someone to want extra press."

Molly's eyes boomeranged between her sisters. "Is that really what you two are thinking? That it's a copycat. Or they're just wrong about the similarities."

Rachel shrugged. "That's what it has to be."

"What about the third option?" Her voice was desperate. "Dad is innocent."

Silence again. Rachel looked at Cara, who was staring at her in the same way. They were debating which of them should break the news to Molly. Cara lost the battle.

"I don't think that's it," she said, her tone soft. "There's no denying Dad was Gemini."

"What do you mean?" Molly's tone was somewhere between a laugh and a cry. "More bodies turning up seems like proof to me. Why are you still so convinced?"

"Because of the pictures. The evidence." Cara was stammering now, each phrase ramming into the next. "I've created timelines. We were out of town each time there was a murder. And the years he couldn't have killed anyone, there were no murders."

"But there could be another explanation. Maybe Dad knew

who the killer was. Maybe he was researching it himself. He was always into local folklore."

"Those pictures weren't research," Rachel said, sensing Cara needed the break. "They were keepsakes."

Molly's breath was shaky. "I know what we found in the shed. I can't forget it. I just don't know why you two can't accept the possibility that the man we knew was real, too. That he was more than what was in that shed. I don't know why you can't give him the benefit of the doubt."

"How can we, Molly? If there was another plausible theory —" Rachel said.

"We've just been given one! The media. The police. They both think Gemini is the killer, which means it couldn't have been Dad," Molly cried. "If you're so convinced Dad did this, what is there to even talk about?"

"I thought the details of the murder were suspicious. And I wanted to check in," Cara said. "None of us have stayed in touch in the past year. I thought this would bring up memories and... I wanted to know that we were okay."

"Yeah, I'm great." Molly slung her purse over her shoulder and headed out of the room. "Nice talk, guys."

Rachel took a step after her. "Wait, we didn't—"

The front door to the apartment slammed shut, cutting her off. With Molly gone, there wasn't anything left to say.

"I did not see that coming." Cara sounded defeated.

"Maybe we should have. We're all dealing with this in our own ways, but she's the one suffering the most from denial."

Cara's eyes wandered across the room to the assorted pill bottles covering Rachel's desk. "And the way you're dealing with it. How's that going?"

Rachel tightened her jaw. "Don't worry about me."

"Do you want to talk about Katelyn?"

"Did I call you about it?"

Cara rolled her eyes. "I wanted to check on you. On both of you. It's not like us to go months without talking."

"It just hurts, you know? We can't be around each other without thinking about Dad. And whenever I think about him, I..."

She didn't want to finish the sentence, or even know how. All she knew was that feeling she tried to avoid was consuming her.

"I know it hurts to think about him," Cara sympathized, "but we're the only ones we have left." She looked at the front door where Molly had just left. "Do you think I should go after her?"

"Give her some time to cool down. She always needs that."

Cara nodded, taking one more look around Rachel's room. "Clean this place up. It looks like shit."

Rachel waited for her sister to turn before slipping her the finger, then she fell back on the mattress, and stared at the ceiling.

A minute later, the door opened again, but this time it was Cindy.

"Those your sisters?"

"Yeah."

"Huh." She looked toward the front door. "They almost seem normal."

"Get out of my room," Rachel said, turning on her side.

"Not until you tell me what happened to my leftovers."

"What the hell are you talking about?"

Cindy slowed her tone, as though talking to a child. "I had food in the fridge. It had my name on it. And now it's gone."

"Well, I'm not the only one who lives here."

"But you're the only one who doesn't have respect for my things."

She had the faint memory of Ryan coming home, sharing a

drink with her on the sofa while they watched an episode of *Key & Peele*. She remembered laughing, the spicy taste of noodles and sickly singe of more beer washing it down. Had Ryan brought her food? Or was Cindy right, and she'd raided the fridge?

"I don't know, Cindy," she admitted, shamefully. "I'm sorry."

"Wow." She laughed. "That's just sad."

Rachel sat up, propelled by embarrassment and lack of sleep, and hurled a pillow across the room. Cindy slammed the door before it could hit her.

TWENTY-FOUR

MOLLY

The fresh air did little to calm Molly's frustrations. Her hands were so shaky, when she pulled her phone from her purse, she almost dropped it. She scrolled through Instagram, looking for something superficial to clear her mind. The first image she saw was a picture of Fiona out with friends last night. Guess she found a second wind after all.

Yet another betrayal. Molly couldn't remember feeling this lonely before. She'd always been an introvert, preferring to have a small circle of quality friends, but most of them had fallen off over the years. Nothing major happened. Just college, then graduation, then embarking on new careers. For some, there had been marriages and children. People outgrow each other, but it didn't matter, because she had two built-in friends for life: Rachel and Cara.

Typical sibling spats and their hormonal teenage years aside, they'd always found their way back to each other. They clung together in the wake of their mother's death. She'd thought they'd do the same after their father died, but it wasn't his death that had torn them apart. It was his life. What he'd done. *If* he'd done it, Molly thought, hopefully.

She checked the time. Great, she'd wasted her lunch break talking with her sisters, and they weren't even willing to listen. They had made up their minds. It was easy for them to accept that their father was a serial killer, to let a box of pictures erase all their other memories of the man.

Easy wasn't the best word. Maybe *easier*. She knew Rachel had been struggling. Katelyn had told her, and after being inside her dank bedroom, it was clear her sister was falling apart. She should have been more alarmed when Rachel decided to leave school. The breakup with Katelyn was the most recent sign; a year ago it wouldn't have surprised her if the two ran off and got married. Now they weren't even together. The contents of the shed had taken their toll. She feared her sister's mental state was deteriorating.

As far as Molly could tell, Cara wasn't holding up much better, even if she was able to put on a more convincing front. She rarely received invitations to her house for dinner, an occurrence that took place almost weekly a year ago. When Molly did talk to Cara, Tate was never mentioned. And where exactly had Cara been yesterday? She believed her sister had cracks in her marriage, and in her life beyond that, but was too stubborn to admit it.

And all her working. *Working, working, working.* She'd not had a book release since before their parents died, and there wasn't one on the calendar. She figured Cara spent most days and nights researching their own father. That's how she operated.

Although she couldn't deny the proof against him, Molly had never wanted to accept their father was a killer. He was a loving father, and none of his other mistakes could erase that. She knew the true Henry, and Gemini was nothing more than an ugly mask he wore, not the other way around. She'd learned to separate the two in her mind.

But now? Another body had turned up, and, if Cara was

right, another letter written by the killer. Sure, it could be a copycat after all this time. Or an over-keen news reporter who floated an idea without evidence. But maybe, just maybe, their father wasn't Gemini after all.

Molly had always been closest to her father. When Cara was busy reading and Rachel was off watching movies with Mom, the two of them would spend time together. He taught her how to hunt when she was ten. Showed her how to read the forest, tune into nature. And it wasn't killing that he stressed to her, but respect. Respect for these animals and the circle of life, in a cheesy *Lion King* sense. This earth and these creatures are our responsibility, and they repay that debt by replenishing our bodies, and on a deeper level, our souls. She carried that message with her, even to this day.

The first time she made a kill—a doe sampling berries in a nearby bush—she cried. Before she pulled the trigger, her emotions were upbeat, her pulse pounding beneath her flesh. But once she pulled the trigger, and watched the animal dart off in fright, she was heartbroken. Ashamed. An activity based on such cruelty couldn't be right.

They followed the trail of blood that painted the leaves and grainy earth. When they found the doe, wide-eyed and still, the animal appeared at peace. Molly let out a sob. Her father placed his hands on her shoulders.

"It's all right, it's all right," he hummed, pulling her closer. "You didn't do anything wrong."

"It feels wrong," she bleated.

"Then you don't have to do this again. Everyone has a different reaction their first time, but I'm proud of you."

And hearing those words, knowing she'd made her father proud, wiped away her shame. And more memorable, was his tenderness in that moment. How could the same person who embraced a crying child be responsible for stabbing over a dozen women to death? It was possible, sure. But Molly didn't want it to be true, and as long as there were other options to explore, she would. The fact someone else was claiming to be Gemini proved she should have trusted her initial reaction all along.

She walked back into the Whitehill Hotel, nodding at customers as they passed. In the center of the room was a circular registration desk divided by three partitions. She stood at the middle desk, checking her email to see if she'd missed anything important while on break.

Not ten minutes passed before a man approached. She didn't know him by name, but she recognized his face. He was one of their repeat guests. Usually did work in town twice a month. He'd earned a reputation for making ridiculous requests and talking down to employees.

"We've got a problem," he said.

Molly put on her most professional smile. "How may I help you—"

"My key card won't work. It's not worked since I got here. All my stuff is in my room, and if I don't get in there, I'm going to be late to a meeting."

"Room number?"

"208."

"We'll fix that for you right away."

"I don't know if you get it," the man continued, not ready to end his tirade. He'd chosen Molly as his target for all his anger at the world. "I'm in this town for business. I have people to meet. This isn't some vacation where I can come and go from my room as I please. I have important commitments, and given the amount of money my company pours into this dump every year, you should be able to make these easy fixes."

Molly kept her eyes on the computer, trying hard not to get flustered. She hated this more than anything, the way people talked down to her. She had a degree in hospitality management and had worked in some of the most prestigious hotels along the east coast, but that wasn't critical at this moment. Getting this person out of her sight was.

"I've reset the code," she said, handing over the new card. "That should take care of everything."

He ripped the card from her hand, and stormed off.

"Is that the guy from 208?" Fiona asked, coming up behind her. The stench of cigarettes clung to her clothes.

"Yep."

"Yeah, he was complaining yesterday about the coffee machine in the lounge. You'd think if his job was so important he could afford a fucking Starbucks."

Molly laughed. "Speaking of which, I feel a craving for caffeine. Cover for me?"

She left the front desk and wandered into the lounge across the way. She actually preferred the coffee at work. She thought it was strong and tasty and liked the mix-ins. Some people were impossible to please.

As she waited on a new batch, she felt her phone buzz in her pocket. She expected it to be one of her sisters offering apologies, but instead it was Ben.

Any plans this week? Thought about catching a movie.

The two had been off and on since college, and he'd been a disappointment since then. He was never around when she needed him—didn't even make it to her dad's funeral—but when he got lonely, or more truthfully, horny, she was the first person he'd call.

She stood there, watching the coffee drip into the pot, questioning whether she should respond, when she heard footsteps behind her.

"Hey, are you the lady from the front desk?" The voice was clipped and gruff, and she didn't have to turn to know it was the guy from 208. "The code you gave me still isn't working."

She turned. "If you go back to the front—"

"I already told you I'm running late. I've wasted another ten minutes with you, and now I'm pissed."

"I'm very sorry for the inconvenience," she said, pouring the coffee into her mug, trying to avoid eye contact. "If you go back to the front desk, we can get you set up in an entirely different room. Sometimes there are mechanical issues—"

"I don't need any excuses. I just don't understand why it's so hard for people to get their shit together."

Holding the mug in her hand, she took a step toward him. With her second step, she feigned tripping, and poured the scalding liquid down the front of the man's torso.

He shrieked in pain.

"What the f—"

"I'm so sorry," she said, putting the mug on the counter and grabbing a wad of paper towels. The man was flapping his hands and panting, then he started pulling at the hot, wet fabric sticking to his skin.

"It's burning," he cried.

"Let me find someone who can help you clean up," she said, walking away before the man had time to respond.

She'd no doubt hear from him several times before he checked out, and she'd probably end up compensating the cost of his room, but it was worth it. Molly smiled.

Sometimes it felt good to inflict pain.

TWENTY-FIVE

When she's not typing on the computer, she's talking on the phone. Back and forth, one device to the next, like a fucking robot. Something that runs off batteries and the brilliance of others, nothing original or organic. Nothing of substance.

She's exactly as I imagined, if not worse. A truly miserable person. When the waitress approaches the table and offers to refill her drink, she brushes her away, as though the poor girl is nothing more than a gnat.

It's clear the restaurant is closing, and yet the woman sits there, making it clear she'll decide when to leave. This is her world, we're all just living in it.

It won't be that way much longer.

At long last, she packs up her bags and prepares to leave. I let her get a few steps in front before I crumple my own paper cup, toss it in the trash and follow her. There are groups of people walking in the opposite direction, away from their cars and closer to the bars with their Saturday night specials. People are reveling in the fact they don't have to work for the next two days, but not her. All she does is work. She's made her career the center of her life, for better and worse, and now it's all she has left.

We've barely walked two blocks before she's on the damn phone again, as though she's a voice of enlightenment, an ambassador to the world. There's nothing unique or important about her. She merely recites what more advanced minds have already summarized. I wonder if she knows that her entire life has amounted to nothing.

People fear death. I used to be one of them. I used to have fears about being hit by a car, being submerged beneath water, being a passenger on an airplane that falls to the ground. Then, I realized death isn't that frightening—it happens to us all, eventually. What's truly terrifying is the amount of people who don't ever live their lives. They never find purpose. They never reach their full potential.

A year ago, my life changed. I vowed to no longer be one of those people. I'm working for something much bigger than myself now, fulfilling my destiny, a cosmic purpose that was handed down to me. I was chosen. Perhaps by the stars.

Unlike the first one, this woman deserves what is coming to her. She has no reason to be afraid because she does not know I'm here. Death comes without warning. There is no grim reaper, just a stranger in the dark.

"Hey," I shout. We've turned the corner, and there's only the two of us standing at the entrance of the alleyway.

The woman turns.

"You dropped something." I bend down, reaching for the sidewalk, although there is nothing there. She looks at whatever precious object she might have left behind, but there's nothing. Just a hand cupping a napkin, now covering her nose and mouth.

Her screams are stifled, her lungs inhaling the noxious liquid on the cloth. By the time I pull her into the alley, she is limp. I wait, making sure no one spotted us.

There is nothing. No one.

Let the fun begin, I think.

And the night rolls on around us.

TWENTY-SIX

CARA

Despite everything going on, Cara could still turn to James, even if it was on the phone. She was relieved he had left White-hill before news of the murder broke. She didn't want to hear him say the word. Gemini. Sometimes she could be like Rachel, too, hoping if she didn't give a topic attention, it would go away.

They mostly talked about family, hers and his. It was nice to revisit the best parts of her life with someone new, leaving out the bad parts.

"Is Tate working tonight?"

She cleared her throat. Tate wasn't a word she enjoyed hearing him say either. And she didn't appreciate how close they were getting to the case she didn't want to think about. "Yeah, he's been covering the same crime scene for the past two days."

James sighed. "I don't see how he deals with stuff like that for a living." He chuckled. "I guess I'm putting my foot in my mouth. You deal with this stuff too, don't you?"

"It's more removed when you're a writer. Seeing pictures and reading accounts isn't the same as being on the scene."

Unless it's your father's victims, she thought. Then it's like you're right there, living each painful moment.

"I do have a surprise," he said, and she could hear the glee through the phone. "My partner at the clinic agreed to cover my appointments so I can have some extra time off. I booked another trip to Whitehill. My flight lands tomorrow night."

"That's great," Cara said, but she wasn't a good actress, and the words came out strained. James being back in Boston meant Cara didn't have to worry about pulling herself away from her own investigation to meet up with him at the Railway Hotel. She didn't need any distractions.

"I guess I should have asked first," he said, having sensed Cara's hesitation. "If you have plans—"

"No, I don't have any plans," she said, correcting herself. "I'd love to see you again." She felt guilty for so much. For making James feel secondary. For hiding the truth about him from Tate and her sisters. Living two lives didn't suit her very well. She wondered how her father had managed to do it for so long.

"I understand. It's not like you can just drop everything whenever I come to town. Maybe you can plan a trip to Boston soon."

"I'd like that. It would be good to get away for a few days."

"You probably wouldn't feel so on edge here."

There was a pause. He was obviously still bruised from earlier, when she'd overreacted to the sight of Beverley Quinn in the hotel lobby. Cara tried to imagine spending time with James in a different city, what it would be like to visit with him without small-town eyes watching their every move. She didn't want him thinking she was constantly trying to hide him, even if she was.

They talked for a while longer, ending the conversation when James decided to go to bed. Outside, she watched as pellets of rain sprayed the windows. She hoped Tate would return home soon; she needed to know if there were any new developments on the Margaret Grace Fulton case. She slid her phone into her back pocket, leaving one life behind, ready to pick up the other.

The next morning, Cara was woken by the screeching of branches against the house and the dropping of rain on the roof. Downstairs, she could hear Tate in the kitchen, likely getting ready for another long day of work. She never heard him climb into bed last night.

It had been two days since Tate received the call about the body by the docks. Two days of infrequent texts and phone calls. Two nights of Tate climbing into bed once Cara was already asleep, leaving again before sunrise.

There was a time when these long absences bothered her. Now she was used to the routine of being a police detective's wife. She knew what their life together would entail when she signed up for it. His job would always be his primary focus, and she was okay with that sacrifice. Tate did important work.

She thought back to when they'd first met. It wasn't long after Cara started writing her first nonfiction book, the one about the murderous wife out in California. It was that book that pushed her to reach out for a source. There'd been a recent poisoning in Whitehill, and she wanted to get a local's take on it, compare it to the one she was writing about.

Her hairstylist's cousin was a newly minted police detective with Whitehill PD, and he agreed to give her a quote. That person ended up being Tate, and less than two years later, they were married.

She winced, thinking back to their wedding day. She'd been happy both her parents had lived to see it. Happy her father had the opportunity to walk her down the aisle, dance with her at the reception, deliver one of his charming speeches to the crowd. He'd always had a gift for pulling people in, a trait he likely used to lure his victims. He clearly had no problems forming a bond with Tate. After raising three daughters, he was thrilled to have a son-in-law, but had any of that affection been real? Looking back, she wondered if her father ever truly cared about him or her or anyone other than himself.

In the kitchen, Tate was pouring the last of the coffee into his to-go canister. When he spotted Cara, he started another pot so she could drink something fresh. It was these moments of consideration that gave her hope their marriage wasn't a complete lost cause.

"Where were you yesterday?" Tate asked, once inside. "I stopped by the house at lunch and you were gone."

"I met up with Rachel," she said. Lying was getting easier, especially if she sprinkled in some truth. She'd seen Rachel, but it definitely wasn't a happy visit.

"You were zonked out by the time I got home. Can't say I blame you. I think it was after two," he said, his voice serious. "There's something I need to tell you."

Cara sat on the sofa, staring up at Tate. A flurry of thoughts whizzed through her mind. James. Gemini. Dad. "What?"

"There was a second victim last night. It's why I'm heading in. The media will probably release a name tonight, but we were trying to keep a hold on it because it's a big deal."

"Who is it?" And why was he making such a show about telling her? Could it be another connection to her?

"It's your old boss," he said, smacking his lips together. "Beverley Quinn."

Cara lowered herself until she was leaned against the back-rest. "Beverley?"

"We didn't know she'd returned to town, but I guess it makes sense if she believed Gemini was back." He waited. "It took us a little longer to confirm the ID. Her face was almost unrecognizable."

But Cara could still see it clearly in her mind. Just the other night, they'd been in the same room, although Cara was quick to duck around the corner. She almost slipped up and told Tate that she'd seen her at the hotel, but she couldn't do that without explaining what she was doing there. And this was not the time to tell him about James.

"Where was she? Where did they find her?"

"In the alleyway behind the *Tribune*. A place significant to the victim."

A place significant to both of them. It's where they'd worked together, before the animosity reached such heights Cara quit.

"Was there a note this time?"

"Not a note from the killer. There was a printout from her book. *Written in—*"

"*—the Stars,*" Cara finished. "She built her career on Gemini, the same person who's taken her out."

"*Someone* has taken her out."

Cara looked at him. Was that a tell? Did he know with certainty, like she did, that this couldn't be the same killer, or was she being paranoid?

"You still think it's a copycat?"

"Hard to say. There's a lot the same, but there's a lot different, too. This person is certainly paying tribute to Gemini, but he's putting his own spin on things."

"Gemini never killed two people so close together."

"I know. It seems important to this guy to get the Gemini name out there. Probably for media attention."

"But Beverley hasn't been in the media."

"Her contact person was out of town, which bought us some time. That person also pointed out Beverley always wore a specific watch. It wasn't found with the body. I'm guessing that's what he took." He sighed. "We thought this was a big story before. Just imagine how wild it will be once word gets out the person who wrote a Gemini book is the latest victim."

"I can't imagine."

"Are you okay? I mean, I know you didn't like her, but it must be weird for you."

"It is."

Her relationship with Beverley had been contentious, even after she left the paper. Her attitude was so fierce, it was hard to imagine her being a victim. And it was even harder because Cara feared Beverley's death was deliberate.

She knew she was no longer being paranoid. This killer was putting his own spin on things, whirling everything in her direction. And now, because she'd chosen to keep her father's secrets, there was blood on her hands.

TWENTY-SEVEN

RACHEL

Rachel and Ryan were at McGuire's, even though her shift didn't start until later that night. The place had a policy about employees not fraternizing there outside of work hours, but Rachel didn't follow it, and no one really seemed to care.

Ryan was starting his first in a series of vacation days from his job as an office manager. Later that night, he'd drive two hours east to visit his brother. She liked Ryan. They had the same sense of humor and laid-back attitude toward life, plus he always paid rent on time and never made her feel awkward, the way some guys couldn't help but doing in the presence of an attractive female. This was supposed to be their last hangout before he left town, but Cara wouldn't stop calling. Rachel had stepped away from playing darts and was leaning against a corner of the room, trying to listen to what her sister was saying over the phone.

"You're saying there's been another victim?"

"Beverley Quinn. My old boss."

Rachel's head felt like it was spinning, and not just from the sips she'd had from the flask in her purse. Normally that name was only mentioned when Cara was retelling her epic take-your-job-and-shove-it tale. Now Beverley Quinn was a Gemini victim.

"Wait, has Gemini ever killed two people so close together?"

"No, but we both know it's not the real Gemini." Cara paused. "I think whoever is doing this knows we know that, too."

"I don't follow."

Rachel listened as Cara reminded her about the note on the body. *He's back from the grave.* And about the first victim's name. Margaret Grace. Yesterday, she'd shrugged off Cara's paranoia as coincidence, but now, with each reveal, Rachel felt a little more unsteady, like she was being knocked over with invisible blows. Sure, coincidences happen, but not in a situation already as bizarre as this.

"... and now Beverley Quinn is dead. Someone with a direct link to me," Cara said, finishing her spiel.

It was Rachel's turn to respond, but she didn't know how.

"What do you think all this means?"

"I think whoever this copycat is isn't doing this because he's after Gemini's fame," Cara said. "I think he's trying to send a message to us. Just like I said yesterday."

"But what's the message? Why us?" None of it was making sense.

"I don't know, but there are too many coincidences. I think the sooner the three of us can get together and talk this over, the better."

"Molly still isn't answering her phone. I've been calling her since last night."

"Well, sooner or later she's going to have to talk to us. What about you? You working today?"

Across the room, she watched as Ryan shot another dart at the board. "My shift starts at six."

"Let's meet up. Maybe we can cover more ground if we work together."

Unlike Cara, Rachel wasn't up for solving mysteries, but it was becoming harder to ignore their connection to this case. "Sure. I'll swing by the house."

"No," Cara said, quickly. "I don't want to worry about Tate stopping by. Let's meet at the library. I'm headed there now."

Cara was right. Something about this reemergence of Gemini didn't feel right, and not just because they knew their father couldn't be responsible. Cara could be known to follow odd theories down the rabbit hole, but if she was right, then the Martin girls were at the center of this.

"Bad news," she said, putting on her jacket. "I have to meet up with my sister."

"Everything all right?" Ryan asked, sliding his glasses up the bridge of his nose.

"Yeah, just family stuff."

Ryan readied his stance again and shot a dart across the room. It pinned to the corkboard with a thwack. "Are things on the mend?"

Right before Cara called, Rachel had been venting about their meeting yesterday, even though, as with everyone else in her life, she couldn't be completely honest. She couldn't say that Molly was living in a world of make-believe, still holding out hope their father was innocent, because she couldn't reveal the truth she and Cara had accepted.

"Who knows," she said, answering the question before throwing her own dart. "We're sisters, so even when we're mad at each other, it's hard to avoid one another."

"What number are you again?"

"Middle child."

"Figures."

"What's that supposed to mean?" She punched him on the shoulder, but all he did was laugh. She smiled. "I guess I can't deny I fit the stereotype. I'm definitely the most free-spirited. Cara, the oldest, is the most analytical. And the bossiest. Molly is definitely the baby. We still treat her like she's helpless sometimes, even though she's an adult."

"That's the thing about stereotypes. We resent them, but sometimes they're true."

"Who is older? You or your brother."

"He is. We're eleven months apart. Irish twins, my mom used to say."

"That's close."

"I was the little surprise that turned up when my brother was practically a newborn. I liked it, though. We're close enough in age I never felt like a baby, and we grew up doing the same things."

"That's fun. I bet brothers don't get into it as much as sisters."

"You'd be surprised." He took a swig of his beer. "What do you think Cindy is?"

In unison, they both answered: "Only child."

They leaned over laughing. Rachel steadied herself against an empty pool table, when she caught sight of a familiar face. *The* familiar face. One that haunted her at night and during the day, and it wasn't her dad.

It was Katelyn.

She was standing by a corner table with another woman, a blonde wearing a black tank top and ripped jeans. They were leaning into each other to better hear over the music pumping out of the speakers.

Katelyn looked up and locked eyes with Rachel. Her smile disappeared.

"Who's that?" Ryan asked.

"Huh?"

"The girl you're staring at."

Rachel raised the flask to her lips. "That's Katelyn. My ex."

"Really." He stared across the room, sizing her up. "So, that's the girl you're all depressed about?"

She punched him on the shoulder again, harder this time.

"Okay, sorry. I get it. I've had my heart broken, too." He waited. When Rachel didn't say anything, he continued. "Are you going to talk to her?"

"I don't know."

Across the room, Katelyn started walking toward them.

"Looks like she's making the choice for you," he said, slipping down the hallway toward the bathroom in an attempt to give them privacy.

Katelyn's face was fresh and clean as always, her hair styled straight and pulled over one shoulder. She didn't seem upset to see Rachel, but she wasn't smiling either.

"What are you doing here?" she asked.

"I work here."

"Since when do you work during the day?"

"I work later tonight. Right now, I'm hanging out with my roommate."

Katelyn nodded. "You have a roommate now?"

"Two, actually."

Katelyn pressed her lips together. She looked Rachel up and down. "You look good."

Anything would be an improvement from the last time she saw her. Rachel was still hungover from a three-day bender, her face swollen from crying, begging Katelyn to come back. The flash of this memory hardened Rachel.

"What are *you* doing here?"

"I'm here with..." She paused, looked over her shoulder, then back at Rachel. "A friend."

Rachel watched the blonde with the ripped jeans. Was she a friend? More? It was hard to tell. All she could think about was the shock of seeing Katelyn again, especially in a place that once held so many happy memories for the two of them.

"We only came here because I thought you wouldn't be working." The words were meant to make the situation better, but they arrived with a painful sting.

"Well, you were right about that," Rachel said, sarcastically.

Behind her, she felt Ryan approaching. He moved closer to the dartboard, acting as though he wasn't interrupting.

"Well, I guess I'll let you go," Katelyn said, her eyes landing on Ryan.

"I thought you already did that." Rachel turned before she could see Katelyn's reaction. She listened to the faint sound of her walking away.

"How'd that go?" Ryan asked once they were alone again.

"About as awkward as you'd expect." She growled in frustration. "Since when did my life have so much drama?"

"Keep your head up, kid," Ryan said, readjusting his glasses before he threw another dart.

"How late will you be in town? You can swing by the bar later."

"Nah, I'll probably head out after this. You gonna be okay?"

"I'll survive," she said, as she left to go meet Cara.

TWENTY-EIGHT

MOLLY

Molly preferred working the weekend shifts at Chester House on her days off from the hotel. The mornings were usually slow, with very few prospective adoptive owners stopping by, which left her plenty of time to sneak into the back and play with the animals. Her favorite part of the job. After the awful day yesterday, the cringing altercation with the man from 208, it was even more important.

She'd always loved puppies, all animals, really, and being entrusted with bathing, feeding and playing with them made her happy. If it weren't for the strict no-pet policy at her apartment complex, she'd adopt one herself. She couldn't take them home with her, but she could love them like they were her own during her time with them.

But she also liked the idea of helping the animals. Some of them had been neglected, left to wander the streets in all types of weather, their fur matted and their bones cold. Others had been abused, arriving at Chester House with sores and open wounds. They needed healing. Molly needed healing. And the time together seemed to benefit both parties.

Molly was sitting by the door in the back room, which gave her a full view of the lobby, letting a Labrador mix named Pumpkin climb over her. Pumpkin had light, fluffy hair and dark eyes. She was cute enough to hopefully secure an adoption by the end of summer. Most people claimed to be animal lovers, but in the year she'd worked there, she'd learned most of them only loved animals that were easy, free from damage. The animals that needed the most love usually had to wait longer for it.

It made Molly happy to think of Pumpkin having a home, and knowing her attention might lead to that. She liked to think her time at the shelter made up for some of the atrocities her father committed. *If* he committed them. Now she was even more skeptical.

Molly's phone buzzed. It was another call from Cara. She silenced it, just as she had all the others. She'd muted the group chat, too. It wasn't hard to guess why she was calling. She'd seen on the news another victim was found, but she'd changed the channel, still not ready to digest any of the information. She wasn't like Cara. Learning about Gemini drained her instead of fueling her.

She did, however, continue messaging Ben. After a few friendly texts, they made plans to meet after her shift. Reuniting with him wasn't the best idea, but she preferred it to spending another night alone. Or to responding to one of her sisters. Even now, when she thought about them, she was angry; they refused to give her or their father the benefit of the doubt.

The front door opened, and Charlie walked inside. He looked around the empty lobby, then caught sight of the open door leading to the back. When he turned the corner and saw Pumpkin, he smiled, but it only took an instant for him to see the anxiety written on Molly's face.

"What's eating at you?"

She laughed, but it sounded fake and forced. "What do you mean?"

"You seem, I don't know, morose?"

She laughed, this time genuinely. "Who talks like that?"

"I guess I do." He crouched beside her, rubbing the back of Pumpkin's neck. "Usually, playing with the puppies is your favorite part of the day. Today you look mad enough to strangle somebody."

She tried and failed to laugh, sound at ease. Molly was never very good at hiding the heart on her sleeve.

"I had a rough day at work yesterday. There's this guest who is always giving people a hard time. He'd just finished blessing me out when I tripped and spilled coffee all over him."

Charlie winced. "Yikes. Did you get in trouble?"

"Not really. But it's never fun to comp someone's room. Especially an asshole like that." She palmed Pumpkin's paw, deciding how much to tell him. "I guess that's not what's really bothering me, though. I'm having some family issues, too."

"Parents are the worst." He sighed, as though in complete understanding. "They can't wait for you to get out of the house, then they want to criticize every choice you make once you leave."

"My parents aren't really the problem."

"Lucky you." He leaned back onto his elbows, kicking out his feet, letting Pumpkin crawl over his torso.

"My parents are dead."

An awkward silence followed. "Molly, I'm sorry. I had no idea. I shouldn't have been going on and on like that."

"It's fine. You didn't know."

She'd made a point not to tell him. It was nice spending time with someone who didn't know all of her problems. Besides, withholding the truth from loved ones was driving her sisters' relationships into the ground. She knew the minute she started talking about her parents, she'd have to start lying by default.

"Was it... recent?"

"Dad died a year ago. Mom died about six months before that."

"That's tough, losing both parents so close together."

"Yeah. It's one of the reasons I started volunteering here. I needed to fill my time with something positive." She paused. Was that a lie? Just partially. "Anyway, I can't blame my parents for my mood. That goes to my sisters."

"You have sisters?"

"Two."

"I've got you beat. I have four."

"Really?" She laughed, finding it hard to imagine Charlie coming from a big family of girls. Perhaps that's why he was so perceptive. "What number are you?"

"I'm the baby."

"Me, too."

"I think I can figure out what's bothering you." He flitted his hands, as though to say *ta-da*. "Baby syndrome."

"What?"

"They talk down to you all the time. Act like they have to treat you with kid gloves."

He'd left out the part about their father being a serial killer, but he was on the right track. "Are you telling me this is common in all families?"

"At least in mine. And it seems like yours."

"Growing up, we were always close. I think ever since our parents died, we've been struggling to get back to that place. And you're right. They treat me like I don't know what I'm doing, and it infuriates me."

"Trust me, I know what it's like to be ganged up on. I've had a slew of sisters against me my whole life."

Molly smiled. It was nice hearing someone knew what it

was like to be in her position. It made her want to share more. "Can I tell you something?"

"Anything."

"When I spilled the coffee on that customer, it wasn't an accident." She waited on him to say something, but he just kept staring at her with curious eyes. "He was being such an asshole to me, and I was already on edge, so I just poured it on him on purpose. I don't really know why. I guess I thought it might make me feel better."

"Did it?" He cleared his throat and restarted. "Did it make you feel better?"

"It made me feel more capable than he was making me out to be. So, yeah. In a way, I guess it did." She smiled to herself, but when she looked at Charlie, she was suddenly fearful. "Please don't think I'm a terrible person—"

He stopped her. "I don't think that. Sometimes it's good to put people in their place, and it sounds like that's what you did."

A horn honked outside. Molly stood and looked through the window, noticed Ben's car pulling up to the curb. He was twenty minutes early, and she hadn't even started her closing duties.

"You know him?"

"Yeah, that's Ben, my ex. We're hanging out after work. Let me just tell him to wait."

"No, you go ahead. I'll cover you."

"Are you sure?"

"Yeah, I'm here until closing. And it looks like I'll have plenty of time on my hands."

His face was strained, and she couldn't decide if it was because of what she'd told him about the man in 208, or, if like everyone else, he had reservations about her being with Ben. Their past relationships had come up before, in passing, and most people didn't have a high opinion of Ben. She wanted to ask Charlie what he really thought, but was afraid of what he might say.

"Thanks," she said, swinging her purse over her shoulder.

Maybe Ben wasn't the best influence, but sometimes a person just needs to pass the time.

TWENTY-NINE

MOLLY

Ben's apartment looked exactly as Molly remembered it. She could see reminders of who they used to be in every corner and crevice. The quilt his grandmother had given him was draped over the old, orange loveseat. His video game console was on, the familiar lock screen on the television. She'd woken up to that image many nights and mornings.

She tried to recall how long it had been since she'd been there. Three or four months. They'd not been a proper couple for over a year, but they continued seeing one another. Each appearing in the other's life when convenient. Or not convenient, rather. It had turned into one of those relationships that got in the way of anything better in the future. She didn't much like the routine they had fallen into, but she hated being alone even more.

"You want something to drink?" Ben sat on the loveseat, propping his feet on the antique luggage case he used as a coffee table.

"I'm okay."

He didn't look like he wanted to move, and the kitchen

appeared like it hadn't been cleaned in weeks. She didn't really want anything from it.

"How've you been?" she asked, walking further into the living room. She sat in an old beanbag chair in the corner. It didn't look any cleaner, but the leather seemed more sanitary than the stained fabric covering everything else.

"Same old same. And you?"

"Busy with work."

They broke up around the time Molly started working at the hotel, the first real job she'd had since graduating college. It was entry-level work, but she was okay with paying her dues. In time, she'd earn a promotion, which would lead to more hours and better pay. Ben wasn't supportive, and the job put a strain on their relationship. He worked part-time hours at his dad's business and had no prospects. Ben was a boy refusing to grow up, a textbook example of Peter Pan syndrome. Still, Molly held out hope that if he did change, it would be for her.

"How's the rest of the fam?"

It's funny how he asked about them now. He was never a big fan of Cara or Rachel. He'd probably be delighted at the fact they'd lost touch in the past year, so she didn't want to tell him.

"They're good. Cara is writing another book. And Rachel is still working at McGuire's when she's not in school." Both statements were lies, but Molly felt the need to defend her sisters. Ben would have too much pleasure in knowing Cara was suffering from writer's block and Rachel had dropped out.

"We went to McGuire's a few weeks back. Too crowded for me. I'd rather stay home and chill, you know?"

She didn't want him to clarify the other half of *we*. They weren't exclusive, but it bothered her that on nights she spent alone, he was likely with someone else. "It's crazy this time of year," Molly said.

With conversation growing stale, Ben grabbed the remote

and turned on the television. The news was on, displaying a bulletin about the most recent Gemini victim.

"No way!" Ben sat forward, a look of pure glee on his face. "Another victim already. Have you been following this shit?"

It was the same report she'd tried to avoid earlier this morning, but now that it was in front of her, she couldn't ignore it. Molly felt like she couldn't breathe. The musty air of the room had filled her lungs and she couldn't puff it out. Her eyes read the bottom of the screen. Locking in on the name Beverley Quinn.

"Beverley Quinn has been killed?"

"Who's that?"

Molly's mouth was open, her tongue turning dry. "She used to be my sister's boss. She wrote a book about Gemini."

"Oh right, Cara writes about this stuff, too. Mysteries."

"True crime. Real stories, not fiction."

"I just can't believe this guy has come back. I mean, I remember hearing stories about him when I was a kid, but I never thought we'd have an active serial killer in Whitehill during my lifetime."

Molly clenched her eyes shut. She didn't want to watch the news report or listen to what had happened, but Ben continued speaking.

"I always thought Gemini deserved more press than he got. I mean, this guy was able to plan all his kills a year apart, and still not get caught. That takes some real brains. He had this whole town on pins and needles. My aunts still talk about how scared they were. Imagine having that kind of power over an entire town."

But Molly didn't want to imagine it. She didn't understand why Ben, or anyone else, would consider a string of vicious crimes entertainment. Until she and her sisters unpacked what was in that shed, Molly avoided crime stories. All mentions of Gemini. She was surprised to hear how much Ben knew about the case, but, then again, maybe she shouldn't have been. He was always into horror films and true crime documentaries. She wondered if, like Cara with Tate, she was fascinated by men drawn to darkness. Men like her father.

"Do you think it's him?" The words shot out without her thinking. She cleared her throat. "I mean, you don't think it's a copycat?"

"Come on, it's the real guy. A copycat couldn't plan it out like this. There wouldn't be enough time. Two bodies in less than a week? Whoever put this together had to really think about it. Spend years planning." He leaned back, his hands folded behind his head. "It has to be him. My bet is he's been in prison for something else. That's why the killings stopped. Probably spent his time behind bars plotting what he'd do once he got out."

Ben had said what she'd been begging to hear. That this had been the same guy all along, which meant her father was innocent. Her sisters refused to believe it, and the media was spinning too many webs for anything logical to stick, but Molly was still holding out hope. She believed the real Gemini was still out there, and that her father would be redeemed.

Ben had unknowingly given her the reassurance she needed.

She stood, walking over to him and kneeling in front of him. He dodged to the left, still trying to watch the television. He forgot about the news broadcast when he registered Molly's hands on his groin, pulling at his zipper.

THIRTY

CARA

When Cara arrived at the library, she scanned the dusty stacks, searching for a copy of Beverley Quinn's book, *Written in the Stars*. She'd read it when it was first published, but bitterness prevented her from keeping a copy at home. By now, news outlets were reporting Beverley's death; they'd even released the detail about a passage from *Written in the Stars* being found on the body.

Cara flipped through the pages, jotting down pertinent details that hadn't already come up in her research. She found the passage that was left with the body in the last chapter of the book:

> *People say Gemini is a monster, and after studying his crimes, I tend to agree. However, a crucial element is often excluded from that assessment. He is a human monster. A living, breathing being, capable of making mistakes. And one day, those mistakes will catch up to him.*

A familiar chill returned. Clearly, this was another message. For her or her sisters. But there was something else about the passage that was bothering her, as though she'd heard those words spoken before.

"Why couldn't we meet at the house?" Rachel said as she approached the table.

"Hey." Cara was so lost in thought she hadn't heard her arrive. "Tate is working crazy hours because of the case. I never know when he'll be home, and I didn't want him interrupting us."

Rachel looked around the room. "So, you wanted to meet here, where anyone could see us?"

"Clearly you don't spend a lot of time at the library. We basically have the place to ourselves." As Rachel sat across from her, Cara got a whiff of something. "Have you already been drinking? I thought you were working later."

"At a bar," Rachel said, defensively.

"A job is still a job."

"Loosen up a bit." Rachel's voice turned playful. "All work and no play makes Cara an uptight bitch."

Cara rolled her eyes, ignoring the jab. She scooted over the book, pointing at the passage she'd just read. "I wanted to come here to read this. The killer left this page from Beverley's book on the body."

Rachel read the words silently.

"What do you think this means?"

"I'm trying to figure out why the killer chose this passage. Maybe he is trying to relate to Dad in some way, focusing on the human element."

"Or maybe the focus is on mistakes. As in, if we'd come forward with what we knew about Dad earlier, none of this would be happening."

Cara bit her bottom lip, looking away. "Yeah, maybe."

She didn't want to admit they'd messed up. Last year, she believed it was best for all of them to move forward. She had no way of knowing someone else knew her dad's secret, and would start killing again. Cara was now determined to unravel this mystery; she didn't want more innocent people paying the price for her mistake.

"When you were doing your research," Rachel started, her voice hesitant, "did you ever find any inconsistencies? Anything that suggests Dad wasn't the real Gemini?"

Cara exhaled. "Are you siding with Molly now?"

"Not necessarily. I mean, I think it is more likely Dad *was* Gemini than he wasn't. But what if she's on to something?"

"Dad was definitely Gemini, and we're not the only ones that know it." Her eyes grew wide. "I haven't found anything which excludes him. In fact, I've uncovered more damning information."

"Like what?"

Cara used to tell her sisters everything. She sometimes forgot there was a lot she hadn't told them in the past year.

"That night, one thing you said kept sticking out in my mind. Aunt Rosemary."

"I think that was the turning point for me, too. I mean, it explains how Dad could be a normal person the rest of the year, then lost his shit when the anniversary of his sister's death rolled around."

"It's funny the things you choose to accept. I've investigated the deaths of dozens of people, but I never thought to look into Aunt Rosemary. I assumed Dad told me everything I needed to know. A month or so after we raided the shed, I decided to google her. Turns out she didn't die in a drunk driving accident."

Rachel sat up straighter, her eyes wide. "How did she die?"

"She was attacked leaving a bar on Memorial Day weekend. Looks like two or three men were involved, but they were never caught. Her body was found in an alley."

"She was murdered and left in an alley. Just like Dad's victims."

"Whatever Dad had going on in his life up until that point, her death must have been what sent him over the edge."

"Don't you think that would turn him away from violence?"

"A normal person with a normal mind. Someone like Gemini? What happened to his sister might have scarred him. Maybe killing is his way of taking back control. Maybe he blamed her for what happened, and he works it out by punishing other women over and over again. Hell, maybe the bastard just had fun with it."

Rachel didn't say anything for a long time. She cleared her throat. "Okay, if we're confident Dad was responsible for the original killings, who is taking over now?"

Cara leaned back, looking at the ceiling. "It has to be someone who knew Dad's secret. Someone who figured out we knew, too. And kept quiet. It can't just be some random person. Whoever this is, we probably know them."

"Okay." Rachel sounded unsure. "Well, who in our lives would do something like this?"

"No one," Cara said. "A year ago, I wouldn't have said Dad could do this, either. I've tried thinking about the people in Dad's life. Maybe a friend or co-worker who figured out what he was doing."

"Sure, they might have stumbled upon Dad's secret, but they would have gone to the police. They wouldn't have a reason to target us."

"True." Cara paused. "I ran into Elias earlier in the week."

"Come on." Rachel laughed. "Elias is not a serial killer. He's like a little mouse with a bad back. He's not capable of murdering two women in two days."

"I'm just thinking out loud. It has to be someone close. Can you think of anyone?"

"I barely see people anymore. My roommates. People at the bar. That's it."

"How well do you know them? Could you see any of them doing something like this?"

Rachel's face turned stiff, like she was offended. "No. Besides, I've known all these people less than a year. They never knew Dad." She waited a beat. "What about you? Anyone new in your life?"

There was a tone in Rachel's voice Cara didn't like, as though the question were more loaded than it appeared. She couldn't know about James, could she? But again, he'd not been in her life that long. He wouldn't have any reason to commit these crimes, let alone the opportunity. He lived in Boston and wasn't in Whitehill when Beverley was killed.

"I know," Cara said, sitting up straighter. "What about Molly's ex?"

"Ben? I mean, the guy's a douche, but if he were capable of killing someone, he'd probably get caught in the first forty-eight hours. Besides, I don't think they are in each other's lives anymore."

"But he knows us. And he knew Dad."

"We could say the same thing about Katelyn and Tate." Rachel waited. "We're not going around accusing them of murder, are we?"

"Of course not."

In reality, she knew very little about her husband these days. She'd thought they'd grown apart because of her own lies, but could Tate have secrets of his own? He'd been close with her father. Could he have uncovered the truth about Henry? Even if Tate did know, he wouldn't go around killing people. And yet, she'd once thought her father wasn't capable of murder, either.

Cara exhaled in frustration. They were throwing out theory after theory, but it was getting them nowhere. "Whoever it is, if they're smart enough to cover up their crimes, they're able to fool us, too. We need to watch our backs."

Rachel shivered, the statement unsettling as it was true. She leaned against the table, her voice a whisper. "I hate to even say this, but what about Molly?"

"You can't be suggesting—"

"I mean, she has anger issues. Has since we were kids. She bottles her emotions until she explodes. The way she's reacted to all of this, it makes me wonder if she knows more than she's saying."

"What do you mean?"

"Well, who was the first one in the shed that night? You or Molly?"

Cara thought back. It was definitely Molly. She was already sorting through their father's things when Cara arrived. "Her." And then, another thought. "And it was her idea to burn the evidence, too."

"Do you think she might have already known? She was always closest to Dad. And since he died, she's done nothing but deny what's right in front of her. She won't even answer our calls."

"Molly has struggled the most with this. But she's not a killer."

"You're right." Rachel leaned back, tapping her fingers against *Written in the Stars*. "If this person knows us, it's likely going to be shocking. Whoever it is."

"We just have to keep looking. Like the book said, this person is human. They're capable of making a mistake. We just have to catch it."

THIRTY-ONE

CARA

The weather remained bleak, storming most of the day and night. James' flight had been delayed, which meant she had a few hours to kill before she picked him up. By the time Cara arrived home, her hair was drenched from the rain. She hurried inside, locking the door behind her. There was momentary peace in the quiet, dry setting of home, then she realized how dark it was in the foyer. She flicked the light switch.

Nothing.

"Cara?" Tate called from the other room. "Watch your step. The power is out."

"Yeah, I can see that."

She walked into the living room. Tate had lit the fireplace and scattered candles on various pieces of furniture, casting a yellow glow about the room. With every movement their shadows danced.

"How long has the power been out?"

"Half an hour or so." He walked forward, handing her a glass of wine. "I thought we might be able to take advantage of the situation."

"What situation?" Only then did she hear the faint music

playing, recognize his button-down shirt and blazer, no tie. "What about the case? You've been working around the clock."

"Which is precisely why the boss stepped in and told us all to go home. She's got the B-group working Gemini for the time being, so we can get some sleep. I'm off for the next forty-eight hours."

"Good," Cara said, trying to dodge him. "You could probably use the rest."

He grabbed her hand, forcing her to stop. "I could use some alone time with my wife. I've picked up food, if you'd like some. It's your favorite."

"I'm soaked—"

"You look beautiful."

"You're crazy." She laughed, pushing him gently, trying to lighten the intensity of the moment. "What's gotten into you?"

"I know we've been..."—he waited, looking for the right word—"distant lately. I want to fix that. I want you to know I'm here for you, Cara."

"Thank you."

He sighed. "I mean, even right now, it feels like I'm talking to a different person sometimes. I miss you. I miss us. And with everything going on at work... it doesn't matter. Tonight is about only us."

She didn't know how to respond. He'd said everything she wanted to hear, what every wife wanted to hear, but that barrier inside her remained. A wall built with bricks of secrecy, one atop the other. Her father and James and Gemini and all of it. She'd lost her confidante, the Tate she was used to having, and she wasn't sure if she'd ever be able to get him back.

The song changed. Tate snapped his fingers and opened his mouth. "I know you love this song."

She smiled as the familiar melody filled the room. She didn't resist when he pulled her closer. She rested her head against his chest, could hear the pounding of his heart, feel every inhale. Oh, how she missed him! How she missed the happiness she felt before there were all these secrets between them. She wanted to weep, because although much of this was her fault, a big part also wasn't. Together, they started swaying, dancing alone in the living room, their shadows stretching across the walls and ceilings.

"This is nice," he said, kissing her cheek. "Sometimes I think we get so caught up in life we forget how it used to be. What brought us together in the first place."

There was so much she wanted to tell him. That barrier remained, even now, thickening with each passing minute. She thought of James. She thought of her dad. She thought of how long it had been since Tate touched her and she didn't flinch. A tear ran down her cheek.

"I can still remember the day I knew I wanted to marry you," Tate continued. "It was right here in this room. Our first Christmas together. You had this glow about you, and I wanted to have it with me every day of my life."

She remembered that moment. Her sisters, mother, father. She thought of all the happy memories they'd had in this space. This was the place they all returned, where her father returned after he committed his awful crimes. The place where he hugged his daughters and made love to his wife, after taking the lives of so many young women. She felt her stomach turning.

Then suddenly, another memory popped into her mind. All of them gathered in this room after her father's funeral. They'd been trading stories and laughing when the name Gemini first re-entered their lives. Of course, this was before they'd searched the shed. But they'd talked about Gemini that night. And Beverley. Both Katelyn and Tate were in the room.

Earlier at the library, Rachel had mentioned the idea of Tate or Katelyn being involved. Cara hadn't really considered it, but what if Tate knew more about her father than she realized? He'd said people like Gemini were the reason he'd entered law enforcement in the first place. And something else he said that night about Gemini. *He's only human.* With a shudder, she realized it was the same sentiment that had been expressed in the passage from *Written in the Stars*, the one found on Beverley's body.

Maybe Rachel was unknowingly onto something. Maybe Tate had already figured out Henry Martin was Gemini. He could have known earlier, as far back as when they were dating, back when he'd decided he'd wanted to marry her on Christmas morning in this very room. It was sick and twisted to think someone would want to latch on to the daughter of a serial killer, but wouldn't it take a sick and twisted person to pick up where her father had left off? Tate couldn't be that person, could he?

Looking out the window, she caught sight of the moon, full and bright amidst the raging storm. Its beauty reminded her of Penny Mayweather. She'd admired a moon like this right before she was mutilated by Gemini. Afterward, her father probably came back to this very room. Cara caught sight of their shadows, which now reminded her of malevolent spirits. A trick of the mind, perhaps? Whatever it was frightened her, and she jumped.

"What is it?" Tate asked.

It was nothing. Just a flicker of light in movement, heightened by the contrasted dark. Still, when Tate touched her arm, she jerked away like she'd been hit. It felt like she couldn't breathe.

"I'm sorry, I just can't do this."

"Can't do what?" Tate asked. He was confused and hurt and worried. "You can't spend an evening alone with your husband?"

What was she supposed to tell him? That her head was filled with images of her father's murder victims? That it was impossible to create happy memories in this room, for it was the same space that housed the monster named Gemini? That she had started to question everyone in her life, even him. She couldn't tell him any of it. She couldn't tell him the truth. So, she lied.

"I don't feel well," she said, averting her eyes. "I need some air."

She headed out the front door, back into the rain. She left Tate alone in the room filled with candles and music and ghosts.

She'd hoped the ghosts might stay there, but as usual, they followed her.

THIRTY-TWO

The rain beats down, slickening the sidewalks. I slip down the alley, waiting to make my move. Right now, everything is going according to plan. I think I've finally piqued their interest—not only the media and the world at large, but the people that matter most.

For the first time in my life, people are actually listening. Taking notice. Amazed at what I've done.

But no one is watching now. I suppose I have the weather to thank for that. Only a crazy person would be out in this mess. Still, some people have routines that must be followed, and I'm relying on her to follow hers.

I stand in the corner, beneath the awning. The sound of raindrops pattering against the metal is pleasant, and if I were a bit warmer, I could probably go to sleep just listening to it. Another sound interrupts that image in my mind, and like a predator in the night, I'm alert. Focused on the task at hand.

It's the sound of footsteps stomping down the stairs of the fire escape. It's the quickest way to make it to the dumpster, and despite the storm, the trash has to be taken out. Again, routine.

She only takes a couple steps before I hear her stumble and curse. I stand back, leaning further into the wall, making sure she can't see me. I don't think she'd notice if I were right in front of her. She's not one to be aware of her surroundings. She's too busy focused on only herself.

She makes it down to the bottom, pulling her coat over her hair as if that will do any good. She puts down her head, and makes a mad dash for the dumpster. I wait until she has lifted the lid to unscrew the light bulb above us.

Now it's pitch-black, and all that can be heard is the sound of heavy rain and more cursing. She's scared, which is understandable. Most people aren't fans of the dark. Usually, it's an irrational fear. But not tonight. Tonight, every fear she's had her entire life is warranted.

I can feel the heat of her body in front of me. She reaches out, trying to grab the railing, but finds me instead. She steps back, but I grab her before she's able to let out a proper scream. I don't even fool with the cloth this time. I ram the knife into her stomach. Once, twice, three times. I almost regret that I twisted off the light. I'd love to see the look on her face, but I can't risk being seen by anyone else.

The attack is so quick she doesn't have time to react. She lets out a single yelp, which is quickly swallowed by the thunderous storm. She's silent now, slumping forward. I'm sure the blood is leaving a mess, but I've prepared for that. My raincoat repels liquid, whether it be water or blood. But before I can strip off my garb and return to my car, I have to heave her up the stairs. I feel certain she's dead, but I need to make sure.

The fun won't be over until we're inside.

THIRTY-THREE

RACHEL

It wasn't even ten o'clock, and Rachel had already cut off her third customer of the night. Holiday weekends were usually rowdy. People wanted to make the most of their time away from work.

She sat on a tub in the storage room, embracing a few minutes of calm.

"Rach," Ivan said, slamming the break room door against the wall. "There's a guy at the bar."

"I'm on break."

"He's requesting you."

Ivan was gone. She exhaled, sick of dealing with drunk people. There were a few regulars she enjoyed, but even their presence had annoyed her in recent months.

Once inside, she noticed the man instantly. His long, stringy hair and crooked back were easy to identify, even from across the room.

"Elias," she said, as she approached.

He smiled, pressing his palms together. "Oh good, you *are* working. I was hoping to catch you."

Elias had come to McGuire's a couple of times in the past,

but it had been months since she'd seen him. She pulled on her memory, figuring they'd only met once or twice since the funeral.

"What are you drinking?"

He leaned forward, squinting to get a better look at the beers. He shrugged. "Anything on draft is fine. I don't know what's popular these days. You pick for me."

She turned, grabbing a frosty mug and tilting it beneath the spout. She looked above, at the clock on the wall. McGuire's closed in an hour, and she couldn't wait.

"How've you been?" he asked her, when she returned with his beer.

"Okay." There was an awkward pause, and she felt the need to keep the conversation going. "And you?"

"You know." He shrugged, holding himself tightly, as though debating whether or not he should continue. "I've been dreading the summer all year, to be honest. I think that'll be the hardest."

She stared at him, unblinking. "Why's that?"

"Your father was off in the summer. That's when we spent most of our time together. Working on different projects. Catching baseball games. Visiting the cabin." He smiled. "I've missed him a lot since he died, but I'm afraid that grief is nothing compared to what is coming. A whole other year without him."

Rachel nodded. What Elias said was true. He did spend more time with her dad during the summer, but there was something else tingling her subconscious, that this time of year was also when Gemini made his kills.

"I guess I just wanted to check up on you girls, is all," Elias said, taking a sip of his drink.

"We're getting through." Her tone was definitive, an attempt to end the conversation, although part of her pitied Elias and his obvious loneliness.

"Say, have you talked to Cara about the cabin?" he asked.

"What about it?"

"I told her there'd been some interest from potential renters. Some couple wants to rent it for July. I told her I'd look after the place, if you girls wanted to start renting. It'd probably turn a good profit for you three, just like it did your dad."

Cara definitely hadn't mentioned that to her. She didn't even tell her she'd seen Elias recently. All she'd talked about for the past few days was Dad and Gemini.

"I'll bring it up next time I see her."

"Sure." He nodded, delighted. "No rush. I know things have been a little crazy here lately."

What did he mean by that? Was he talking about the residents of town in general, or about the Martin girls specifically? After all, the craziness had been heightened just for them. Rachel's mind went back to the library, their attempt to narrow down a suspect list. Meek, lonely Elias seemed like an unlikely suspect to her, but it was suspicious he'd tracked down both of them the same week the killings had resumed.

Elias patted his jacket, reaching for his wallet. He took out a twenty and placed it on the bar.

"Well, it was good seeing you," he said, standing. "I'll let you get back to work."

She waved, watching him as he walked away. She pocketed the cash, noticing his beer was almost full.

THIRTY-FOUR

RACHEL

Rachel sat on a metal bench inside the waiting area of Molly's apartment block. Someone had decided to buzz her in on the way out. Normally, people would be too cautious to do that sort of thing, especially with a serial killer on the loose, but it was one hell of a storm outside.

She liked listening to the sound of rain hitting glass, and that's what she did as she waited for her sister to turn up. Molly had been ignoring texts and phone calls for days, and Rachel wasn't used to being pushed to the side. Usually, she was the one with better things to do, but everything that had happened in the past week—the new bodies turning up—worried her. She at least wanted to make sure her sister was okay.

A car pulled up to the curb and stopped. Rachel stood, cupping her hands and peering through the glass to try and make out who it was. Then the door opened, and Molly climbed out of the passenger seat. Beyond her, Rachel spotted Ben behind the wheel.

She was comforted her sister was safe, but now her irritation had renewed. Ben was the last person Molly needed to be with during a crisis. He fed off her, like a tick off blood, stealing the best parts of her. Molly deserved better, and Rachel planned on letting her know it.

"Are you fucking kidding me?"

Molly jumped back, having not expected anyone to be waiting inside. Her reaction slowed when she recognized her sister. "What are you doing here?"

"You've been ignoring us. I wanted to make sure you're okay."

"I don't think you're the best person to be making house calls. Isn't it usually the other way around?"

"Clearly you're not in your right mind either." Rachel nodded outside to where Ben's car was in the process of driving away. "How long has he been back in the picture?"

"It's none of your business."

If they'd been together a while, Rachel wouldn't know because she'd been avoiding Molly. But Molly's reunion with Ben made her uneasy. She thought back to her afternoon with Cara again. If Ben had re-entered their lives recently, she wondered if it was at all connected. He hadn't even made it to their father's funeral—but what if that was deliberate? What if he'd been avoiding them, waiting for Gemini's kill cycle to come around again before making his presence known. She wanted to warn Molly about the possibility, but was afraid of pushing her farther away.

"We used to tell each other everything, Molly."

"Well, it's not been like that since Dad died. We've all been in our own worlds. I don't press you about what happened with Katelyn. Or Cara about what's going on in her marriage. Don't start making comments about Ben."

"You're right." She looked down, acknowledging she was to blame for her part in avoiding her sisters over the past year. "We've fucked up. We've let Dad come between us. I just don't get why you're ignoring us now."

Molly leaned against the window, watching the glaring

lights on the wet streets. For a long while, she didn't say anything. "You two wouldn't even hear me out the other day. You've already decided that Dad... is who you say he is. It upsets me you won't look at other possibilities."

Rachel suddenly felt claustrophobic, longing to be outside, breathing in the cool air, walking in the damp darkness. She pushed her shoulders back and inhaled slowly. "Okay. I'm willing to hear you out. You think there are other possibilities?"

"I've never thought it made sense. Dad was a lot of things, but he wasn't a..." Molly lowered her voice to a whisper, "killer. I know we found all that stuff in the shed, but maybe it didn't belong to him. Maybe he knew who the killer was, but didn't feel he could say. And now this person has started killing again."

"But the letter—"

"I know about the letter!" she shouted, then lowered her voice. "I know the letter looks bad, but I don't think Dad would write that. The handwriting was similar, but not exactly the same."

"We have no way of knowing for sure." Rachel's cheeks warmed with anger. A big part of the reason she'd distanced herself from her sisters was because they had burned what was found in the shed without her consent. They had robbed her of the opportunity to do what she thought was right.

"We couldn't let you accuse Dad without knowing." Molly fidgeted, like maybe she did regret the decision. "And even if Dad did write that letter, someone could have made him. The real killer."

"Do you really think that's a possibility?"

Rachel could see Molly's demeanor changing. It was obvious she so desperately wanted her theory to be true, but still didn't quite believe it. "Maybe. Maybe Dad was tracking the case like Cara, and that's why he had all that stuff. And whoever he was following found out and decided to make him look guilty."

Rachel wanted to bring up the jewelry they found again—the items belonging to the same women in the photos—but she didn't. "I don't remember Dad having a hobby of tracking serial killers."

"That doesn't mean he didn't do it! There are all different sides to a person. Just because we didn't see them all doesn't mean those sides didn't exist."

"That's my point." It only took one look for Rachel to see how much that comment wounded her sister. Molly folded into herself like a child. She went on. "Cara has a theory about that."

"That the real Gemini is still out there?"

"Not exactly. She thinks that whoever is killing these latest victims knew Dad was Gemini and is trying to send us a message."

Molly laughed. "She brought this up the other day, and you shot her down. What changed your mind?"

Rachel laid out Cara's theory. She told her about the first victim's name being the same as their mother's and the note found on the body. *He's back from the grave.* The second victim, Beverley Quinn, and her undeniable connection to Cara. When she finished, Molly didn't seem convinced, but did appear slightly startled.

"So, you think whoever is doing this knows Dad is the real Gemini. He knows we know about it. And now he's punishing us for covering it up?"

"It's a possibility," Rachel said. "With Cara it's hard to tell if she's reading into things. If she wants there to be a connection or not."

"That's what I've been saying all along."

"Neither of us *want* Dad to be Gemini, Molly. I just can't deny what we found. Maybe none of us really knew him, but that doesn't mean we don't have each other."

Molly shook her head. "I just need some time to figure

things out. I thought we'd spent enough time apart over the past year, but I guess I was wrong."

Rachel stood. It didn't appear like Molly was going to invite her upstairs, but she couldn't leave without at least asking. "Are you and Ben back together? If you want time away from us, fine. But don't go back to him. He's not good for you."

Molly brushed past Rachel, using her key to unlock the mailbox. She turned back. "Stop telling me how to live my life."

There was so much Rachel wanted to say to her younger sister in that moment. She wanted to tell her she understood her grief, that she missed Mom more than words could express. She wanted to tell her that she was falling apart without Katelyn in her life, that she needed her sisters more than ever, that she was reluctant to ask for help because she didn't want them to see her struggle. She wanted to tell Molly how much she missed her.

But she didn't say any of that. Every now and then, she figured, it was better to just let a person be angry. She walked outside as the rain began to slow. For the short walk to her own apartment, there was little more than a drizzle. Her top was sticking to her skin and her hair was frizzy. She was planning on going inside and taking a hot shower, then finishing off the bottle of wine she opened yesterday. She might crush up a Xanax to ensure a good night's sleep. This had become her regular plan of late, her idea of a good time. Because no matter who she was with—her sisters, Ryan, Katelyn—she no longer found comfort in the presence of people; she found it in the clutches of substances.

Rachel had always been more of a partier than her sisters, but she had never let it get out of hand. In some ways, she'd lived most of her life with other people's expectations at the back of her mind. First, her parents. Then, Katelyn. Now, she was free to do whatever she wanted, and she was beginning to realize how dangerous a position that was to be in.

But what else could she do? This was the way she was

wired. She couldn't drive herself crazy with research and analysis, like Cara. And she was too pessimistic to try and save the world like Molly. She needed to drown out the same thoughts and memories that were plaguing all of them, and drinking was the only way she knew how.

Rachel unlocked her front door and walked inside.

The lights were off, and there was a rancid smell hanging in the air. She hadn't been at the apartment since noon, and Ryan had already left town. She figured the stench was courtesy of Cindy's latest raw food diet, or some other health kick.

She flicked on the lights.

Cindy was at fault for the smell, all right. Her body was sprawled across the kitchen floor. There was an unnatural grayish hue to her skin. Her eyes were open. Blood covered her torso, trickling from the exposed gash in her neck.

After a few seconds of wide-eyed awe, Rachel jumped back. She tripped over the threshold, falling into the hallway. She covered her mouth, trying to stifle her own screams, but she couldn't stop looking.

Couldn't stop staring at Cindy. Dead. Her body posed on the floor of Rachel's apartment.

THIRTY-FIVE

MOLLY

The water thundered over Molly's head, running down her shoulders, washing away her shame. She had been annoyed when Rachel started lecturing her, mainly because she knew her sister was right. Ben had been an asshole to her in the past. But she still turned to him because it was painful to go through life alone.

What Rachel wouldn't consider was that people did change. Ben had been kinder today, more attentive. He had even agreed to join her at the Chester House function on Tuesday. That proved he still cared for her. Ben had failed to be there for her in the wake of her parents' deaths, but maybe he realized that and was trying to be better. Molly tried to see the good in him, just as she tried to remember the good in her father.

As she was exiting the shower, her phone began to ring. She wrapped a towel around herself, spying Cara's name on the screen. She silenced the call, walking into her bedroom. The phone rang again, and Molly decided she didn't want to play this game all night. Rachel had already tracked her down; she might as well hear what Cara had to say in order to avoid a face-to-face confrontation.

She answered. "I'm not in the mood—"

"Molly, listen," Cara cut her off. "I'm at the police station with Rachel. Her roommate, Cindy, died. The police think she was murdered by Gemini."

"What?" Molly sat on the bed, the damp towel falling around her feet. "I saw Rachel tonight. She was just here."

"She found her when she got home." There was a pause, rustled background noise filling the silence. "She's talking to the police right now. I think she's pretty shaken up."

Molly had wanted to avoid her sisters, refuse to engage until they agreed to hear her out. But in that moment, all the resentment she had toward her family and the rest of the world fell away.

"I'm on my way."

As she got dressed, she thought about the strange closeness she felt to the situation. She'd just seen Rachel, and Rachel had just seen a dead body. Molly didn't know Rachel's roommate—Cindy, Cara had called her—but she'd just seen her a few days ago. Cindy had let them into the apartment the morning of their fight. Only yesterday she was alive, and now she was gone.

Then Molly thought about what Rachel had said, Cara's theory that this killer was targeting them. She didn't want it to be true. She wanted to believe the original Gemini killer had started up again. She didn't want to think a copycat had picked up where her father left off. Of course, if her idea about the letter was true, that her father had uncovered the identity of the true Gemini killer, maybe that was why they'd been targeted.

Perhaps this person had sat around for a year, waiting, expecting the Martin girls to come forward. To announce Henry Martin as the Gemini killer. When that didn't happen, maybe he decided to lash out, killing in quick succession, ensuring all the victims had a connection to them.

There were numerous possibilities, but Molly could no longer ignore the connection between her family and these recent kills. And she could no longer ignore her sisters. They needed her.

She had to go.

She rushed back downstairs, back into the night and the rain, which had picked up again. Her hair was already wet from the shower, but she didn't care. The only thing that mattered was getting to the police station.

"Molly?"

It took her a few seconds to register someone had said her name. For a moment, she'd thought it was her imagination. But when she turned, she saw Fiona standing near the entrance to Molly's apartment. The hood on her jacket was raised, making her difficult to recognize at first.

"Fiona?" She looked around. It was past midnight. The only people on the street were hopping from one bar to the next. Seeing her outside her apartment was unexpected. "How do you know where I live?"

"We passed your place after work one time. Don't you remember?"

Molly didn't. Where Fiona lived was a mystery to her. Every time she'd tried to make plans with her outside of work, Fiona had blown her off. And yet here she was, standing outside in the rain.

"I was hoping we could talk. Charlie and I got into a fight."

"Why didn't you just call?"

"My phone died. I went outside to blow off some steam, and I figured I'd come over. I think I've messed things up, and I really need your advice."

Fiona had picked the worst night to try and build a genuine friendship.

"Now really isn't a good time. Maybe I can give you a call later or we can talk about it at work." Molly turned, continued marching in the direction of her car. The sound of footsteps in puddles followed, and she realized Fiona was still there.

"Please. I really need a friend."

Fiona had plenty of friends. She'd heard her talk about them. Seen pictures of their exploits online.

"I'm more Charlie's friend than yours."

"What's that supposed to mean?"

"We never hang out outside of work, not that I haven't tried. And you only talk to me when you need something, this moment included. You're the most self-involved person I know, and if you're really after my opinion, it's that Charlie could do much, much better."

Fiona was stunned. As Molly tried to pass, Fiona grabbed her arm. The pressure of her hand on Molly's arm was unwelcome, even threatening.

"Is there something going on between the two of you?" This time, Fiona's voice sounded more calculated than confused.

Molly was taken aback by the question. "Why would you even think that?"

"You work together. I mean, I'm his girlfriend, and sometimes I feel like he prefers you over me."

"That's between the two of you. It has nothing to do with me."

With one quick movement, Molly pushed her. Fiona slipped, landing on the slick sidewalk. Molly rushed toward her, but she realized she didn't want to help her up, like any other person would. She wanted to hit her again. She wanted to release all her anger and anxiety on Fiona this very instant. She clasped her hands together to stop herself.

Fiona stood shakily, her pants soaked from the wet sidewalk. Her face was pale, and she looked at Molly with frightened eyes. "You are such a freak."

By now, a few other people had started to gather around them. It was hard to tell whether they thought Fiona simply slipped, or if there was a bigger altercation taking place. Molly felt her phone buzzing in her pocket. Another message from Cara, wondering where she was.

"Fiona, I'm sorry."

She took off down the street before Fiona or anyone else could speak to her. She couldn't think about what had just happened. She couldn't think about anything, other than getting to the police station.

THIRTY-SIX

MOLLY

By the time Molly arrived at the station, Rachel was done being questioned by investigators. She was sitting in the corner of the waiting room with Cara, and together they were waiting on instructions from the police. Tate had joined them.

When she saw Rachel balled up in a flimsy plastic chair, she forgot their fight from earlier. They embraced, and her body felt heavy in Molly's arms.

"Are you okay?"

"I don't know. I've never seen something like that. Not in that way."

The sisters looked at each other, then averted their eyes. Sure, they'd seen photos of the Gemini crime scenes, the ones hidden beneath the floor of their father's shed, but none of them had ever seen something so brutal up close. Molly couldn't even imagine.

"We can set you up with some counseling, if that will help," Tate said. He was standing with both hands in his pockets. He was trying and failing to be professional, his brotherly love taking over.

"I never liked her," Rachel said, staring blankly ahead.

Molly didn't think she'd been listening to Tate. "But to see her like that... She didn't deserve that. No one does."

"I wouldn't go around telling people you didn't like the dead girl in your apartment," Cara said, her voice low.

"Surely, they don't think she had anything to do with this?" Molly said.

"Right now, it appears the victim was likely killed while you were still at work. Then you went straight to Molly's," Tate said. He looked at Molly, and she nodded. "No one thinks you're involved, but they'll have to follow up over the next few days."

"Do they think it's Gemini?" asked Cara. She was the only one brave enough to ask, Molly thought.

Tate looked around the room. "That's the working theory, yes. It's a little different from his other crimes. I don't think there has ever been a victim found inside her own residence before."

"Kamryn Shelton. Summer of 2001," Cara said. "She was found inside her dorm."

"Maybe I'm wrong. I'll check into it." Tate appeared taken aback by her ready answer. "Cindy wasn't actually killed in the apartment, either. It looks like she was killed outside near the dumpster. The killer brought her body back inside through the fire escape, but we don't know why."

They knew why. Because the killer wanted Rachel to find Cindy's body.

"I know you weren't great friends, but you lived together, so you might know. Did she have any jewelry she'd wear often? Anything that sticks out."

Rachel closed her eyes to think. "She wore a necklace with her name on it."

"We'll look into it," Tate said.

"Was there a note?" Molly asked. "Cara said the last two victims had a note."

Tate looked around the room again, as though maybe it was

against protocol to share this part. "There wasn't a written note, but someone left a message."

"What was it?" Cara asked.

"They carved the Gemini symbol into the victim's torso post-mortem."

Cara looked at Rachel. "You didn't say anything about that."

"I didn't see." She stood suddenly. "I think I'm going to be sick."

She stomped past the row of chairs and ducked into a hall bathroom. Cara followed her.

"Shit," Tate said. "I do this for a living, but I've forgotten how close to home this is. I can't believe Rachel has been brought into this. I shouldn't have mentioned the Gemini symbol. She's already traumatized."

"Why do you think this guy has returned after all this time?"

"I couldn't tell you. Honestly, I don't even know if it's the real guy." There was a commotion behind them, and he looked back. "All I know is I want nothing more than to catch him. I need to go. Will you tell Cara to call me?"

"Sure."

Molly waited by the bathroom. Cara walked out, gently closing the door behind her.

"How is she?"

"I've never seen her like this. Between Dad and Katelyn, she's already fragile. I don't want this pushing her over the edge." She looked back at the bathroom, then at Molly. "Look, I've got this work commitment... I can't really get out of it."

"At this hour? Our sister just found her roommate murdered."

"I know. I have to finish something urgent." Cara bit her bottom lip, a common habit when she was on the verge of disappointing people. "Can you just stay with her? Let her sleep at your place tonight?"

"Sure. Someone needs to be there for her." She couldn't believe Cara was doing this now, when Rachel needed her most.

"Good. I promise I'll meet up with you guys in the morning."

"Tate wanted you to call him," Molly called after her.

Cara bit her lip again. "Thanks."

Molly leaned against the wall, trying to ignore the sounds of Rachel retching. It must have been horrifying, finding her roommate like that. She thought of the symbol that had been carved into Cindy's flesh. That must have taken some time. Rachel was lucky she hadn't arrived sooner. She could have been another victim.

Of course, Gemini had never been known to kill two women at one time. And now she was thinking of Cara's theory. Was this killer targeting people they knew? Rachel's roommate winding up dead certainly suggested that. And where was Cara running off to anyway? What could be more important than being here for Rachel?

She heard the sound of the toilet flushing, then something else. Rachel was sobbing.

Molly closed her eyes. It was going to be a long night.

THIRTY-SEVEN

CARA

Cara fought back tears as she slammed the car door shut. Even though Rachel had just experienced something truly awful, even though she needed her, Cara had promised to pick up James from the airport, and his flight had landed almost an hour ago. She couldn't fulfill her promises to one person she loved without letting down another.

This was exactly why she had to stop doing this. Sneaking around with James. Lying to Tate. Abandoning her sisters when they needed her most. She was deceiving everyone in some way, and that made her sick.

Knuckles rapped against the window, making her jump. Tate stood in the rain outside her car.

"Where are you going?"

"I'm running some errands for Rachel," she lied. James was already waiting. She could have told him something had come up and to get his own ride, but she didn't want to do that. He'd flown in to see her, and she felt guilty ditching him.

"I wasn't trying to upset you earlier."

"I know that."

"Where did you go?" Tate asked. There was a sharp tone to his voice she couldn't ignore.

"I just needed some space," she stammered, not capable of coming up with another lie so quickly. And why was he pressing her about it? He almost sounded suspicious. "I went for a drive, and then Rachel called. I came here."

He watched her for a second longer, then looked back at the police station. "So much for having the next two days off."

Three murders in three days. Not only was this an extreme pace for the Gemini copycat, it was pushing the Whitehill PD to their max. "She seems really shaken up. I want her to be okay."

"First Beverley, now Rachel's roommate. What are the odds you'd both know the victims personally?"

There it was again. That suspicious tone. She wondered what he'd been doing tonight after she stormed out of the house, before he got the call about another victim. Was her paranoia so strong she was starting to suspect her own husband?

When Cara tried to speak, it felt like something was caught in her throat. "I guess I hadn't thought of that."

He nodded and frowned. "Better get back to work."

Cara watched Tate walk back inside before pulling out of the parking lot. She sped in the direction of the airport, the rain tapering off with each passing mile. When she arrived, James was waiting outside beneath a cement awning.

"You've done me a favor getting out in this," he said, looking up at the sky.

"Sorry for taking so long. I can't believe you're already back."

"Well, since my schedule opened up, I figured what the hell?" He smiled. "I can never pass up an opportunity to see you."

Cara smiled but it didn't quite reach her eyes. "I'm not going to be able to stay long tonight."

His excitement dimmed in an instant. "Why?"

"It's already so late and my sister... Rachel. She needs me."

"Did something happen?" he asked, his voice filled with concern.

Cara thought about Rachel, but not the emotional wreck she left at the police station. She heard Rachel's voice in her head, asking if anyone new had entered her life in the past year. James was the only person, but it was impossible for him to be involved. He lived in Boston, only visiting Whitehill when his schedule allowed. Beyond that, he knew the least about Gemini and the dysfunction in her family. She'd shielded him from it.

Cara chose her words carefully, watching his reaction. "Her roommate died."

"My God." James ran a hand through his hair, looking out the window. "How?"

"It's not clear what happened," Cara lied.

"Was Rachel close to her? I mean, is she upset?"

"She's the one who found the body. It's been a lot on her."

Cara waited for him to ask more questions. She figured if James, or anyone else, was behind this, they'd like hearing about their crimes, but James remained silent, his eyes on the road ahead.

"I wish you'd called me," he said, at last. "I could have rescheduled my trip."

"Everything happened so quickly. You were already on the plane by the time I heard about Rachel."

"She needs you right now, and I understand that." He looked into his lap, his jaw tightening. "But I can't shake the feeling that there's not enough room for me in your life."

"That's not true."

And yet, ever since the Gemini kills had started up again, it appeared that way. James wasn't involved with what was going on, and she hated herself for even considering it. He wanted only to be a positive presence in her life, but she was blocking him out as she was everyone else.

When they arrived at the Railway Hotel, he grabbed his luggage from the back seat. She wished she could say something to him to ease his disappointment, but she didn't know what.

"I'm not sure I can keep doing this."

"Doing what?"

"I make you a priority, Cara. I got on a plane to spend more time with you. And you treat me like I'm an option."

"That's not what I'm trying to do," she pleaded. "I can't control what happened tonight—"

"I'm not talking about tonight. It's been six months, and I'm still no more a part of your life than when we met up for the first time. That's not what I wanted and you know it. I need more."

"Just give me some time."

Now was the worst possible time for James to become a bigger part of her life, but she couldn't tell him that. She couldn't let him into the secrets of Gemini and its impact on her family. All she needed to do was figure out who was targeting them, so she could end this. Then, maybe, she could give James everything he wanted.

As she drove off, she felt like she was sinking, letting down yet another person in her life. On her way home, she called Molly to see if Rachel needed anything.

"She's fine. We're at my apartment," Molly said. "She took some sleeping pills and she's already passed out on the couch."

"How did she seem?"

"Exhausted. I am, too." She paused. "I hope you finished up your work."

It was clearly a dig at her for leaving. Cara didn't respond, because she knew she deserved it. She'd failed them both, all to try and make James feel important. And she'd disappointed him by leaving early, only to be too late to support Rachel.

At the very least, she hoped Tate would be around. She wasn't happy about how she'd left things with him, either.

But when she arrived home, the rain finally at a standstill, the driveway was empty.

THIRTY-EIGHT

RACHEL

Rachel woke up to the sounds of Molly rummaging around the kitchen. She opened her eyes, taking in a living room that was far different from her own. Clean. Modern. The windows were bare, welcoming in bright rays of sunlight. Molly's place looked barely lived in, while Rachel's apartment was the opposite, bearing too many signs of life.

And now death. Rachel wondered if she'd ever be in her home again without thinking of Cindy's dead body.

"Sorry," Molly said when she saw Rachel moving on the sofa. "I didn't mean to wake you."

"You weren't doing a very good job of being quiet."

"I'm used to being alone." She looked down at her coffee. "How did you sleep?"

"Better than expected." Rachel hadn't had any nightmares, but it took her a long while to fall asleep, her mind revisiting the horror of Cindy gutted and limp on the kitchen floor. Her open eyes eternally watching her. Finding her like that was far worse than seeing the pictures in her father's shed. Real flesh. Real blood. She didn't know one human could inflict so much pain onto another, and she feared the memory would haunt her the rest of her life.

"You're welcome to stay here as long as you want."

"Tate will let me know when I can swing by the apartment and grab a few things. I'll stay at Cara's for a while. There's more space there."

Suddenly, she felt guilty for the things she said about Molly yesterday. Sure, Molly could be unpredictable, especially when it came to their father, but here she was, supporting Rachel when she needed it most.

Rachel propped up on an elbow and began scrolling through her phone. She had over a dozen missed calls from Ryan, and several messages.

I heard what happened.

Are you okay?

Rachel, talk to me.

I'm coming back.

Molly looked at the clock. "I have to be at work in ten, but if you'd rather someone stay with you, I can call in."

"No need. I'll be fine." She continued scrolling through messages. "It looks like Ryan came back to town. I should probably meet up with him."

"Who?"

"Ryan. Our... *my* other roommate."

"Oh." Molly looked away, awkwardly. "You told him what happened?"

"I gave his phone number to one of the police officers last night. I'm sure one of them reached out. I wasn't in the right headspace to talk to anyone."

"You don't have to push yourself. Call out of work the next few days. Take some time to relax."

"No, it will be good for me to see Ryan. He's more than a roommate. He's a friend, I guess."

Molly had a strange look on her face, close to a grimace. "I need to run. Lock the place up when you leave."

Rachel grabbed an Uber and met Ryan at the pub across from their apartment building. There were still police positioned outside the front doors, their home still an active crime scene. The idea made her shiver.

Tate had said Cindy was killed outside, near the dumpsters. For some reason, imagining that frightened her even more. She'd always had the creeps whenever she ventured to the back of the building. It was too dark, too narrow. She'd psyched herself out more than once thinking someone could easily hide in the foliage, and she'd been right. She wondered if Cindy had even noticed someone there with her before it was too late.

And then, if that wasn't awful enough, the killer had dragged Cindy's body back into her apartment. He posed the body in a place personal to the victim, and to her. Cara was right, she thought. He was targeting them, and he was too many steps ahead.

Rachel's thoughts were interrupted by someone barreling into her. It was Ryan, his embrace almost toppling her over.

"Thank God you're okay." His arms held her so tight she struggled to breathe. "You scared the shit out of me when you didn't answer your phone."

"It was a rough night. I wasn't thinking straight." Her mind went back to the scene. *Those eyes.*

They found a table outside on the patio and sat. Ryan waved over a waitress and ordered them drinks. "None of this feels real. I mean, poor Cindy," he said. "I know we weren't always the nicest to her..."

"I know. Trust me, I've been on my own guilt trip. But there's no way we could have known what would happen." She stopped, wondering if that was true. Hadn't Cara tried warning her? "There's no way I would have *wanted* this to happen."

The two never got along, and Cindy was often annoying and openly rude, but she didn't deserve what happened to her. Rachel couldn't imagine anyone deserved to die like that.

"I hate that you were the one who found her." He pounded his fist against the table. "I should have been there."

"Who knows, one of us could have been in danger had we been there at the wrong time." Unless, Cara was right and this had been planned out. The killer didn't want Rachel there when it happened, he only wanted her to find the body. He wanted to send a message. "You didn't have to come back."

"I wanted to make sure you were okay. I can't imagine..." His words trailed off, as though he were trying to picture the scene. Rachel knew no prediction would do the reality justice. "Do the police have any theories? Was anything missing from the apartment?"

Ryan and Rachel had never discussed Gemini before, an added benefit of their friendship. Even though the local press had been talking about the new string of victims nonstop, Ryan was more likely to scroll recent events on CNN. He probably assumed Cindy's death was a robbery gone wrong.

"The police think Cindy's death might be connected to two other recent murders."

Reluctantly, Rachel filled him in on the Gemini killings. Ryan sat in front of her, almost completely still. Eventually, he leaned over, his hands rubbing at his forehead, as though he could somehow erase the information.

"You're telling me they think a *serial killer* murdered Cindy? In our apartment?"

"We don't know anything for sure yet." She didn't tell him about the Gemini symbol etched into her skin; whenever she thought about it, her throat filled with bile. "But considering the timing of the other murders, it's at least a possibility."

"But I mean, why *her*?"

"I... I don't know." Another swarm of guilt filled her lungs. *Because of me*, it whispered.

"Do they think she was targeted? Was she connected to the other victims? I mean, I thought serial killers followed some type of pattern or something."

"I'm not sure. I don't know many details." Another lie. She knew all the details. And she knew Cindy's death was her fault.

"Maybe you should ask your sister about it. The one who writes crime stuff. She might be able to fill you in."

"Yeah, I'll do that. Speaking of my sister, I'm going to be staying with her for a while. I'm not sure when they'll release the apartment as a crime scene, but even when they do, I just don't think I can live there."

"I understand."

"I'm not trying to kick you out."

"Don't even worry about it. I don't think I could stay there either, knowing what happened."

"The officers said we can swing by later and pick up a few things."

"That's good to know. I'll probably head back to my brother's place for the time being." He paused. "Unless, you want me to stay around—"

"No, I'll be fine. Really." She twirled the empty beer bottle in her palm. "Maybe after the dust settles, we could find our own place."

"I'd like that. Can't say I'm big on living alone after this."

"Trust me, after a week at Cara's I'd probably rather live at a crime scene." She paused. "That was a joke."

"I know it was." He pulled her in for a hug. "Just let me know if I can do anything."

"I will."

The waitress came over with another round of beers. He lifted his up. "To Cindy."

"To Cindy," she echoed, then she drank. Right now, she needed to erase the trauma of what happened; Ryan and the drinks would help her forget. Starting tomorrow, she vowed to do whatever it took to keep another innocent person from being hurt because of her.

THIRTY-NINE

MOLLY

Molly was finishing up her evening shift at Chester House. They'd secured all the animals for the night, and deep-cleaned the foyer and waiting area for the upcoming party.

"You want me to stay until you close up?" Marsha asked.

"I'm fine."

"I can stay with her," Charlie said, leaning the broom and dustpan in the corner.

Marsha nodded, glancing at the calendar on the wall before she left.

"You'll both be at the fundraiser, right?" she asked.

"Wouldn't miss it," Charlie said.

"I'll be there," Molly said.

"Bring a date. Or a friend. Anyone you think might commit to helping us out." She shrugged on her jacket. "Sure could use the extra hands. Have a good night."

That was why the upcoming fundraiser was so important. Not only would it bring in large donations, but it would also likely result in a few more volunteers coming on board, at least for the summer. It had felt like a revolving door lately. There were tons of high school and college students who liked to volunteer, but they didn't really last. The only real staples were Marsha, Molly, Charlie and a few guys who worked morning shifts.

"Who knew Marsha cared about our social lives?" Charlie joked.

"I guess she's not always a drill sergeant." Molly smiled. Being here for the past couple hours had almost made her forget about the trauma of last night. She'd actually been thankful Marsha had been there, serving as a buffer. Charlie hadn't mentioned what happened with Fiona last night. Molly wondered if he even knew.

"So, are you bringing anyone tomorrow?"

"Ben is coming with me."

"Are you two dating again?"

"I don't know." She could feel her cheeks blushing. "It might be headed in that direction."

Charlie remained quiet, which made her think he wasn't happy for her. She'd dropped enough details about Ben in the past to leave a bad impression. Or maybe he was gearing up to confront her about Fiona. She was embarrassed about what happened and feared Charlie would label her just as Fiona had. A freak.

"What about you? How are things with Fiona?"

He hesitated. "We've been fighting lately. With summer around the corner, she's been pressuring me to introduce her to my family. I don't know if I'm ready for that."

"Oh." He didn't act like he knew about last night. And it also explained why Fiona had tracked her down. Maybe she wanted some honest advice, or she might have been hoping Molly would put in a good word for her. The latter seemed more likely.

"She's a sweet girl. Truth is, I don't know how serious she is about me. Or anything, really. I'm not ready to introduce her to my family until I know." When Molly didn't respond right away, he pressed further. "She is a nice person, right?"

"We work together, but..." Molly didn't really know what to say. Fiona was civil with her, chatty, but she'd pretty much shut down any chance of the two of them being friends, which is why Molly had lashed out at her last night. It was obvious she was pestering Molly for her own gains, and Molly was tired of feeling used.

"Please, tell me." He leaned across the table. "We've been together a few months, and nothing is exactly wrong, but I can't shake the feeling I'm one of her playthings. If she's a truly awful person, I'd like to know it now. Especially before she meets my family."

"She's not awful." Molly laughed nervously. "She's just a little self-involved. I don't think she sees much past herself. She's not like—"

"Us." He smiled. "We see the problems in the world and try to fix them. It's why we volunteer in the first place."

"Yeah, she's definitely not like that." Molly paused. Should she tell him about last night? How she'd pushed Fiona? He'd probably find out soon enough, but she didn't want to ruin the moment. "I'm not saying you shouldn't go out with her. She's nice and funny when she wants to be. Maybe she just has some growing up to do."

"Well, it's not like I'm trying to marry the girl." He shook his head. "I guess what I'm trying to say is people like us are rare. It makes it hard sometimes, because we care about things others don't. It can make us lonely. It's also why we have to stick together."

Charlie was right. Maybe these thoughts and experiences she'd labeled as burdens were actually gifts. It separated her from the Bens and Fionas of the world, and made her more sensitive than the Caras and Rachels.

He sighed and stretched his arms. "After this week, I'm exhausted. Is it wrong that I want tomorrow night to be over?"

"Marsha said last season's event brought in a lot of extra sponsors." She forced a smile, avoiding eye contact. "It's one of those necessary evils, I guess."

"I'm looking forward to next weekend, at least. My family took some time off, and we're having a little reunion. We've booked a cabin in the woods. Should be a good time, if Fiona stops pressuring me to bring her along." He saw Molly's face and stopped. "You okay?"

"Not really." It felt nice to be honest about at least that much, even if she was still holding back. Charlie was good at picking up on others' emotions, especially hers. He'd opened up to her about his problems, and now she wanted to reciprocate. "I've got some family stuff, too. It's just not as happy as yours."

"Why don't we go grab a bite to eat? We can talk about it."

"You were just talking about how tired you are. I'm sure you'd rather go home. You've put in enough hours for charity this week," she tried to joke.

"It's not charity." His tone was serious, sincere. "You're my friend and I can tell something is bothering you."

The loneliness that had been plaguing her for the past day—for much longer than that, if she was being honest—slid away. Someone cared. Not out of duty, like one of her sisters, or out of personal gain, like Ben and Fiona. He was genuinely concerned, and it felt nice.

FORTY

MOLLY

They walked down the street to the Midnight Diner for burgers and shakes. It was there she finally opened up with him about what she'd experienced in the last twenty-four hours. Rather, what Rachel had experienced, and how it was difficult watching her pain, like watching a tragedy unfold behind a glass wall and not being able to do anything.

"I can't imagine." Charlie was staring over her, at nothing, it seemed. "I feel like an ass."

"Why? None of this is your fault."

"I was giving you a hard time about Gemini when it first hit the news. Like it was a joke, or something. I never stopped to think real lives were being torn apart. And now here we are, and your sister—"

"You couldn't have known that." Sure, he'd made a callous joke, but he wouldn't be the first person to put his foot in his mouth. Or the last. Most people didn't stop to think about how devastating these cases could be. They had the luxury of distance, something Molly once had, and she wished she could go back to that time.

"You're the only person who has cared to ask about my life

in general," she continued. "You're a great person. And, if I'm being honest, my only friend."

"That can't be true."

"It is. You know, growing up I was always close with my sisters. They were my best friends. That all changed when our father died. We've grown apart this last year, and without them, I feel like I have nobody."

"Grief can do that to people."

"It's more than just grief." Being honest felt so good, Molly wanted to tell him everything, but she couldn't. It would be a betrayal. So, she paraphrased. "My sisters have this idea our father wasn't as good a person as we thought. They've made some accusations about him in the past year that I can't fully wrap my head around. And he's no longer here to defend himself."

"Like what?"

"It's hard to explain."

She knew who her father was to her: the man who took her hunting, taught her about life, loved her unconditionally. Then there was the person Cara and Rachel believed him to be: Gemini, a monster who murdered women and toyed with police. The two identities couldn't exist in the same space, and Molly wanted, with every fiber of her being, for the man she knew to be the real one.

"I don't want to pry." His hands fidgeted with his straw. "You don't have to give me the details."

"We found some things in my dad's house, after he died. Stuff he didn't want us to find. My sisters would rather focus on what we found than the person we knew, and something about that doesn't sit right with me. It's pushed us away from—"

"Excuse me."

It took Molly a moment to realize someone else, not Charlie, was talking to her. She turned, caught off guard by the man standing beside their table.

"Elias?" She stood.

"I thought that was you." He moved toward her like he wanted a hug, but held out his hand instead. She shook it.

"How are you?" Fear climbed her spine, and she couldn't decide why. Probably because she wasn't expecting to see anyone she knew at the Midnight Diner. And she was still shaken from yesterday.

"I'm good, good." He looked around the restaurant, and then as though reading her mind, he offered an explanation. "I've got a couple of rentals around this part of town. I'm checking up on them, and what not."

"I didn't know you were still renting."

"Yeah, you know, your dad was always giving me tips on real estate and stuff." He smiled genuinely. "I miss him a lot, you know. And I've been thinking about you girls."

Saliva stalled in Molly's throat.

Elias' gaze wandered around the room, and landed on Charlie. "Is this your boyfriend?"

Molly turned, blushing. "No, this is my friend. We work together at the animal shelter down the street."

"Hello." Charlie offered a friendly wave, then went back to drinking his milkshake.

"Animal shelter, huh?" Elias pressed his chapped lips together and nodded. "Your dad would be proud of you. He always said you did the most for others."

"I'd hope so."

"Well, I don't want to take up your time." He paused, as though he wanted to say more, but was reluctant to do so in Charlie's presence. "It's good running into you."

"You too."

She continued gritting her teeth as she watched him walk away. Elias often appeared at random moments, but she felt like this run-in might have been planned. She'd not noticed him when they walked into the diner. Had he even been eating? But why would he be following her around now?

"Who was that?" Charlie asked.

"Elias." She sat back down, still looking over her shoulder, as though the encounter wasn't yet finished. "He is... was my dad's best friend."

"He seems a little..."

"Strange?"

"I was just going to say quirky, but yeah, I guess you're right."

"Yeah, he's always been like that. He can be socially awkward, but I think that's because Dad was his only real friend." She looked in Elias' direction, even though he was gone.

Charlie took another sip of his drink. "Anyway, we were talking about your sisters. You were saying you wanted to prove them wrong."

Molly's mind was still on Elias, her eyes on the window where she'd last seen him. "Right. I just don't know how to do that."

"You have to present your own theory."

"What do you mean?"

"Well, clearly they see one side of your father. You have to make them see another. Make them see he's the good person you remember him being."

Charlie didn't know the whole story, but his advice made her think. Instead of showing her sisters another side to their Dad, maybe she needed to present a new suspect altogether? Prove to them someone else had committed these crimes. Prove their dad wasn't Gemini.

Maybe she wasn't crazy to suspect her father wasn't the real Gemini. Maybe someone else was to blame, and for whatever reason, her father had vowed to keep the secret.

Elias' secret perhaps?

She never considered it before. Whoever framed her father

had to be close to him, and Elias was his best friend. They were around the same age, which meant Elias would have been young and healthy during the years Gemini was most active. Even the way he'd run into her right now seemed intentional; she wondered if Cara and Rachel had seen him lately.

"You know what?" she said to Charlie. "I think that's exactly what I should do."

She needed to investigate further.

FORTY-ONE

CARA

Cara tried reaching out to Rachel and Molly throughout the day, seeing if they needed anything. Molly was busy working. Rachel was in artificially good spirits, having gotten drunk at lunch with her other roommate. Her *living* roommate, a morbid thought Cara couldn't shake. Rachel still hadn't been allowed inside her apartment, so she decided to sleep off her hangover at Molly's another night before moving in with Cara.

Since both her sisters were safe, she tried reaching out to James. She wanted him to know that he was a priority to her, but he was giving her the cold shoulder. When she suggested they meet at the hotel, he said he already had plans with a colleague who lived nearby. She didn't know if she believed him, or if he was simply punishing her. She didn't blame him for being upset, and decided it was best to give him space.

Cara tried not to think about the many people she had let down, and instead, turned her attention to Gemini. She devoted the rest of her afternoon to doing what she did best. Trying to make sense of the obscure.

As a child, Cara enjoyed puzzles. She would sort the pieces, then spend careful time analyzing each carved-out detail, never losing sight of the big picture. Sometimes she would complete the entire board in her mind before placing the pieces where they went. And no matter how long it took her to complete the project, she got it right. Speed always took a backseat to accuracy. She wondered if this was similar to how her father felt plotting out his kills.

That might also explain why she was drawn to mysteries. Both fictional and real. She liked gathering information from various sources, photographs and clues and witness statements, then she'd lay everything out on the table, literally. She'd stare at her separate collections until they made sense, then she'd bring them together, creating a coherent story. Finding the truth was often impossible, but Cara got close.

She was doing that now. She had printed out everything she could about the most recent Gemini kills. She had the names of all his victims—Margaret Grace, Beverley Quinn, Cindy Reece —and their connections to each one of them.

Their mother's name.

Cara's former boss.

Rachel's roommate.

And she had the other clues, too. The message: *He's back from the grave*. The passage plucked from Beverley Quinn's book. The symbol carved into Cindy's flesh. There was a common theme in the madness, something that would point her toward who was doing this. She just had to find it.

Cara's eyes scanned the documents, devouring each detail like a ravenous animal on a binge. All the connections led back to them, which confirmed what she already feared. The person who was doing this—this new Gemini—knew who the original culprit was.

This person knew about them.

This person knew about their father.

This person knew they had kept his secret.

And now this person was toying with them, leaving subtle

clues. They couldn't go to the police without revealing the truth about their father, and she couldn't turn to Tate without unveiling all her other secrets.

Lies upon lies, secrets upon secrets. This was their inheritance. When she looked at her father's smiling face, still sitting in the frame on her desk, it took all her strength not to hurl the picture across the room. Instead of focusing on what she couldn't do, she focused on what she could, forcing herself to rework the puzzle until the picture was clear in her mind.

And she felt like she was getting closer.

She barely registered the sound of the front door opening, then slamming shut. She didn't have the wherewithal to be afraid; all of the little mysteries surrounding this new string of murders were coming into focus, making her feel, for the first time since that fateful night in her father's shed, like she had the upper hand. She was so very close.

Then there was the sound of something clattering against the hardwood floor, and she was forced to look up. Tate was standing in front of her. He had knocked over a stack of books, not even trying to retrieve them. His gaze was locked on hers.

"What the hell, Tate?" She was more annoyed that he had interrupted her quest for answers than she was by his behavior. She started putting away her research, hoping Tate wouldn't notice anything Gemini-related.

"We need to talk." His words were overflowing with annoyance, much like his stare.

"I'm in the middle of something." It came out like an excuse, but it was true. It was so fucking true, and she wished now more than ever he'd leave her alone.

"Now."

One word, harsh and final. He dropped a folder onto her lap. She looked up at him, for the first time willing to take in his demeanor, the way he was swaying from side to side, like a flimsy tree caught in the wrath of a storm. She flipped open the folder, and felt her stomach clench.

There were pictures of her with James. At the hotel bar. At the park. Last night, in her car.

"It's really come to this?" he asked. The question was rhetorical. For a relationship built on openness and trust, neither one of them would have predicted another man would come between them.

"I knew there was something going on with you. I've tried talking to you about it. Wooing you. I was willing to move into this house." He spread his arms, as though he could reach out and touch all the memories in the space. Their life and history together on full display. "And you do this to me?"

Cara didn't want him to find out about James like this. She wanted to be the one to tell him, when the time was right. Thing is, there was never a right time to unveil a truth so large, a truth which rattled the foundation on which they stood. He was forcing it out of her now. She started to speak, her words shaky, still trying to buy herself time.

"You've been following me?"

"I had one of my co-workers follow you."

She looked down at the pictures. Each one was taken from a distance, zoomed in enough that you could see both faces with precise clarity. He'd been onto her for weeks. Maybe even a month. It was embarrassing he'd dragged other people into this.

"This isn't what you—"

"Don't insult me with excuses." He raised a trembling hand. "Did you really think you could cheat on *a cop* and he wouldn't have the resources to find out?"

"Tate, you need to listen to me." She stood, reaching out for him, but he stepped back, like her touch was toxic. His sheer anger brought tears to her eyes.

"I'm done listening. I'm done trying, Cara. I would do so

much for you, but I'm not going to stand by while you have an affair."

"I'm not having an affair!" she shouted, but Tate was in no state to listen.

"It's right there." He extended his hand towards the photo, just barely missing Cara's shoulder. "I have proof of it. Pictures of you and your lover—"

"He's my brother!" she shouted, louder this time, trying with all her might to drown out his accusations.

Tate stumbled, first physically, taking a step that didn't quite land, then with his words. "He was... What?"

"He's my brother," she said, calmer this time. "James is my brother."

FORTY-TWO

CARA

Tate sat on the couch balancing his elbows on his knees. He rubbed at his head like he could somehow dislodge the thoughts inside. Or perhaps, piece it all together, like one of Cara's puzzles.

"Since when do you have a brother?"

"Most of my life, it seems." She tried to smile, but it felt false. "I just found out about him six months ago."

"How?"

"After Dad died, I started looking into his history. Going through his belongings..." She stopped herself, thinking now might be her chance to unload everything. And yet the words wouldn't come. They sat stubborn on her tongue. *James*, she warned herself. *Focus on James.*

"I think it's something most people do after their parents die. Both of mine were gone in less than a year, and I was searching for a connection to them. I went as far as submitting a DNA test to one of those ancestry sites. Turns out, James had submitted his DNA, too."

Tate was in awe. "Did your father know about him?"

"If he did, he didn't make any attempts to be in James' life."

She looked away, could feel shame spreading across her cheeks. "James is the same age as Molly, which means he cheated on my mom. It's probably why he never had anything to do with him."

Tate stood then, pacing across the room. "I can't believe this. Henry cheated on Margaret Grace?"

Tate had always respected his father-in-law. Witnessing the shock to his uncovered affair made Cara shudder; she could only imagine how Tate would react if he found out the whole truth about Henry Martin, as ugly as it was.

"What did your sisters say?" he asked after several minutes of silent thought.

She lowered her voice, the shame all but consuming her. "I haven't told them. They don't know anything about him."

He rubbed his face, then let out a laugh. "This explains everything. Why you've taken your dad's death this hard. Why you've pulled away from all of us in the past year. You found out this horrible secret and you've been keeping it to yourself."

She coughed, then added, "Yes."

Tell him now, a voice inside said. *Tell him the truth, that your father's affair is nothing compared to the secrets you're really keeping. Tell him your father is a monster, a murderer. Tell him Henry Martin is Gemini.*

The thought of confessing filled her with both sickness and relief. How painful it would be to share the truth, but how comforting it would be to stop all the secrets.

But the words wouldn't come. She thought of the way Tate looked at her at the beginning of their conversation. He thought she was having an affair, and in that moment, everything he'd ever felt about her and their lives together had changed. What would he do if she told him his father-in-law was a serial killer? How would he look at her then?

"I can't believe you've not told them about this."

"I wanted to get to know him first. It didn't feel fair to intro-duce them without having an idea of what kind of person he was. The last thing I want to do is cause more pain for our family."

James had been pestering her about introducing him to Tate and her sisters for weeks, but she kept stalling. He was desperate to be reunited with the family he never had, but, self-ishly, Cara enjoyed having him all to herself. Every moment of her life before finding out Henry Martin was Gemini had been shared with her sisters, and every moment since then had been stained. Her time with James made her feel new, clean, like a happy family was still attainable.

"And is he a good guy?" Tate asked.

"Seems to be. He's a veterinarian based out of Boston. He's been flying in when he can to meet with me. His mother married and he has a decent relationship with his stepfather. Still, I guess you never want to pass up the opportunity to get to know your family. That's why we've been at the hotel so often."

"I can't wrap my head around all this," Tate said, sitting back down. "When I saw those pictures, my mind went to the worst possible scenario."

"I can't blame you for that. I've been lying to you. Lying to Rachel and Molly. Lying to myself, in some ways." Cara forced herself to look at Tate. "But I'd never cheat on you. You're the most important person in my life, and I'm sorry I've kept so much from you."

Tate placed his hand over hers. "It's a lot to process. To find this out and not even be able to ask your dad about it. Or your mom. You must have so many questions."

Cara let out a dry laugh. "I do."

"Thank you for telling me now. And I think you need to tell Molly and Rachel, too."

"You're right." And he was, but what she couldn't tell him was that they already had too much on their plates right now. While Tate and his friends on the force were chasing a killer, she and her sisters were chasing a trail left behind by their father, and James was only a small part of that. The most inno-cent part.

That was something else that had been bothering her over the past few months. In all the conversations she'd had with James, he understandably wanted to know about Henry Martin, the father he'd never met. She'd told him the truth up to a point, but how could she tell him half his DNA belonged to a serial killer? She couldn't, thus carrying on the lie that Henry Martin was a decent man.

"You need to tell them," Tate said. "Not just because they deserve to know, but because you have to share this with some-one. You can't keep all this inside, trying to shield them from it. All it's doing is tearing you apart. You can't torture yourself over the mistakes your father made. He wouldn't want that for you."

Cara didn't know what her father would want for her. She didn't know if he ever cared about her at all. But Tate was right about telling her sisters; they needed to know about James. She should have told them much earlier, before this new round of killings even started. Who had she been trying to protect in this past year? Their marriage? Her sisters? Her father?

"I'll tell them," she decided, her fingers trembling.

Cara had to stop being the keeper of Henry Martin's secrets.

FORTY-THREE

RACHEL

Rachel didn't think she could take another night sleeping on Molly's lumpy sofa, and she was happy she didn't have to. An officer had called her early that morning and told her the apartment was clear. She'd swung by her place and grabbed a few necessities, taking great care to avoid the kitchen. It was strange being there, breathing in the familiar woody incense mixed with the scent of blood.

She'd packed enough clothes for a week, and asked another co-worker to cover her upcoming shifts. There was only one more obligation she had to complete before she settled in at Cara's place: meet with Katelyn.

She wasn't surprised when Katelyn reached out. After all, Cindy's murder had been all over the news, linked to the other Gemini killings, although the grizzliest of details were left under wraps. The address hadn't been released, but Katelyn must have realized the crime had happened at their old apartment. She must have looked behind the reporter at the graffiti-covered parking sign, the speckled railing leading up to the front door.

They agreed to meet at the park. Rachel would have

preferred to not meet at all, but Katelyn was persistent. It was painful to see her name appear on Rachel's phone, and she didn't want to deal with any further harassment. It somehow hurt her more to know that Katelyn was only reaching out because Cindy was dead, and for no other reason.

Katelyn was already sitting on the park bench when Rachel arrived. She was wearing her favorite red tunic and leggings alongside the buffalo-checkered Keds Rachel always gave her a hard time about. Normally, Rachel would have cracked a joke, but she didn't. She was already in enough pain.

"Hi," Katelyn said. She stood, moving toward her for a hug. Rachel accepted, but then quickly stepped away. "Thanks for meeting me."

"You didn't really give me much of a choice."

"I wasn't going to just let you avoid me after what happened. I had to see you. Are you okay?"

"Not really." The vulnerability she was so used to displaying around Katelyn made her uncomfortable now, so she changed direction. "Clearly, I've not been okay for a while. That's why you left, remember?"

"I don't want to get into this right now—"

"Then what do you want to get into? Do you want to hear all the details? How I found my roommate's body carved up in my own kitchen? Steps away from where we used to—" She stopped, raising a hand to her mouth to stifle her sobs. "I still don't want to think about it, let alone talk about it. My goodness, Katelyn, you're no better than the reporters hanging around the apartment."

That last sentence clearly hurt, but Katelyn refused to snap back. She sucked in her cheeks, opting to be the bigger person, something that irritated Rachel more.

"I don't want to hear about the details," she said. "I just want to check on you. I can't imagine how terrifying it must have been."

"It was something." She looked at the fallen leaves on the sidewalk, anywhere other than Katelyn's piercing stare.

"What are you doing now? Are you staying at the apartment?"

"I'm bunking up with Cara for a while."

"That's good. You should be around family at a time like this."

Family. That's what Katelyn had been to her once, but now it felt like talking to a stranger. A stranger who knew all of her secrets. Well, most of them anyway. It was the one secret she didn't know that had torn them apart.

"Look, I appreciate you checking on me, but there's no need. I've been managing just fine on my own."

"I'm sure you have." She looked down. "While I'm here, I thought I'd let you know I'm leaving town for a while. I'm staying with Mom over the summer."

"Why?"

"She's trying to fix up the house and sell it. She wants to buy a smaller place by the beach somewhere, and I thought it would be good for us to spend some time together before the move."

"I meant, why did you feel the need to tell me?"

This time, Katelyn couldn't disguise the hurt Rachel's words caused. She clenched her eyes shut, like she was trying not to cry.

"Believe me, I wanted things to work out between us, and I'm heartbroken it didn't, but I don't understand why you have to be so mean to me."

"I'm not being mean. I'm being rational. You're the one who chose to end things. That means I don't need you checking up on me, and you don't have to tell me your plans for the summer."

"Fine, Rachel. I'm sorry I suggested meeting."

She stood, gathering her bag and slinging it over her shoulder. Rachel felt hollow. She didn't like being cruel to Katelyn, but she resented her for walking away. Still, with this recent string of Gemini murders, it was probably best for Katelyn to distance herself as much as possible.

"I'm sure you'll be happier there," she offered.

"It's better than staying here where there are so many memories."

Katelyn started walking down the sidewalk, then she stopped and took a few steps back.

"You know, when I first saw the news and realized a murder had taken place at our apartment, I was terrified something might have happened *to you*."

Rachel hadn't thought of this. That Katelyn might have been afraid of losing her. In her mind, she was already lost. Rachel considered telling her now, in this moment, how she really felt. That she still woke up every morning expecting to feel Katelyn's feet pressed against her shins. That she still thought of Thursday as date night, even though she hadn't been on a date in months. How even now, in this moment, she was in awe of Katelyn's beauty.

When she opened her mouth, all that came out was, "Good luck back home."

Katelyn nodded and walked away.

FORTY-FOUR

CARA

When Cara woke up, Tate was asleep beside her in bed. She considered waking him, but decided he'd get a call from the station soon. For the first time in a long while, Cara actually felt refreshed. Sure, she'd kept her biggest secret, the truth about Henry Martin hidden, but at least she'd told Tate about James. There was a lightness she could feel now, and it made her smile.

Tate stirred, squinting when he turned to see light beaming in through the bedroom windows.

"What time is it?" he asked, looking at his watch. He sat up straight. "Oh shit, I have to get going."

"Sorry, I should have woken you."

"No. I needed the rest. It was a long night."

"I'm sorry about that, too."

He climbed out of bed, taking careful time to kiss her on the head. "You don't have to apologize. I only wish you had felt like you could come to me with this earlier."

"I'm still processing it all," she said, leaning her head against his chest, so she didn't have to look at him. *It all*, of course, meant more than her father's affair, more than the realization she had a brother. It encompassed the full extent of her father's darkest actions.

"I can't believe your dad would do this to you and the girls," Tate said, his anger peeking through. "To your mom! Do you think she had any idea?"

"I think there were a lot of things about my dad she never knew."

He looked at his watch again. "I really need to leave. If you need me—"

"You've done more than enough," she said, smiling.

"Think about what I said. About your sisters. You can't keep this to yourself anymore."

She knew he was right, even if she wouldn't say it.

"I'll call you later."

With that, he got dressed and hurried out of the house.

Cara lay in bed alone, listening to the hum of the house settling around her. She thought about their conversation from last night. Rachel and Molly deserved to know the truth, and James deserved to know his entire family, not just her. And now that he was back in town, they had the opportunity.

She pulled out her phone and sent a text.

I'm going to tell them.

Minutes later, James called back.

"You're right," she said. "Rachel and Molly need to know."

"Are you serious?" His tone was a mixture of nerves and excitement. "When?"

"Tonight."

She heard him exhale on the other end of the line. "Are you sure? I don't want you to do this because I'm pressuring you."

They went back and forth, Cara assuring him she'd come to the decision on her own. She didn't tell him about her conversation with Tate.

She said Rachel and Molly would be over later that night. They agreed James would be on standby, could possibly even come by the house and meet them in person, depending on how they digested the news. She sent him her address, just in case. She'd be quick to let him know if they needed more time, but she was hoping her sisters would react positively. James had already waited long enough.

"I don't even know what to say," he said. "I never imagined I'd have three sisters, and now it's all happening. Do you think they'll handle the news okay?"

"They'll be fine." All of them had accepted painful truths in the past year. The existence of another sibling should be something to celebrate. And she hoped James would no longer feel like he wasn't important to her. "Yesterday, did you really have plans with someone else?"

"Yeah, I did. Did you think I was lying to you?"

"I don't know. After our conversation, I figured you didn't want to see me."

"I was angry last night, but this... this makes up for everything."

As they ended the phone call, Cara felt the weight lifting from her shoulders. Tate was right. Carrying all these secrets was too much for her. She'd already been carrying enough of Henry's secrets.

With the plans in place, Cara put away her phone. Right now, what she needed to do was figure out who was behind these new killings, and why exactly he was targeting them.

As usual, she had all the pieces—the evidence, the clues— she only needed to study them a little harder, until the entire picture made sense. She went into her study and sat behind the desk. She unlocked the bottom drawer, the one that contained all her folders and notebooks on Gemini.

But when she pulled open the drawer, it was empty.

She stared, blinking at the empty space. This couldn't be

right. Had she been so tired she left it out last night? She could have sworn she put everything away after Tate came storming in. She looked at the desk, checking the other drawers to make sure. Still no sign of her research.

She stood, pacing across the room and pushed the bureau forward. Her corkboard, with all its timelines and photographs, was not there. She was always most careful hiding this component of her research, on the off-chance Tate went looking around her office. But the entire board was gone.

A clammy sweat was spreading across her chest, but she continued breathing, slowly and deep. She opened up her laptop. At least she'd have the digital backups of everything she'd found thus far. She'd scanned most of the photos and witness statements, hiding them under cryptic names on her computer. Hawaii 2013 marked the Millie Rothenberg murder. Charleston 2017 marked the Kamryn Shelton case.

Both files were gone, along with all the others. In fact, her entire computer had been wiped, reverted back to factory settings.

All her pictures and timelines and articles...

All the research she'd spent the past year uncovering...

Everything proving Henry Martin was Gemini... was gone.

FORTY-FIVE

RACHEL

Rachel stood in front of Cara's house, which would always be *their* house in her mind. It was the place she grew up. Her childhood home. She'd not been inside since they uncovered the boxes.

It should have been easy for her to walk in, find a comfy spot on the sofa, binge watch Netflix, but there was a heavy air around the house now, around everything associated with her father and her family.

Even though she knew where the spare key was located, Rachel knocked on the front door. She listened to Cara's feet thudding down the stairs. When she opened the door, Cara's cheeks were flushed. Her eyes were wild.

"What's wrong now?" Rachel asked, not really wanting to know.

"Come inside."

Rachel did, dropping the two duffel bags that contained her belongings for the next month by the wall. She crossed her arms, waiting for her sister to tell her the latest development.

"Follow me."

Cara led her toward the back of the house, sliding open the

doors to her father's study. Cara's study now, she supposed, and yet she couldn't ignore the sensory pull of being back in this place: the intimate sights, familiar smells, as though even the dust had been waiting on her to return.

Cara raised her hands. "All of my Gemini research is gone."

"What do you mean *gone*?"

"For the past year, I've been looking into all the old cases. Putting together timelines of Gemini's kills and Dad's where-abouts at the time. Someone has taken it all."

"Maybe Tate did something with it."

Cara narrowed her eyes. "Tate doesn't know about any of it. I've kept it all hidden from him." She walked over to the book-case against the wall and pushed it forward. "I stored most of it on a board back here, some of the files in the desk. He rarely comes in here, but when he does, he doesn't mess with my work."

"So, what are you trying to say?"

Cara walked closer, crossing her arms. "Someone broke into the house and took it. They even wiped my computer."

"Are there signs of a break-in?"

"No." Cara pinched the bridge of her nose. "But my research is gone. Someone has been inside the house, and they've stolen my work."

"Why would someone do that?"

"For the same reasons they murdered someone with Mom's name. And your roommate and my former boss. They're trying to send us a message. *He's back from the grave.*"

Rachel looked around the room, picturing how much research her sister had likely collected over the past year. She imagined it all disappearing with the snap of a finger.

"You think that the killer has been in here?"

"That has to be what happened. No one knows I've been looking into Gemini, but if this new killer knows as much about us as I think he does, it wouldn't be hard for him to figure out I was studying the cases."

"When is the last time you were around your research?"

"I know it was here yesterday." She turned quickly, as though she didn't want Rachel to see her face. "I was working on it when Tate came home. Someone must have broken into the house while we were asleep."

Rachel shivered. The idea of someone creeping around downstairs while Cara and Tate slept unsettled her.

"Would someone really be that brazen? To sneak around a cop's house in the middle of the night just to take your research?"

"Well, this stuff didn't disappear on its own." She paused. "Maybe they plan on exposing Dad as the real Gemini killer?"

"If that were the plan, I don't think they'd be piling up bodies of their own." Rachel thought for a minute. "Maybe this copycat wants all the credit for himself. He may not *want* anyone finding out Dad was Gemini."

"I don't know what they're after, but it freaks me out someone has been inside the house. Our house." She waited. "And if this person planned on taking all the credit, I'm not sure why they'd target people we know."

Rachel looked around the room again, tried to imagine a stranger sifting through Cara's things. She couldn't quite picture it. "Since there are no signs of a break-in, I think we need to consider who might have access to the house."

"Obviously, me. Tate." Cara sounded defensive.

"And me. Molly." She made eye contact with Cara, looking for a reaction. "Who else would have a spare key?"

"Elias would know about the spare. Hell, he might even have his own copy. He sometimes looked after the house when Mom and Dad were away." She paused, as though really trying to think. "Someone could have taken one of our copies, which brings us back to who is close to us."

"When I stopped by Molly's apartment the other night, she had been out with Ben. Do you think he could have stolen her key?"

"Anything is possible. Whoever is doing this has access to us. They could have made a copy of the key months ago without our even knowing."

They were back at a standstill. Too many possibilities, but not enough evidence pointing them in the right direction.

"Maybe it's time to bring Tate into this—"

"No. If I tell him Dad is Gemini, it will change everything between us. He's not the type of person who can just sit on information like that. I mean, look at what it's done to us this past year. I don't want him to be in a position where he has to choose between supporting me and doing what's morally right."

"You think it's morally right to tell people the truth about Gemini? About Dad?" When Rachel had made that same argument a year ago, Cara had pushed back the hardest.

"I don't think people would be dying now if we had."

Rachel knew this was the closest Cara would ever come to admitting she was wrong. Her regret was almost palpable.

"There's something else I should tell you," Cara continued. "The day we burned the pictures in the shed... we didn't burn all of them."

"What do you mean?" Rachel asked, dryly. "Molly said you burned them all."

"She thought we did. But I kept some, without her knowing."

"What? After making such a fuss about going to the cops without evidence—"

"I didn't want you going to the cops then. And I wasn't keeping them for that reason. I wanted them so I could investigate the crimes."

"What about the jewelry?"

"It's all gone. The flames caused too much damage."

Rachel had been angry with her sisters for burning the evidence for an entire year; it was what pushed her away from them more than anything. Now she was learning that those same pictures still existed and had been stolen all at once.

"You don't think Molly would have taken my research do you?" Cara asked.

"Molly? You said she didn't know you had it."

"Right, but what if she found it. She's adamant Dad is innocent. What if she stole my research so that we wouldn't be able to prove it?"

"I don't think Molly would go that far—"

"You're the one who suggested she might know more than she was letting on. And you also pointed out she has a key to the house."

"That was before Cindy died." And just like that, Rachel was back to seeing the body. A shiver climbed her spine. Her own sister couldn't do that to another person, could she?

"I'm not saying Molly is killing people. But what if she knows who is? She might be holding back because she wants to clear Dad's name. Maybe Ben is helping her."

Rachel pondered Cara's theory. Molly would do anything to prove their father's innocence, but she didn't believe she'd deceive them in the process. She hoped she wouldn't.

"If Ben is behind this, he's doing it on his own," she said. "She's loyal to Dad, but she's loyal to us, too."

"Right," Cara said, but something in her voice sounded less than genuine. "She's coming over later, you know. I told her to stop by after the Chester House fundraiser."

"Good."

But Rachel now had an uneasy feeling. About what, she couldn't quite explain.

FORTY-SIX

MOLLY

Chester House was the one place that could make Molly forget about her problems. She had started volunteering as a way to repent for her father's sins. Gemini had haunted her long before the new round of killings started. For a year, she'd fought the evidence in front of her.

The man who taught me how to ride a bike is a killer.

The man who used to proofread my essays is a killer.

The man who was supposed to walk me down the aisle is a killer.

She had never wanted to believe it, and now it appeared that her apprehension was warranted. Elias had as many red flags about him as their father did. And he was a more appropriate suspect, she figured. Perhaps she was right after all and Henry Martin had caught onto his friend's actions before his death. She only needed to find proof.

Molly had plans to investigate further, but she had to get through the Chester House fundraiser first. She slicked her hair into a ponytail and slipped into a black dress. She wanted to look her best, but she was also using the event to her advantage. She'd invited Elias to come.

As she expected, he was one of the first people to arrive once the doors opened.

"Molly," he said, walking toward her with arms wide. She tried to act as natural as possible when they embraced. "I can't tell you how happy I am that you invited me. It means a lot."

"After we ran into each other yesterday, I realized it's been too long. There's free food and drinks. Not a bad way to spend a Tuesday night." She had multiple reasons for inviting him, actually. First, she wanted to see how he would react. She also wanted to know where he would be that evening, for later.

Marsha walked by wearing a purple sweater and slacks, a departure from her usual hoodie and jeans. She nodded at a few of the early guests, waving when she caught sight of Molly.

"Let me introduce you to the director," she said, pushing Elias in her direction. He was never one to turn down an influential person. And Marsha enjoyed hearing the sound of her own voice. She figured if she could get the two of them together, they might distract each other long enough for her to sneak out and take on the next part of her plan.

"Thank you so much for having me," Elias said, extending his hand to shake Marsha's.

"It's always nice to meet new faces," she said. "Come. Let me give you a tour."

Molly smiled as they walked away, pleased to see her plan was working. She shooed the thoughts of Gemini away and focused on making the night the best event possible. She made her way around the room, making small talk with familiar faces and strangers alike. She listened as Marsha presented Chester House's mission statement to the crowd.

Molly should have enjoyed the evening, but she was also disappointed Ben still hadn't arrived. She'd not pressured him to come, and he'd acted as though he wanted to. Maybe Rachel was right. Ben was an asshole who wouldn't change. She'd wanted to believe otherwise.

He could be in danger, she thought. Gemini had already gone after people connected to Cara and Rachel. Of course, Gemini had never killed a male victim. She checked her phone. There were no messages from Ben. She took a deep breath and tried not to think about it.

"There you are," Charlie said, standing next to her. "We were looking for you earlier."

"Marsha had me offering tours of the kennels. We must have missed each other." Molly noticed Charlie was dressed up; it was the first time she'd seen him in something other than a T-shirt and jeans. "Nice outfit."

"I picked it out," said Fiona, walking beside them. Her two-piece ensemble was fire-engine red and eye-catching; Molly was surprised she hadn't noticed her earlier. It was the first time they'd seen each other since their argument.

"Having a good time?" she asked.

"The best. Charlie gave me a tour of the animals in the back. I might just steal one for myself." Fiona stepped closer to him, resting her hand on his chest. She seemed desperate to prove their relationship was on the mend.

"Looks like Marsha could use an extra hand." Charlie hurried across the room, where Marsha was busy replenishing the buffet table, leaving the two of them alone.

"Fiona, about the other night," Molly started. "I want to apologize. I shouldn't have pushed—"

"It's fine." Her words were clipped. "Let's just forget about it."

"I had a lot on my mind—"

"Charlie told me about your sister. You were dealing with something much bigger than my problems. I'm sorry for not even asking what you were going through."

Molly swallowed hard. "Did you tell Charlie—"

"No. It was late and we were both emotional. I'm too embarrassed to tell him about it, really. Keep it between us?"

Her cheeks blushed with relief. "I'm happy you and Charlie patched things up."

"Me too. I think we're moving in the right direction. I'm introducing him to my parents next week." The smile fell, and she looked away. "I'm sorry for accusing you of having feelings for him. And I'm sorry for the other things I said."

"It's fine. Really."

"It's sometimes hard for me to accept when a person is being genuine. You've been a good friend to Charlie. And me. It's time I start returning the favor."

Fiona was complicated, but who wasn't? Maybe she needed someone like Charlie to bring out the best in her. Seeing them together only made her long for Ben more.

Another hour passed. Molly had filled up on miniature hot dogs and cheddar biscuits. She'd served punch and made small talk with a dozen or so attendants. She kept scanning the crowd, but there was still no sign of Ben. Elias, on the other hand, was sitting at a table with Marsha, deep in conversation. The plan was working.

"Everything okay?" Charlie said, standing beside her.

"Yeah." Her eyes darted to the door. "Look, I think I'm going to have to get out of here. I promised my sister I'd head over to her place."

"Man, we were going to see if you wanted to grab dinner with us. Is Ben here?"

"He's around here somewhere," she lied, not wanting to admit she'd been stood up. "Next time, okay?"

"I understand. We'll probably head out, too. One of your sisters works at McGuire's, right?"

"Not tonight. But it's a fun place. You two should check it out." In reality, Molly had only been there twice, and was miserable both times. Bars weren't really her scene, but she would have made an exception for Charlie and Fiona. And Ben, if he ever turned up. She tried not to think about it. Tonight was about tackling bigger problems than Ben.

Across the room, Elias was still in conversation with Marsha and a few others. They'd barely spoken since he'd arrived, and she wanted to leave before he saw her again. She worried, briefly, that if her suspicions were right, and Elias was Gemini, that she'd put Marsha in a dangerous position, but she pushed the thought away. Marsha didn't fit the profile of Gemini's victims.

Molly hurried outside before Elias could see her leave.

The colors in the sky were dimming from blue to gray as night set in. She made it a few steps when she noticed Ben's car pulling up to the curb. He slammed the driver's side door.

She froze, waiting for Ben to meet her on the sidewalk. "You're late."

"I know." He looked up and down the street. "I got held up with some things."

"The party is practically over. I'm just now leaving."

"I said I'm sorry." He wrapped an arm around her waist, pulling her closer. "Come on, the night is young. Let's grab some drinks. That's still part of the plan, right? We can head back to my place after."

Molly pulled away. "I'm not going anywhere with you."

"Don't be like this." He was giving her that smile, the one that tried to magically pacify her, but this time, she wasn't having it.

"I can't depend on you for anything, and you still expect me to be there when you want me."

"I've got a lot going on—"

"It doesn't matter. When you care about a person, you make time for them. You keep your promises. You show up when they need you." She paused, changing her tone. "When their *parents* die, you're there for them."

He looked down. "Are we really going to hash this out again?"

"No. We're not." She pushed past him, walking away. "We're done."

He scoffed. "You think you're *breaking up* with me? I mean, this isn't even official."

"Whatever this is, it's not happening anymore." She turned, pausing long enough to get a good look at his face. She felt a finality that had never been there before. "Have a nice life, Ben."

"Molly, come on. You're overreacting."

He grabbed her arm. She tried shaking him off, but he refused to let go. She didn't like the feeling of his hands on her skin, the way they were pressing into her, trying to squeeze something out. When she looked into his eyes, she wondered what else he was capable of doing.

"Let go of me, or I'll scream," she said, as plainly as she could. There were several people on the sidewalk, and she wanted to use their presence to her advantage.

After several seconds, he let go. He seemed more than just embarrassed. Disappointed, maybe. After she got a few steps ahead of him, he shouted after her.

"Whatever. Like I need a clingy bitch like you."

Molly kept walking ahead, her shoulders back, her head high. She didn't turn, didn't give him the satisfaction of letting him think his words bothered her. In fact, she wasn't bothered at all. If anything, she was proud. Instead of her eyes filling with tears, she smiled.

Confidence was blooming inside her chest, and she very much liked the feeling.

FORTY-SEVEN

Just look at her, walking along the sidewalk without a care in the world. She's smiling, like she's got some fantastic story taking place in her head. For a brief moment, she looks invincible. But it's only a moment, and it's also a fraud.

No one is invincible. Everyone has their time, and tonight is hers.

She wouldn't know that, parading down the street. So full of life. So full of promise and possibility. It will soon be stripped away, but she doesn't know it, and there's something beautiful about that.

I let her lead the way, waiting for the precise moment when I can strike.

See, I've been a fraud this whole time, too. So few people have ever seen the real me, the monster lurking inside. She is about to be next, and I can feel my body tensing with excitement.

She isn't alarmed that I'm walking beside her. What is there to fear? It's a wonderful Tuesday night, the moon casting a spotlight wherever we turn. Ah, the moon. It's so enchanting, like her. She stops, craning her head to look above. She's smiling, taking in the beauty for what she doesn't know will be the last time.

"Have you ever seen anything so beautiful," she says to me, or herself, or to no one.

I wrap my arms around her, covering her mouth with the cloth. She's too mesmerized by the sky to be alarmed at first, but once she is, her eyes turn wide. She tries to scream, but it's useless, and the car driving past with the heavy bass drowns it out. She struggles, her chest heaving rapidly, and then she goes limp in my arms.

I make another cursory check of the sidewalk, this way and that. No one, only us, embracing beneath the light of the moon.

I pull her in the alley and begin.

It's so very close to being finished.

FORTY-EIGHT

CARA

Cara couldn't shake the creepy feeling she had when she thought about someone entering her house without her permission, snooping through her things, the research she'd kept hidden from everyone, including her husband. It was a violation. Just like this new round of murders had been a complete violation. Gemini was supposed to be her secret, her burden to bear, and now she had to listen as the whole world talked about it, knowing only she held the answers.

Adding to her frustration was the fact James wasn't responding to her messages. She thought he'd pester her with follow-up questions. What should he bring? What should he say? He'd gone silent since they last spoke. It wasn't like him.

Rachel burst through the front door. She was sweaty and breathing hard after her evening run. She peered into the study.

"Aren't you afraid to be running around the neighborhood at night?" Cara asked, putting away her phone.

"If this person is after me, I don't think it matters where I am," Rachel said, a look of displeasure on her face. "Any idea when Tate will be home?"

"Nope."

"I really think you should tell him someone broke into the house."

"And what will I say they took? My research proving our father is a serial killer?"

"I don't know. Tell him something. And if you think it's someone we know, you should change the locks. Obviously, this place has been compromised. The whole reason I'm staying here is because it's supposed to be safe, but that's not really the case if people can come and go as they please."

Rachel was right. Cara knew she was, but she didn't want to deal with it. There was already so much she was holding back from the world, her sisters and husband included, and beginning the process of letting people in was difficult.

If Rachel was worried about Molly, she was trying hard not to show it. She was walking around the room, her eyes scanning the bookshelves and pictures on the wall. Almost all of it had changed since their father died.

"How do you do this for a living?" Rachel asked. "Follow these cases. Write about nothing but murder and death."

"It's just a job. It was never personal until now." She turned away from her sister, who was still walking around the room. "Sometimes I think that's what I inherited from Dad, you know?"

"I have no idea what you're talking about."

"Come on, I'm sure you've thought about it in the past year. We're related to a serial killer. Don't you ever wonder how Dad could be so messed up and we turned out normal?"

"Normal is a bit of a stretch—"

"You know what I'm saying." Cara's voice conveyed she wanted to be taken seriously. "Our parents pass things down to us, whether we want them to or not."

Cara was rambling, vocalizing the thoughts and fears she had kept inside for the past year. She knew Rachel was only half listening, but she didn't care. It felt good to say the words out loud.

"I think all of us inherited something from him," she continued. "I know I didn't get any of Dad's anger or his fury, but maybe he's the reason I was drawn to these stories in the first place. Maybe that's why I'm so focused and methodical about things. Serial killers are like that, if they don't want to get caught. Which Dad never did. Maybe that's what he passed down to me."

"I try not to think about it," Rachel said, as though she was barely listening. "I won the genetic lottery that kept me from being a psychopath, and I want to leave it at that. I'm nothing like him."

Cara's phone buzzed with a notification. She'd added Google alerts for anything related to Gemini, and there was a hit. "Oh shit."

"What is it?"

"Police Respond to Possible Gemini Crime Scene," she said in a mock reporter voice. "I guess that answers whether Tate will be working late."

She stood and walked across the room. She opened the bureau, which contained the television she used to watch documentaries and interview tapes for work. Now, she turned to the local news channel, waiting to hear what reporters had to say about Gemini's latest victim.

"… arrived on the scene in the past half hour. A local was out walking their dog when they stumbled upon the body in this alley behind where I stand," said the reporter. Bright ribbons of caution tape shone in the background.

"What makes them think that it's Gemini?" Rachel asked.

"I'm sure it's the cause of death. And maybe the body was dumped in a significant place to the victim." She exhaled. "How can this be happening? We go our entire lives barely thinking about Gemini, and now it's all we hear about."

"Someone is making it that way. At least, that was your theory in the beginning. I didn't believe you at first, but after finding Cindy..."

Rachel was back in that moment, it seemed, staring at a dead body on the floor. Cara knew it was different from seeing that same image in a photograph. More brutal. Then she noticed something familiar on the screen.

"Isn't that close to Chester House? The place where Molly volunteers. When is the last time you talked to her?"

When Rachel spoke, she tried to hide the fear in her voice. "She texted me before the fundraiser started. She said she was coming by tonight."

"I'm going to call her."

"I already tried before I came home," Rachel said. "Her phone is off. She never keeps that damn thing charged."

Cara tried not to psych herself out. It wasn't yet ten o'clock. Molly could still be on her way. Besides, if the killer was targeting people the sisters knew, he wouldn't go after one of them, right?

As she was dialing Molly's number, another thought crossed through her mind. James. He wasn't responding to messages either. If this person knew about the Martin girls and their secrets, did he know about James, too?

Molly may not be the only person who was in danger.

FORTY-NINE

MOLLY

Molly had only been to Elias' house once in her life. Usually, it was Elias turning up at the Martin family home. During hunting season, he'd venture out into the woods with Henry, coming back with various animals whose fur they would strip until late into the night. He'd often come over on weekends, watching football with Henry in the den or woodworking with Henry in the shed.

Always, always with Henry.

As she got older, it was hard for Molly to understand what it was her father saw in Elias. The two were different in so many ways. Henry was an academic; he'd met Elias, the school custodian, when he first accepted his position at Whitehill High more than four decades ago. Henry was a family man, whereas Elias had no children, had never married. Perhaps that's why he'd clung to the Martin family over the years. And yet, it must have been their hobbies—hunting, woodworking, sports—where they found common ground. Since neither Margaret or Henry had siblings, Elias was the closest person the Martin girls had to an uncle.

The only time Molly went to Elias' house, she was twelve.

Elias' father had died. She had no way of knowing whether or not they were close, but she doubted it. It was as though no one was important to Elias aside from Henry. Her father had picked her up from soccer practice and told her to sit in the back. There was a steaming casserole sitting in the passenger seat.

"We're stopping by Elias' house," Henry informed her, then told her about the sudden passing. When she asked why they were bringing food, he replied, "People need each other most in the wake of loss."

It was one of those familiar lines she'd heard so often during her childhood. As they drove, farther and farther into the country, he talked to her about life and death and how humans try to manage the time in between. When they pulled up to Elias' house, an uneasiness took over. Molly had never seen a place so desolate.

The home was small, made of sun-weathered siding with a tin roof. The yard was littered with various items—gardening tools and paint cans and deflated tires. She spotted a machete leaning against a nearby tree. It was the first time she'd been confronted by someone who had far less, and it was her father's best friend. She remembered this moment as the first time she appreciated her family's wealth. They weren't rich, but to Elias, the Martins must have been kings.

"Would you like to go inside?" Henry asked her. She shook her head, still mesmerized by the paltriness of the place. Her father nodded. "I'll only be a minute. It's best not to linger."

She watched him exit the car, one of Margaret Grace Martin's homemade casseroles in his hands, and enter the rustic home, not even taking the time to knock. Molly waited in the car. Thinking of Elias. Thinking of death. Thinking of her own father, and how she was grateful to have him. After they left, the two got ice cream, as though sweetness could somehow banish the world's sadness.

All these years later, Molly could still remember how to get to Elias' place, even though it was night. She doubted he'd moved. She figured if someone called a place that measly home, they'd never put in the effort to find somewhere else. It suddenly struck her as odd that Elias was renting apartments to other people. Surely, even the most rundown apartment would be better than the shack he called home. Maybe that had been a lie, an excuse for running into her at the diner.

There was a narrow gravel road splitting the rows of trees. She'd never been this far into the forest at night, and it chilled her to think Elias lived here all alone. Then again, maybe that was what he preferred.

Her headlights illuminated the old shack, which looked even worse now than it had fifteen years ago. The house was small, but the grounds were huge. The property was unkempt, trash and unused tools scattered about. It looked like the perfect place to hide something, to hide people, to hide yourself from the world. Only the trees stood witness to what went on here.

Before entering the house, she checked her phone. No service. A tingle of fear climbed her spine when she realized how alone she was. Whatever she was looking for, she needed to hurry. She pushed on the front door, which swung open with ease. There was only one bedroom inside the house, no attic or basement she could find. There was a cupboard full of canned foods, but little else inside the kitchen. Most shelves and drawers were bare. The most up-to-date piece in the entire place was a large flat screen tacked to the living room wall, with a collection of DVDs stacked beneath. She didn't find anything connected to Gemini. In fact, there was only one personal element anywhere: a framed photograph of Elias at Fenway Park, similar to the picture of Henry he'd gifted them after the funeral. It was hanging by the front door.

Outside, Molly wanted to end her search before she started. The sky was full dark, the light on her phone dim by comparison. There was simply too much. It wasn't like she expected to find a body inside one of the barrels or a bloody weapon stabbed into a tree. Elias wouldn't be that careless. She just needed something to prove Elias was a worthier Gemini suspect than her father, and then maybe her sisters would take her concerns seriously.

At the edge of the forest stood a small shed. It looked barely big enough to hold a riding lawn mower. The sides of the building were splintered and sun-stained, and the metal roof was leaning dangerously to one side. A rusty chain was wrapped around the handles. Upon further inspection, she saw it was simply hanging there, unlocked. Perhaps Elias wasn't worried about visitors stumbling around his property after all.

Molly unfolded the chain and pushed open the doors.

A jolt of déjà vu hit her like a lightning bolt. She stepped backwards, falling hard against the dusty ground. She'd been here before, experienced this exact moment, a year earlier, with her sisters. And yet, the time and place were different. She was alone now. And she was staring at Elias' shed, not her father's.

Still, everything was the same. The pictures of the victims. Some eyes shut, some eyes wide. All throats slit, blood drenching the clothes on their bodies. The exact same evidence they'd found in Henry Martin's shed was here, too. And there was more of it. Paring knives and pocket knives and even a butcher's cleaver. Molly looked around, but only crickets and trees surrounded her.

She stood, too afraid to walk inside the shed. She took out her phone, snapping pictures of what she'd found. Something to show the others. There's no reason Elias would have all these pictures, including the weapons, unless he were the actual Gemini killer. Perhaps her first thought had been right all along. Henry, like them, was only searching for Gemini's true identity. He discovered it was Elias, his best friend, and that's why he had copies of those same photographs.

She had to get out of there. She had to tell the others.

Finally, she'd be able to convince them their father wasn't Gemini.

Elias was.

FIFTY

MOLLY

Molly's heart was beating fast as she drove to Cara's house.
Once she made it out of the woods, her phone blew up with
messages from her sisters, wondering where she was. She didn't
take the time to respond. She wanted to meet them as quickly as
possible so she could tell them what she'd found.

Her sisters might be hesitant to believe her, but they never
had the same connection she had with their father. The bond
between Molly and Henry was special. They were cut from the
same cloth, one that was no longer bloodstained, in her mind.

Finally, she could make Cara and Rachel see. Sure, having
pictures of dead women was suspicious. But Elias had those
same pictures. And weapons. And who was more likely to
commit multiple murders spanning two decades, Henry
Martin, the family man, or Elias, the recluse?

Molly unlocked the front door using her key. She could hear
her sisters' voices coming from her father's study. It sounded
like they were arguing.

When Cara caught sight of her, she exhaled. "Oh, thank
God."

She wasn't sure why Cara was so happy to see her, and she

didn't know why her sisters were fighting. The news report behind them caught her attention, and she was drawn to the screen like an insect drawn to light.

"We were worried ab—"

"Guys, wait," Molly said, cutting Rachel off and moving to the television. She turned up the volume using the button on the side. "Let me hear this."

"Gemini has another victim," Cara said.

This was all new information to Molly. She listened to the newscaster in wide-eyed amazement.

"... the body was found in this alley," the reporter said. She abruptly stopped, touching her ear and looking down. "We are now able to confirm the name of this latest victim. Fiona Sheraton..."

Molly covered her mouth with her hand, still unable to look away. "No, it can't..." she said, her words muffled.

"What is it?" Rachel said, finally taking her eyes off Cara. She stared at Molly, concerned.

"I know her," Molly cried. "Fiona. We work together at the hotel. I... I just saw her."

She'd only seen her an hour ago. She'd been wearing a vibrant outfit and trading smiles with Charlie. They were supposed to be on their way to grab dinner. How could she be dead when there was so much life ahead of her?

"It looks like all three of us have been hit now," Rachel said, and Molly knew she meant the victims were being plucked from each of their social circles. "I'm just happy you're okay. For a minute, we thought it might have been you."

"Me?"

"Take a look at the street," Rachel said, pointing at the television. "The body was found near Chester House."

"Was she connected to Chester House in any way?" Cara asked.

"I just told you she was there with me."

"Yes, but did she volunteer there? Usually, Gemini leaves the victims in a place that is significant to them. Beverley was left outside the *Tribune* headquarters and—"

"And Cindy was left inside our apartment," Rachel finished the sentence.

"Her boyfriend. Charlie. He volunteers there with me." Again, Molly was lost in combing through memories of the night. Suddenly, she wondered if Charlie was okay. She pulled out her phone and called him, each unanswered ring raising her pulse.

"Maybe the body was dumped at Chester House to send a message to us," Rachel said. "That this is more about us than the victims."

"We're the only ones that would understand that message," Cara said.

Suddenly, Molly remembered why she was so determined to be there in the first place. She pushed away thoughts of Fiona and Charlie.

"There's something I need to tell you both." She took a deep breath. "If Dad wasn't Gemini, I kept trying to figure out who it could be. There had to be a reason those pictures were in his shed."

"We've already gone over this," Cara said.

"Just listen." She stomped her foot, demanding attention. "Only one other person made sense. Elias. Maybe Dad found out what his best friend was up to shortly before he died, and that's why all the stuff was in his shed."

She braced herself for their denial, but instead, each sister tensed.

"Have you thought that, too?"

"Elias came by the house," Cara said. "Right around the time the murders started."

"He came into McGuire's, too. Said he wanted to check in on me."

A morsel of hope burst inside of Molly, sending tingles of euphoria throughout her body. "See, it's not totally out there, is it? That's why I went by his house just now."

"You did what?" Cara asked, outraged. "You're telling us you think Elias might be behind all this, so you went to his house without even telling us?"

"You're the last person who can chastise me for getting involved. You look into this type of stuff all the time. Anyway, I wanted to have a look around his place when he wasn't there. You want to know what I found?" She waited. "All of it. Just like in the shed. Pictures and evidence. He had it all there."

"My research," Cara said, looking at Rachel. "I was freaking out earlier today because someone had stolen it."

"Would Elias do that?" Rachel asked.

"Or *maybe*," Molly said, her voice heavy with irritation, "Elias has been Gemini all along."

"Someone still stole my research. And Elias would know where Dad left the spare key."

"What if Elias knew we were on to him?" Molly felt her anger rising, upset Cara was still refusing to consider the possibility.

Just then, Cara's phone started ringing. She looked down, the color draining instantly from her cheeks. "It's Tate."

She tucked her chin low, wandering across the room like she didn't want the others to hear. Or maybe she didn't like feeling the pressure of what they wanted her to tell him.

Molly could only hear muffled whispers. Cara's voice was rushed, even scared.

"What is it?" Molly pleaded, but Cara held up a hand, ignoring her.

After a few more simple exchanges, she ended the call and looked up.

"The police think they know who Gemini is," Cara said. The room went silent.

Molly felt like she was on the precipice of falling. One word, one syllable, one breath, might be enough to topple her over the edge. "Who?"

Cara's eyes were filled with tears. She looked at Rachel, then Molly.

"Elias."

And then it was like all the confusion and sadness that had filled Molly's world for the past year drifted away, and she felt peace.

FIFTY-ONE

CARA

Cara wasn't sure what to think, what to feel. For more than a year, she'd believed that her father was Gemini, a notorious serial killer. It was what the evidence said. It was what her research suggested. But now? Molly's theory, which Cara had assumed was derived from emotional desperation, just might be true.

"What exactly did Tate say?" Rachel asked.

"He said they received an anonymous tip about Elias. They're executing a search warrant for his place as we speak. They must have found everything Molly just told us about."

"I told you," Molly said with a childish smugness.

"Were you the anonymous tip?"

"No! I came here as soon as I left his place. I wanted to tell you both what I found."

"I believe you found that stuff at Elias' place, but everything else in the past year has pointed directly to Dad," Cara said. Then, suddenly remembering, "What about the letter?"

"If Elias knew Dad was on to him," Molly said, her breath growing shallow, as though she were at the tail end of a long race, "he might have forced him to write it. Maybe Dad's death wasn't accidental at all. Elias could have done something to him."

"But why would he do that?" Rachel asked. "It's not like he sent the letter to the police. He left it in Dad's shed, with everything else."

"Maybe he wanted insurance. Proof in case the police ever came after him, or if Dad told anyone about what he found," Molly said. "Or maybe we found the evidence before he could destroy it. Remember, he was the person who stayed the longest after the funeral. And he came by the next morning. Gave us that picture of Dad at Fenway Park. What if he was trying to find a way to get it?"

"You really think Elias was Gemini this entire time?" Cara asked, still unsure.

"He's a more likely suspect than Dad," Molly said. "He lives alone. Has no family. Fits the profile, or whatever it is you say."

Of course, Cara wanted it to be true. She'd rather anyone be the killer than her own father, but something about the scenario wasn't connecting in her mind. There hadn't been anything in the shed that pointed to Elias. Sure, he might have gotten rid of anything incriminating around the time Dad died, but if Elias did that, why wouldn't he get rid of everything? And how had the police decided Elias was a suspect at the same time Molly searched his place?

"If Elias is Gemini, then why did he start killing again?" Rachel asked.

A good point, Cara thought. Elias was around the same age as their father, and he had an equal number of ailments. He likely stopped for the same reasons: old age, poor health. But why start killing again now? And why with such renewed fervor?

"Maybe being found out, going to such lengths to cover up his crimes, made him nostalgic. Maybe he just couldn't resist killing again."

"What do we do now?" Rachel asked, and Cara wondered if, like her, this all seemed too simple.

"We'll wait on Tate to call back," Cara said. "That's all we can do. And it's good that we're all here together. We can come to terms with Dad and what he was or wasn't once and for all."

"That's not why we're here, though," Rachel said. "You said you had to tell us something. It's why you wanted Molly here. Tate only just told you about Elias, so it can't be that."

Before Cara could answer, her phone pinged with a message. Finally, James had responded. The excitement of labeling Elias a suspect had made her forget. James. Her brother. Their sisters.

Are we still on for tonight?

Relief spread through her body in warm waves. He was safe. The whole time she'd been convinced this killer was targeting them, she hadn't considered they might be after all of Henry Martin's children. Every minute he spent in Whitehill was a threat, and she figured they'd all be safer if they stuck through this together.

Come on by, she texted back. *We're talking now.*

"What did you want to tell us?" Molly asked.

Cara exhaled. She wasn't sure now was the right time, but she didn't think she could push it back any longer. She had to keep them all safe, and they deserved to know the truth.

"No, I had something else I wanted to tell you," she said, looking away from her sisters.

As quickly as she'd rejoiced in confessing one thought, her body clenched at the idea of sharing another. Her biggest secret, in some ways as earth-shattering as the shared one about their father.

They weren't alone in the world, the three of them. Not

really. There was another sibling out there, and she'd been keeping him to herself.

"Is it about Dad?" Molly asked.

"No. Well, a little, yes."

"Something about Gemini? Or the case?" Rachel added.

"Maybe we should all sit down," Cara said, wandering into the living room. She sat in front of the fire.

Rachel remained standing. "Just spit it out all ready, Cara. Nothing can be more shocking than our father maybe being a serial killer."

"She's right," Molly said. Her eyes were wide, fixated on Cara. "Just tell us."

"You know I've been researching Gemini for the past year. Looking into Dad's past. Well, I found something. We have... I found..." Cara exhaled again. She knew what she had to say, and yet finding the right words seemed impossible. "Dad had another child. A son."

The room fell silent, all the air and words and sounds sucked out. Cara looked at each of her sisters. Rachel's cheeks were red, her lips pursed. Molly's mouth was open. She looked like she might cry.

"We have a brother?" Molly whispered.

"Yes."

"How?" Rachel asked. "Do you know this for sure?"

"I've spent the last year trying to learn as much as possible about our dad. His crimes, but stuff before that, too. What his life was like before he married Mom. Before that. I used one of those ancestry websites, and that's how I found out about him. James."

"When?"

"I found out six months ago."

"And you're just now telling us?" Molly was standing now.

"I wanted to meet him first. I wanted to make sure we were

actually related. And that he was a decent guy, before I let him into our lives."

"You wanted to keep him to yourself," Rachel said.

"It's not that—"

Molly wouldn't let her finish. "Did Dad know about him?"

"No. I don't think he did."

Cara's phone pinged with a text: *Five minutes away.*

"How old is he?" Molly asked.

"He's the same age as you."

Molly looked down. "Dad cheated on Mom."

Rachel's cruel laugh trilled across the room. "Really, Molly? That's your biggest concern here? For the past year, we believed Dad had a hobby of butchering women, but you're upset that he was unfaithful?"

"I'm upset about all of it," Molly said, through gritted teeth.

Cara understood. Even if their father wasn't a serial killer, he still wasn't the man any of them believed he was.

FIFTY-TWO

RACHEL

Rachel was so angry, she wanted to leave the room.

The revelation she had a brother momentarily eclipsed everything else, even the reemergence of Gemini. It was unbelievable. And even more infuriating was that Cara had known about him for six months and kept it to herself. Rachel felt the same way she had when she realized her sisters had destroyed the Gemini evidence without her consent, although not all of it apparently. That was yet another lie Cara had told.

"When are you going to start being honest?" she asked. "You didn't tell us we had a brother. You lied about burning all the evidence in the shed."

"What?" Molly asked.

"Oh yeah, she didn't tell you either. Turns out she kept some of the pictures, and that's part of what was stolen from her office."

Molly looked at Cara. "We burned it together."

"Not everything," Cara said, unwillingly. "I couldn't destroy it all until we had more answers."

"And what's your excuse for hiding the fact we have a brother?" Rachel asked.

"I knew it would be just one more blow."

"Tell us about him," Molly said, sounding more interested than angry now.

Cara forced herself to smile. "His name is James. He's a veterinarian based out of Boston."

"Who is his mother?"

"I don't know much about her. James didn't know about Dad until last year, after she died." She paused. "He's been wanting to meet you both—"

"Not happening. I've had enough of confronting Dad's secrets," Rachel said.

"That's not fair," Molly said. "Based on what Cara said, this guy wasn't trying to disrupt our lives. You can't blame him for wanting to reach out to his family."

"It's not his fault Dad was such a lowlife," Cara added.

"Did you tell him what Dad was?" Rachel asked.

"Of course not."

"There you go again!" Molly stood and stomped across the room. "The police are searching Elias' home as we speak, but you're still placing all the blame on Dad."

Cara exhaled as though gearing up for a rebuttal, but she fell silent when there was a knock at the door. Rachel looked toward the front of the house.

"Who is that?"

"I told you," Cara said, standing slowly. "James wants to meet you both."

"Tonight?"

"He's only in town for a short while," she said. "And now that Gemini has targeted all of us, he's safer here than at the hotel."

"A brother," Molly said under her breath, chewing on the word like she liked the taste. Her demeanor was curious, hopeful.

But Rachel couldn't hide her anger. "Do what you want. I'm grabbing a hotel for the night."

Cara exhaled in frustration, just as there was a second knock at the door. She started walking to the front of the house.

Rachel stood hurriedly, grabbing her coat. She didn't want to be rude, but she couldn't handle introductions right now. She needed to let her anger and shock at the revelation simmer before she met him. She hoped to leave through the side door before seeing him, but she was too late. She stopped when she caught sight of him in the foyer.

"This is James," Cara said, standing by his side.

Rachel's anger was quickly replaced with confusion.

"Ryan?" Rachel said, staring at his face, totally familiar except for the absence of his glasses.

Molly, walking a few steps behind her, stopped. "Charlie?"

The confusion seemed to multiply as Rachel looked around the room, at the perplexed looks on her sisters' faces. It was then she realized they were all looking at the same person, but calling him different names.

FIFTY-THREE
CARA

Cara felt a strange heat climbing up her neck. Her sinuses felt clogged, like a migraine was settling in, and the more she tried to think, the more her head hurt. She'd hoped this introduction would be positive. But each of her sisters had looked at James with surprising recognition.

"Ryan, what are you doing here?" Rachel asked, but he didn't respond.

Ryan, she knew, was the name of Rachel's other roommate. The one she'd never met.

"This is Charlie," Molly said, as though proving a point. "We work together at Chester House."

"You work with Ryan?" Rachel asked Molly, clearly still confused. Each one of them stood frozen in place, prisoners to their own understanding.

James, however, was smiling, pleased with the disconcertment he'd caused. He locked eyes with Cara, his smile growing wider. "I told you I couldn't wait for a family reunion."

Rachel looked from James to Cara. "*This* is our brother?"

"Yes." Cara struggled to process the little she knew about her sisters' lives in the past year. Molly had been volunteering at

Chester House for six months. The same amount of time Rachel had lived with Ryan and Cindy. Six months. That was how long James had been in her own life. She struggled to understand what it meant, or maybe her mind was simply stalling, trying to avoid the awful truth that was emerging.

"What the fuck is going on?" Rachel roared, backing away from the front door. "You live with me and work with Molly? Cara thinks you're our *brother*! Why have you given us all different names?"

"Isn't it obvious?" Molly sat down, staring blankly ahead. Even in the chair, her posture was unsteady and stiff, a statue at risk of toppling over. Her expression mirrored Cara's now. Her eyes empty. "I already told you Charlie was with Fiona tonight."

Cara looked away, covering her mouth with the back of her hand. She had lost control of her emotions. She wasn't sure if she wanted to cry or throw up or scream.

"What are you saying?" Rachel cried. Her anger was so fierce it blocked her from being able to see. She needed someone to piece it together for her.

"James, Charlie, Ryan... whatever his name is," Cara said, her stomach tossing with nausea. "He's the new Gemini."

FIFTY-FOUR

Before entering the Martin family home, James stood outside, watching his sisters flit about their father's office, addressing each other with raised voices and dramatic hand gestures. From his viewpoint, it was almost comical. Watching everything unravel in real time.

More than once, he'd worried they would uncover the truth before this night. Portraying three different people was a difficult task, but a necessary one in order to get what he wanted from each sister. He longed to be close to them, but how was he to do that when they were estranged from each other? He had to lure each of them in different ways.

Cara had been the easiest to entice, but also the hardest one to fool. If he'd given her some type of false backstory, she'd have found him out in the time it took someone to say Google. So, he gave her his real name, his actual hometown, his real profession. Everything he told her could be easily verified with a quick Facebook search, something he figured she'd done at least a dozen times since they'd met. All he had to do was lie about when he was flying in or out of town.

He knew Cara was on the search for answers, so that was

what he gave her. She'd moved into the house not long after the funeral, and for weeks he watched her, waiting for a moment to connect. Many nights, he'd watch as the lone light in the downstairs study stayed burning. She was driving herself mad with guilt and rage and questions.

She needed to know she wasn't alone, that he was out there, too. But how?

That was when he got the idea to slip an advertisement for the ancestry website into the mailbox. She could have already considered it, but needed a nudge. He placed it in between fliers for cheap cable and local cleaning services. It was a long shot, but maybe not so long. After all, he knew his sister, the esteemed true crime writer, was on the hunt. She just needed something to find.

Henry Martin would never have submitted his DNA to a place like that. Firstly, because he was a selfish bastard with no desire to find connections. Secondly, because a recorded sample of his DNA could pose a problem for someone like him. One slip-up at an old crime scene, and his identity as Gemini would be revealed.

DNA was how they caught the Golden State Killer.

DNA was how they caught BTK.

Curious family members had a habit of giving things away.

Sure, Henry Martin's DNA wasn't in the database, but James' was. For weeks, he waited, wondering how long it would take Cara to bite the bait, submit a wad of saliva and get her results.

A month later, he received that standard phrase that put everything else into motion.

You have a match.

A half-sibling, out there living in the world. It wasn't a shock to him, of course. But Cara? It took a whole other month before she built up the nerve to contact him. Once she did, they began their frequent meetings at the hotel. Getting to know each other, even though he already knew everything he could about her. In some ways, he knew her better than she knew herself.

Rachel was a little harder to track down. Tough exterior, that one. For weeks, he watched her at a distance. She was the beautiful, bossy bartender at McGuire's. From corner booths and pool tables, he'd study her. He witnessed her outward appearance deteriorate, her frame growing paler and lankier by the shift. Through the bar grapevine, he listened to what regulars said about her.

Her father had died, you know.

Her boyfriend broke up with her.

Wait a minute, not a boyfriend. She was into girls.

She can't make rent. She's looking for a roommate.

James' ears perked up at the last one. It was the perfect way for him to connect with her. He'd been out of Boston for more than a year, not that his Facebook profile hinted at that. If they were living together, he could get to know her even better than the others. And keep an eye on her. It was clear she was becoming a danger to herself. As Ryan, he could be there for her. Protect her.

Molly was the easiest. She was so lonely, he probably could have shown up at her place out of the blue, a complete stranger, and she would have let him in. It was clear his younger sister had very little self-worth. He wanted to fix that.

Instead, he decided to volunteer at Chester House. There, he was Charlie, a new Whitehill resident. That was partially true, although he'd had to come up with some other lies to keep his character going, feigning interest in that dreadful Fiona. Charlie made it his mission to build Molly's confidence, reconnect her with the family she'd lost.

That had been his end goal. Bring them back together. Reunite the family he'd never had but always deserved.

James watched them through the window, wondering if, in

between their shock and confusion, his sisters would take the time to consider how kind he'd been to them.

As he walked to the front door, he was confident he'd succeeded in giving each one of them the very thing they needed.

FIFTY-FIVE

CARA

Cara's skin was pale, her eyebrows arched. She was afraid. James was smiling. She looked from his face to his body, registering his stance. He was holding something inside his jacket.

He tilted his head to the side, the way one might look at a beloved pet, and smiled.

"I'm sorry I have to do this to you."

He grabbed her then, turning her around so that her back was against his chest. He pulled a knife from his coat pocket, aiming the blade at her neck, and kicked the door shut behind them. Rachel and Molly jumped back, in fear and disbelief.

"Charlie!" Molly shouted. "What are you doing?"

"What do you want?" Cara whispered, her cheeks and neck warm with the blood pumping beneath her flesh.

"Your phones." From his other pocket, he took out a cloth bag and tossed it across the room. "Throw them in there."

Rachel and Molly did as they were told. They couldn't move fast enough, and yet each movement was rigid, paralyzed by fear.

"Where is yours?" he asked Cara.

"In my pocket." Her words struggled to escape with his arm tight across her collarbone.

He looked at Rachel. "Grab it. Put it in there."

Rachel moved closer, reaching into Cara's jeans and pulling out the phone. She scurried back to the bag and threw it in.

He turned to Molly. "Kick it over."

She did as she was told. James bent down, grabbing the bag, his knife barely moving from Cara's throat.

James gave the room another once-over, making sure there weren't any other threats. There were no security cameras inside the house, and Cara had gotten rid of the landline after her father's death.

He dropped his arms to his sides, freeing her. She stumbled forward, falling into her sisters' arms. She looked back at him, fear mingled with hatred in her stare.

"What are you doing here, Ryan?" Rachel asked, her arms wrapped around her sisters.

"I just want to have a talk." He moved further into the room, the girls cautiously stepping away from him. He waved the knife in the air. "I apologize for the dramatics, but I had to make sure I had your full attention. I don't need anyone getting the police involved until we've finished our discussion."

"What discussion?" Rachel spat.

He leaned against the desk in the room. "I guess I should start by re-introducing myself. The real name is James. I should get that part out of the way, even though we've all had plenty of time to get to know each other." He snickered. A high-pitched, sickening sound. "I've got to say, this isn't the family reunion I'd been anticipating."

"You need to tell us what you're doing here," Cara said.

"You know I've been wanting to meet them for a long time. Meet them as their brother, that is. Of course, you kept putting me off."

"Is that why you did all of this? Because I waited too long to introduce you?"

"No. I don't want you to blame yourself. I knew how important it would be to get this right. That's why I approached each of you in a different way, gave you each what you needed. I had to make sure you could trust me. I didn't want you throwing me away like Dad did."

"Dad knew about you?" Cara asked, realizing, with each passing second, that everything they'd talked about in the past six months was a lie. All the times he'd asked questions about Molly and Rachel. When he'd wanted to know what their father had been like.

He already knew all the answers.

FIFTY-SIX

How do you put a price on a man's life?

A woman's life?

A child's?

Henry Martin had done so quite easily. Six hundred dollars a month. That's what he'd agreed to pay James' mother in order to keep their son a secret. Their mistake a secret, rather. It was never part of Henry's plan to have a son.

James still wasn't sure how his parents met, but he imagined there wasn't very much romance involved. Henry Martin frequented Boston bars during his trips away from home, usually taking his best friend Elias with him. That must have been where he picked up his mother, Cassandra, the local barfly.

She must have had proof Martin was the father, and that's why she contacted him. It was a risky move, reaching out to a serial killer, but it's not like she knew what he was. No one did. Henry didn't want to make a big mistake all the messier, so they'd made an arrangement. Six hundred dollars a month. That had been the value of James' life from the start.

Much like the Martin girls, James hadn't put it all together until after his own mother had died. All his life, she'd told him she didn't know who his father was, and that whoever he was, he wasn't much account. As he'd gotten older, and seen the trollop his mother was, he believed it.

It wasn't until she died and he was cleaning out the remaining boxes in her apartment that he found the bank slips. Dozens of them. Six hundred dollars every month, from the time he was an infant until right after he turned eighteen. His mother was a packrat and also a troublemaker; she likely held onto the receipts on the off chance they'd hold some benefit to her.

Henry Martin. That was the name written on each check. He googled him, but it was a common name. There were dozens in the Boston area alone. He started looking elsewhere. He noticed some of the earlier checks came from a small bank, not one of the commercial ones in the area. In fact, it was a maw and paw branch that had gone out of business years ago, but before that, it was based in Whitehill.

A quick Google search showed that there was a Henry Martin living in the area. He taught history at the local high school. A recent obituary revealed his wife of over thirty years had just died, leaving behind Henry and... three daughters.

For James, three sisters.

His childhood had been lonely. Often times, his mother was abusive. She'd clearly become pregnant by mistake, and a child had put off love interests and required his mother to work harder than she preferred. James was a special child, after all. Incredibly smart, but volatile, as though his mother's anger had imprinted onto him.

Many nights, he'd pretend he lived in a different house, with a different family. He imagined having a brother close to his age, someone who could participate in the same activities he did. He imagined what it would be like to have older siblings, sisters whose lead he could follow. He imagined having a stepfather that loved him, a caring mother. All these stories hadn't been lies; they'd been real to him once, if only in his mind.

None of that seemed to matter now that he knew he had a family. A better family than the one he'd ever been given or dreamed of having. And clearly his father knew of his existence. It stunned him a bit that his father never reached out, but then again, he was married. James tried to think of his father as a whole person, not just in his relationship to him. He was a man who made a mistake, which resulted in pregnancy. He probably feared losing his wife, his daughters. That was the reason he'd kept James a secret. It was a hurtful reason, but James understood it.

But now, Henry's wife had died. James' awful mother had died. The lanes were clear for a relationship, and James was excited to ask.

He traveled to Whitehill. He found Henry Martin almost instantly—his father was a big fish in a rather small pond. He had a beautiful home where his daughters still joined him every Sunday evening for family dinner. He imagined being there with them, at the table, holding hands and trading stories. He envisioned family holidays in the downstairs den, a big Christmas tree by the window in the study. He saw the shed in the backyard, and pictured all the weekend projects they could tackle together.

When he finally worked up the nerve, he followed Henry to the hardware store and engineered an introduction. Henry mentioned he was looking for someone to help him complete renovations on the house, and James offered his services. They agreed to walk across the street for a cup of coffee, at a place called the Midnight Diner, and talk over the arrangement.

James was humbled in the presence of his father, taken aback by his kindness and manners. He'd never interacted with such a gentleman, almost blushed when passing strangers waved at Henry, and him too, out of politeness. Henry was kind and respected and the exact type of person he'd always wanted to call his father.

He should have waited, worked harder at building a relationship, but he couldn't hold back anymore. After a lifetime of being alone, he was more than ready to be part of a family.

"I need to tell you something," James said, his voice beginning to quiver. "I'm not just a handyman."

"I figured that much," Henry said, chuckling. "But as long as you can get the job done."

James stared ahead, unsure of where to go next.

"What is it?" Henry asked after several awkward moments.

"Don't you recognize me?"

Had he not wondered, even noticed the resemblance? It was clearly there. The jawline. The eyes. The hands, even.

"I'm sorry, are you a former student?" Henry was desperate to be polite. In a town this small, to not remember a student would be an embarrassment, but he kept staring ahead. Clueless.

"No, I'm not a student." He looked away, almost ran out of the restaurant that very moment. Then, a wave of courage or fear took over. "I'm... I'm your son."

Just like that, Henry changed. Those kind eyes turned black, like an interior light had been flicked off. He leaned back, his jaw tight. "I think you have the wrong person."

"Cassandra Summers. She was my mother." He pulled out his wallet, his hands shaking as he tried to unfold the photo. "I don't have many pictures of her from before I was born. But this is what she looked like. She died recently. That's when I found the bank receipts. They had your name..."

When James looked up again, the expression on Henry's face was almost frightening. He didn't like being the subject of his stare, like an ant beneath a magnifying glass in the sun.

"That proves nothing."

"She kept record of all the payments," James continued.

"Six hundred dollars a month, every month, until I turned eighteen."

"I don't want any part of this."

Henry tried to stand and leave, but James grabbed his arm, stopping him.

"Are you saying I have the wrong person? If that's what you think, we could get a test—"

"No!" Henry yelled, quickly looking around the room to make sure no one had heard. The place was nearly empty. "No, that's not what I'm saying. I couldn't care less if you're my son, but whatever you are, I want nothing to do with you."

The words were so painful. James swallowed. "I understand why you had to keep me a secret. You have a family. A wife—"

"Leave my family out of this."

"I know your wife died a few months back. Just like my mom. That's why I'm reaching out now. I thought maybe we could make up for lost time."

"There will be no making up of anything. I have my family. I have a life here." He jerked back his arm, defiantly. James didn't dare to stop him this time. "You'd best head back to wherever you're from and forget about this place. Forget about me."

Henry walked away. James waited a beat before chasing after him. He caught up to him in the hardware store parking lot, just as Henry was entering his car.

"Henry, please. Maybe I didn't go about this in the best way, but all I want is to get to know you. Let you get to know me."

Henry looked around the street. "If I wanted to know you, don't you think I would have reached out by now?"

"I've never had a father! I've never had sisters! Or a family—"

"And you still don't." He jerked the car door open. "Don't contact me again."

James stood, heartbroken, watching as Henry Martin drove away.

FIFTY-SEVEN
RACHEL

"Dad knew about you?" Rachel asked.

"He always did. He never wanted anything to do with me, but once I got older, I thought that might change. I tracked him down, tried to build a relationship." James' stare turned dark. "Needless to say, it didn't go how I wanted. I had to do something different this time around."

Rachel kept staring at him, finding it hard to believe that the man she'd been living with—one of the few people she considered a friend—was actually her brother. Seeing Ryan's face in her childhood home was so unexpected. And her sisters were next to him. They'd always been separate in her mind, and yet, here they were. Together.

"When I found out about you, I didn't turn you away," Cara said. "I welcomed you into my life."

"But you kept me as your little secret, didn't you? You had to make sure the others knew about me on your terms." He paused, looked at them quizzically. "Not that I can't relate to the need for control. Can you guess what I had to do to keep things under my control?"

"We've put it together," Rachel said, dryly. "You're the new Gemini."

As the words left her mouth, her stomach clenched. She couldn't believe Ryan or James or whoever-the-fuck could deceive her like this. Just yesterday, he'd comforted her in the wake of finding Cindy's body. They'd spent the afternoon getting drunk together, throwing darts at McGuire's. All the while, he was the same person who had butchered Cindy. He'd been goading Rachel and her sisters, taunting them with the secret they'd kept.

He laughed. "Isn't it ironic? Dad tried his best to keep me out of his life. He never would have guessed I'd be the one to carry on the family name. All I wanted to do was know more about him, build a relationship. When that didn't happen, I had to look into things myself. That's how I stumbled upon Dad's little secret."

All the times she'd talked with Ryan about her family, felt she had to hold back from telling him the entire truth, he already knew. He knew her father—his father—was Gemini, and yet, it hadn't wrecked his life in the same way it did hers.

"When did you find out?"

"Not long before he died. And finding out who Dad truly was, that he was the Gemini killer, didn't sicken me. If anything, it made sense. It gave me a purpose. Something to aspire to. I just had to get him out of the way first."

FIFTY-EIGHT

James had no plans to return to Boston after his confrontation with Henry. He refused to retreat to the same, lonely life he'd always known—no family, no structure, no care. He'd thought Henry Martin might treat him with a modicum of decency, love even, but he didn't. He'd shunned him, managed to instill more shame in a matter of minutes than his mother had his entire childhood.

He waited outside the Martin home, day after day, trying to make sense of this man who wanted nothing to do with him. Whenever Henry left for the day, he'd follow him, learn his routine. He spent a lot of time at the local hardware store. Most evenings were spent at Elias' house. Sometimes he'd visit one of his three daughters. Occasionally, he'd go to the cemetery to put flowers on his wife's grave.

After a couple of weeks, he began using Henry's absences from the house to explore. He found a spare key beneath the paving stone by the door, making it easy for him to get inside. He walked around the various upstairs bedrooms, wondering which room belonged to each sister. Had they shared rooms? Did Cara sleep in the top-floor bedroom, the one with the eye-like window peering down on the lawn below? Was Molly's room closest to the master bedroom? Had Rachel slept downstairs, by the back door?

He raided the medicine cabinets. Learned Henry Martin had been taking sleeping pills and antidepressants in the wake of his wife's death.

His visits inside the house were all quick; the last thing he wanted was to be caught.

Then, he started to explore outside, mainly the shed. He imagined the projects that might have been completed here, wondered if any of the furniture in the house had been crafted by Henry Martin's own hands. He imagined his sisters working in the heat, swatting away flies, Margaret Grace coming outside with a pitcher of lemonade to quench their thirst.

He wondered what it might have been like to be part of a normal family, instead of growing up in that drafty apartment, his mother entertaining random suitors on the other side of the wall.

An anger began to grow, pulsating. As though anger had formed its own heart inside him.

In a rage, he grabbed an old Polaroid camera sitting on a shelf, and threw it across the room, the glass and plastic splintering into pieces. He quickly found a broom and a dustpan in the corner and cleaned up his mess. He made sure to get every last piece—he didn't need his father knowing someone had been snooping around. He even pushed back the storage cabinet, and that's when he saw it.

The indent in the floor.

A door, rather. He opened it, curious to know what was underneath.

Having lived his entire life in Boston, the Gemini case was something he'd only heard about in passing. Like Zodiac or Green River or Son of Sam. It didn't feel like a real thing, didn't feel urgent or close.

When he first saw the pictures and jewelry, he didn't realize he was staring at the keepsakes of a serial killer. That's how unfamiliar he was with the case. But something clearly wasn't right. No one kept close-up photos of dead women. They definitely didn't store them in a secret hole beneath the ground. Some were so detailed; he could see the jagged flesh on their necks. He stared at the camera he'd broken, and another thought occurred to him.

When he left, he started reading. Hunting. Trying to make sense of what he found. It didn't take him long to uncover similar pictures online, although they weren't the intimate ones he'd discovered in the shed. He read news articles about Whitehill's very own serial killer. Gemini. He continued reading, devouring the information like a person who had been denied sustenance.

He came to the conclusion that his father, Henry Martin, was the Gemini killer.

And in that moment, everything made sense.

The coldness staring back at him in his father's eyes.

His own proclivities as a child, then a young man.

His anger, which might have originated from his mother's treatment, but felt like it had been there all along. He hadn't inherited his mother's cruelty, but his father's. It had been born into him, destining him for darkness.

When he thought back to the pictures, he didn't feel sickness or shock.

He felt inspired. As though a neon sign had turned on inside him, lighting his path, showing him who he really was. Who he was put on this earth to be.

Henry Martin had already been given his chance. James thought about confronting him, telling him he knew his secret, that unlike his wife and daughters, he understood.

Then he remembered his father's words at their first and final meeting.

And he decided maybe Henry Martin's days needed to end, so his could begin. A king can't take the throne until their predecessor has passed.

He waited until it was late at night. He took the key hidden beneath the paving stone, the same one he'd used to explore the house a dozen times before, and went in. He crept to the back bedroom.

Henry Martin kept a glass of whiskey by his bedside table. Earlier, when Henry was at the hardware store, James had added a few crushed-up sleeping pills to the liquid. Enough to make sure Henry would sleep soundly while James wormed his way into the house.

He watched his father sleeping in his bed, the quivering rise of the old man's chest as he breathed. He could have already ended him, added more to the carafe than would have been possible for any man to withstand, but he wanted a few more moments with his father, with Henry.

And he wanted Henry to know he hadn't died peacefully in his sleep, the way most aspire to go. He was being ended. By his son. By James. By the person he'd tried to pretend didn't exist.

Henry's eyes were wide when he opened them and saw he wasn't alone in the house, but the drugs in his system made it hard to react. He could do little more than move his arms.

"I need you to do something for me, Dad," James said, placing a notepad and pen on Henry's chest. "Write exactly what I tell you."

"What's this?" Henry pushed out. "I'm not—"

"You will do whatever I say, otherwise I'll go after Cara and Rachel and Molly."

Henry's eyes were wide then, his trembling hand struggling to reach for the paper. They always say psychopaths are incapable of love. Maybe it was true, because James had felt very little love in his own life. But in that moment, Henry showed he had at least some affection for his daughters, otherwise he wouldn't have obliged. If only he could have shown the same concern for James, they wouldn't be in this situation.

"Are you ready?" he said, helping Henry steady his hand. "Okay, write: I am the Gemini killer."

Henry dropped the pen, his eyes growing wider.

"Oh, you thought it was a secret? Just like you thought I was a secret," James said. "Well, I found out who you are. And it's only a matter of time before the rest of the world does, too."

"No," Henry said, shaking his head, but he had too little strength to do much else.

"For once in your life, you need to do what's right. You need to be honest."

"What are you going to do with it?"

"Your daughters deserve to know the truth about you, and they're only going to believe it if you tell them yourself."

"I'll tell them. Bring them here right now, and I'll admit what I've done."

James shook his head. It was pathetic, watching a man beg. He wondered how many of Henry's victims had done the same thing.

"They're not coming, Henry." His voice was stern, menacing. "Write the letter, or else I'll have to tell them myself, and it won't be pretty."

Henry picked up the paper again, writing exactly what James told him. It was only a few sentences, but it was in his handwriting, as shaky as that might be. In order for his sisters to connect with him, they had to know the truth about their father. That he'd deceived them as easily as he'd abandoned James.

James took the letter, folding it inside an envelope and placing it on the bedside table. He poured more whiskey into Henry's mouth, forcing him to take another heavy gulp. And he sat there the rest of the night, until the old man's shallow breaths ceased.

By the time Elias arrived the next morning for their scheduled fishing expedition, Henry was dead, and James was gone. Word started to spread around town that their beloved community member had died. In his sleep, it seemed. An accidental overdose. He wasn't used to taking the pills, and he'd never really been the same since his wife died.

Now, the Martin girls were orphaned.

And they had a funeral to plan.

FIFTY-NINE

MOLLY

Molly could barely register what was going on around her. White noise was building in her head, buzzing, and the world felt very far away. When she'd first pieced together Charlie was her brother, she hadn't quite believed it. Not dissimilar to how she felt when she learned their father was Gemini.

She was dimly aware that her hands were shaking. In anger or in fear? No, it was sadness. She was mourning the loss of her closest friend, who had been replaced by James. Her brother. A murderer. Just like her—their—father. She had confided in Charlie, told him things she couldn't share with anyone else, including her sisters. To think he'd been lying to her this entire time, betraying her trust... And worse than that, he had done the unthinkable.

"What do you mean you had to *get him out of the way*?"

"I snuck into his house, made sure he had enough medication in his system to overdose, then I set the scene." He smiled. "I killed him."

Molly was full on crying now. She'd been betrayed on so many levels, her hopes climbing high, then plummeting right in front of her. She'd believed her father was innocent. She'd believed Elias was guilty. But now? Not only did she have to reckon with the fact that her father was Gemini, Charlie, her only friend, had picked up where he left off. Her brother! *Charlie* was her brother. That person couldn't be responsible for murdering Cindy and Beverley. And Fiona! His own girlfriend.

Just hours ago, Fiona and Molly had buried the hatchet. Whatever flaws she had, Fiona didn't deserve what happened to her. Molly only had to close her eyes to imagine it. Charlie leaving Chester House, holding her hand as they strolled down the sidewalk. Pulling her into an alley. Likely ripping the necklace from her throat, replacing it with a deep cut. She trembled at the horror of it, and the knowledge that Fiona's life was only taken because of the connection to her. Had dating Fiona, then murdering her, been his plan all along?

And yet, the hardest death to accept was the one he'd just admitted committing. He'd killed their father, robbed Molly of the chance to ask him why he did the awful things he did. He'd robbed her of the relationship she thought she'd had with him, even if none of it was ever true.

"Why did you have to kill him?" she cried.

"Because the bastard deserved it." He paused. "And so we could be together."

SIXTY

James couldn't remember the first time he wanted to hurt someone—it was an instinct for as long as he'd been alive—but he often recalled the first time he actually did it.

Growing up, James was the target of bullies. Maybe it was because he was pale and scrawny, the result of a lifetime of poor dinners. Maybe they could smell the poverty coming off him like it was one of his mother's heady perfumes. Whatever the reason, he was often ridiculed during elementary school, but he was smart and kept to himself, so he made it through all right. He would rather be the weird kid in class than back home listening to his mother and her male callers.

By high school, something changed. He changed. He was now tall with thick dark hair and a blemish-free face. Some girls had even begun calling him cute and cool. There wasn't anything cool about him, really. But his overnight attractiveness was something new, different from the meathead jocks who had been popular since kindergarten.

James was sixteen when he started dating his first girlfriend, Marie. They were in the same grade, and, like him, Marie was smart, which meant they had several Honors classes together.

They got to talking more and more in between lectures, working on group projects. When he became convinced that Marie did actually like him, he took the plunge and asked her to a movie. She said yes; he'd never heard a more wonderful word in his life.

For almost a year, the two were inseparable. They went to school functions together and dances, date nights every Saturday. He hung around with her friends and their boyfriends, all of whom were more popular than him. Marie was his first kiss, his first everything. And he'd never been happier.

For the first time in his life, James felt like he belonged. He was accepted. Even his mother treated him better, as though she finally acknowledged she'd produced a son more intelligent and likable than she could ever be. She almost bowed in his presence, and he loved it.

But he also genuinely cared about Marie. She was kind and beautiful, and most importantly, she'd chosen him. Because of that one choice, James' entire life had changed.

Until it changed again. Marie threw a party at her house after graduation. Everyone came wearing the colors of whatever school they planned on attending. Marie wore orange and white for University of Tennessee. James wore red and black for University of South Carolina, where he'd received a full ride. The distance didn't bother him, and the two had rarely talked about it. He knew they'd see one another on visits home, and they could make it work.

As the hours grew longer and the music grew louder and the drinks became easier to down, James felt the urge to leave the crowd and find a place to rest. Really, he wanted to find Marie, who he'd lost sometime earlier in the night. He went upstairs to her bedroom, but the door was locked. He jiggled the handle. He could hear voices on the other side of the door. Heard whispers and laughs and giggles.

When the door flew open, Marie wasn't alone. Ray was

with her, one of their classmates. He wore the same orange and white colors that she did, and refused to make eye contact with James as he exited the room. Marie's cheeks were blushed, and it wasn't just from the alcohol.

"It's not what you think," she said, but James didn't want to listen to her excuses. Hearing her try to talk her way out of what he'd seen angered him even more, and before he knew it, the two of them were on the bed together, James on top, his hands squeezing Marie's neck.

Marie's eyes were wide and her face grew increasingly red, like a plump fruit you could pop with a pin. James kept squeezing, unfazed by the broken sounds she made. It felt like an eternity and a second all at once, until a noise downstairs startled him, and he let go.

Marie fell back onto the bed. At first, he thought he might have killed her, but then he saw the gentle rise and fall of her chest. He left, afraid of what might happen to him, afraid of what she might think when she woke up.

But the next day, she called him, wanting to talk about what he'd seen. It was as though she'd forgotten about what had happened between the two of them in the bedroom. Or maybe she wanted to forget. Maybe this was the trade-off. She'd forgive him for what he did to her if he could forget what had happened with Ray.

James never talked to her again.

And yet he thought about her. More specifically, he thought about that night where he'd almost killed her. A more sensible person would simply be thankful nothing came of it, but James found himself wondering what might have happened if events unfolded differently. What if he'd kept squeezing a little longer? What would it feel like to watch the life leave those pretty brown eyes?

James, good-looking and smart as ever, had several different girlfriends while at USC, and even more after he graduated. He tried to choose girls that he felt wouldn't hurt him, and some he even cared about. But even in those relationships, he thought of his close encounter with Marie. He thought about it when he was having sex with other women. He thought about it when he was pleasuring himself. And it was such a dirty, dirty fantasy to have, he knew he could never tell anyone about it.

When he found those pictures in Henry's shed, memories of his night with Marie returned again.

That sick fascination returned, and he found himself wondering what it would feel like to inflict that kind of pain on others, to follow through with it, not chicken out as he had when he was an unsure teenager.

When he realized Henry had been successful at not only committing those crimes but getting away with them, the lights around James seemed to shine brighter. As though everything finally made sense. This was the missing piece, the part of his life that was meant to make him feel whole. And it had taken a parent he'd barely known to show him the way.

And now he was trying to share the same path with his sisters. It was clear they all felt unfulfilled in some way. Maybe, like with him, this was what was missing.

The hardest part for them to understand would be how he was like Henry. How they were like him too. That together they could live out their full potential, honor their father's legacy and make him proud in a way they never could when he was still alive.

SIXTY-ONE

CARA

The knot in Cara's stomach refused to untangle. She stood there, her arms wrapped around a trembling Molly, trying to hold back a fuming Rachel. And she was listening as her brother tried to explain the unjustifiable horrors he'd committed.

"Why did you have to kill him for us to be together?" she asked.

"Dad wasn't a good person, Cara. I know he put on a convincing front. It appears he was certainly kind to the three of you, but it was all a sham. If he'd been a real parent, a true father, then he wouldn't have slammed the door in my face. He didn't care about his family, he only needed a convincing role to hide who he really was, and he chose the three of you for the parts."

As far-fetched as James' reasoning was, it pained Cara to admit some of it was true. It had to be. After all, how could the caring, thoughtful man she'd loved be the same monster who tore those women apart? It was the question she'd been asking herself every day since they found the pictures in that shed.

"But why did you have to kill him?" asked Rachel.

"I guess I didn't have to do anything. I wanted to kill him. You would understand if he'd treated you the way he did me. After I found those pictures, learned what kind of a monster he was, he thought he could just ignore me? He didn't realize that he'd passed the worst parts of himself on to me. All that cunning and rage. It was time someone gave him what he needed, and who better than the prodigal son?

"Of course, I hoped it would bring *us* all together, too. He wasn't willing to let me near you while he was still alive. We're all orphaned now. I figured with Henry out of the picture, we would have no one but each other, at least that's how I pictured it. Then, after the funeral, the strangest thing happened. Instead of pulling together, you fell apart. You started ignoring each other. I had no option but to approach each of you separately."

"Had you been planning this all along?"

"Not at first. There's this strange thing about killing. It stays with you, long after your victim has taken his or her last breath. Maybe it's different if you get caught for the crime, but I didn't. Even though I was getting to know each of you, I couldn't shake this feeling. This urge. It's like a part of Dad stayed with me, haunting me in a sense. I didn't know what to make of it, then it hit me. I could bring Gemini back. Finish what he started."

"Why?" asked Rachel. "What he did was awful. It changed the way we all thought about him. You could have been close to the rest of us without picking up where he left off."

"Did he ever leave us, though? See, I have this wild theory that there is a part of Dad in all of us, it just shows itself in different ways. But we all have that darkness within. I've seen it in each of you. The three of you try to suppress it, and I decided to embrace it."

"You're sick," Rachel said.

"I'm sick? Sicker than drinking and drugging yourself every night? Sicker than inflicting pain on those around you to feel a little better? Sicker than lying to those closest to you, using others' pain as a way to glorify yourself?"

His descriptions of them hurt, but Cara refused to give him a reaction. "Nothing any of us has done compares to you."

"That may be true, but none of us are innocent here either. In case you haven't noticed, I've been doing this to help you. I'm getting your problems out of your way."

Cara squinted. "What are you talking about?"

"The former boss that tried to wreck your career before it even started. You told me about her during one of our first meetings, when we were bitching about our old jobs. I gave her what she deserved."

He looked at Molly. "And Fiona was no friend to you. She was a leech, and you couldn't even see it. I'm telling you, Molly, you've got to stop surrounding yourself with people that treat you like shit."

He turned to Rachel. "And don't even get me started on Cindy. We lived with that bitch. You might try and make me feel guilty about the others, but you and I both know I did the world a favor by getting her out of the way."

"Cindy got on our nerves, but I didn't want her to die! No one deserves this." Rachel closed her eyes, and Cara knew she was picturing the body again. "You can't go around murdering people."

"Dad did," he said, plainly. "And life seemed to turn out okay for him."

"What about Elias?" Molly asked. "You killed him, too?"

"Let's not get ahead of ourselves," he said. "We won't have much of an opportunity to get to know one another if I'm behind bars, will we? I needed someone else to take the fall for my crimes. And Elias seems like the perfect fit. All I had to do was steal Cara's research and plant it at his place."

"You think you can frame Elias and all of this will go away?" Cara asked.

"No, the fun isn't over yet."

"What does that mean?" asked Rachel.

"I need more than just pictures to implicate Elias, which is why Gemini needs another victim."

"Who?" Cara asked.

"I'm not done trying to improve your lives," he said with a smile.

Fear pumped through Cara, almost doubling her over. And anger. At herself. She had reached out to James, making her responsible for the lives that had been taken. She thought of Tate, of all the time they still needed together. James better not hurt him or anyone else she loved. "Who is it?"

James' eyes landed on Rachel.

"Katelyn."

SIXTY-TWO

RACHEL

Rachel stormed forward, stopping directly in front of James' face, only because Cara and Molly were holding her back. For the first time, she felt the urge to harm another person. She wanted to hurt James, kill him even, if he did anything to Katelyn.

"You better be lying," she said, as a wave of emotion pulsated through her body. She regretted the way she'd treated Katelyn earlier, remembered the heartbreak on her face. That was nothing compared to the pain she would feel if James got a hold of her. It didn't make sense, though. James had already framed Elias for the murders. Why would he take another victim now? Why would he take Katelyn? No, he was saying this to test her.

"I can assure you I'm not," he said, plainly.

Rachel wriggled her arm from Molly's grasp. She was about to strike James when Cara wrapped her arms around her waist, pulling her toward the window.

"Don't do that," she said. "It's what he wants."

"He has Katelyn!" Rachel shouted, looking from her sisters to her brother. "We have to do something."

"Well, that is the plan," James said, crossing his arms. That sick smile was on his face, and he leaned against the desk like he didn't have a care in the world.

Cara marched forward. "I don't know what you're trying to do. But this isn't a game, and it's certainly not the way to bring any of us closer to you. You can't go around hurting the people we care about—"

"The people you care about?" he said, astonished. He rubbed his forehead with two fingers. "I thought we already went over this. I'm not going after people that love you. Only people who've hurt you. The people that weren't as loyal to you as they should have been. I'm giving them what they deserve."

"No one deserves to be stabbed and discarded like trash."

"Maybe not," he said. "But some deserve it more than others. And I know it must have felt good, just a little bit, to know the people who irritated you are no longer in the picture."

Rachel's head was pounding hard, her fear even more. It was nauseating, listening to James' twisted reasoning. And frightening, because this deranged man was dangling the person she cared about most right in front of her.

"Why Katelyn?" she asked, her voice breaking. "She's not a problem. I love her."

James scoffed. "Love her? Come on, Rach. Now you sound like Molly, groveling at the feet of people who treat you like shit. Katelyn abandoned you when you needed her most. She knew you were grieving, hurting. And what did she do? She left. She walked away so you could keep poisoning yourself. And who was there to help you pick up the pieces? Who was there to help you move on?" He waited. Then, "Me."

"I swear, if you hurt her..." Rachel was marching toward James again, her finger out in front of her body as though she could use it as a weapon.

"Just take a minute to think things through." He looked around the room, at each sister. "That's been your flaw this past year. You won't take the time to look at life through each other's perspective. That's why I'm here. To help you see."

Rachel raised her arm again, was about to bring her fist down on James' head, when he grabbed her wrist. He twisted her body around and raised the knife, pointing the blade at her stomach. Cara and Molly jumped back.

"Don't do this," Molly said. "Just let her go."

"I didn't want it to go this way," he said, softly. He was moving backwards, dragging Rachel with him toward the door.

Rachel wanted to fight back, to hurt him until he told her where Katelyn was, but her fear stopped her. She was frozen, dead weight in James' arms, the tip of the knife so close to her skin. In the horror of this moment, another terrifying memory broke through: Cindy's mangled body on the ground. *Those eyes*. He'd done that to her.

James was at the door now. He reached a hand behind him, and twisted the knob. The door swung open, letting in the cool night air. A few leaves blew in, dancing around their feet. For several minutes, they all stood still, and no one, James included, seemed to know what might happen next.

"Are you going to hurt her? Kill Katelyn?" Cara asked. Her voice cracked when she spoke. "You have to tell us."

"I'm going to finish what I started," he said. "It's up to you if you want to get in my way, or join me."

With one quick movement, he pushed Rachel to the ground. Immediately, he ran outside, leaving the door open. Rachel crashed hard against the floor, scraping her knee. Molly and Cara ran to her. When Rachel tried to stand, her ankle felt like it was firing, and she yelped in pain, but she kept trying to move forward.

"We have to find him. We can't let him leave."

Cara ran outside first, while Molly helped Rachel find her balance. Each step she took on the swollen ankle hurt, but she didn't care. She hobbled outside and down the front porch steps. It was dark and the streetlights had already turned off for the night. The wind was whooshing in the trees, but that was the only sound she heard.

Then Rachel saw a figure, a black body moving closer in her direction. When the figure came closer, it was only Cara, and Rachel's shoulders fell in defeat.

The street behind her was empty.

SIXTY-THREE

MOLLY

Molly ran after her sisters, barely able to see them in the dark, but she could hear them. Cara's panting. Rachel's despair. Her own heart, pounding inside her chest.

"I don't see him anywhere," Cara said.

"Keep looking. There has to be something."

But there was nothing. They were alone in the dark, and all of Rachel's wailing wouldn't change that.

"He must have been on foot," Cara said. "Maybe he parked his car somewhere else."

"Well, we have to find him." Rachel's tone was short, and it was obvious she was trying hard to hold back tears.

Sure, none of James' victims deserved to die the way they did, but Katelyn was different from the others. Rachel cared about her. They all did. If something happened to her, they'd never forgive themselves.

"We have to find out where he's going," Cara said. "He made it clear that wherever she is, she's still alive. He must be holding her somewhere."

"He said, join me," Molly added. "He said it like a dare. Like we should know where he's going."

"I have no fucking idea where he went," Rachel said, running back toward the house. Every few steps, her left leg would buckle, but she kept moving. "He can't be at Katelyn's place. And our apartment is still a crime scene."

"Every time I saw him, it was at the Railway Hotel. He wouldn't take her there," Cara said, barely loud enough for them to hear.

A flare went off in Molly's mind, and her eyes went wide. "The cabin."

"How would James even know about the cabin?" Rachel asked. "We've not been there since Dad died."

"He knows everything else about our lives," Cara said.

"When I met with him yesterday, he said something about getting away this weekend. For a family reunion at a cabin in the woods. That has to be where he's going."

"We need to call the police," Rachel said.

"And what will we tell them?" asked Cara. "That we think our brother is a killer and he might have your ex-girlfriend and is maybe at our old vacation home?"

"We have to tell them something," Rachel said. "He has Katelyn. We can't play around anymore."

She ran back inside the house, but stopped abruptly in the foyer. "Our phones. He took them with him."

"We're going to have to head up there ourselves," Cara said.

Molly reached in her pocket and grasped her keys. "We can take my car. He can't be that far ahead of us."

"Let's go," Rachel said, charging past them, each step seeming to do more damage to her injured ankle.

"Drop me off at the police station," Cara said, sliding into the back seat.

"We don't have time," Rachel said.

"If you want the police involved, I need to get ahold of Tate. You know how winding the roads are around the cabin, and there's no reception. He can tell the first responders where they need to go. He'll have the entire department there as fast as possible."

"What if James panics?" Molly asked. When she tried to imagine James at the cabin, she didn't know what to expect. "He wants us to follow him, but not the police. What if he does something to hurt Katelyn?"

Rachel winced.

Cara said, "We'll do what we can. Whatever he has planned, he's keeping her alive for a reason. There's still hope."

Rachel nodded, looking ahead through the windshield.

Molly squeezed her hands around the steering wheel, and floored the gas pedal.

PART III

SIXTY-FOUR

James wondered which of them would put it together first. Definitely not Rachel. She was operating on pure emotion. Cara was usually the most logical, but she wasn't thinking straight either. She was still reeling from the big reveal, and she seemed the most wounded that he had deceived her.

His money was on Molly. He'd given a hint when he told her about his plans for the weekend. It wasn't a total lie. Any other place of relevance was a crime scene: Chester House, the apartment. The Railway Hotel was too enclosed. If he was going to finish this thing, he needed some peace and quiet. What better setting than the Martin family cabin? He couldn't think of a more fitting venue for a family reunion.

James had parked his car three blocks away from the Martin home. It didn't take him long to cross the street, start the engine and merge onto the highway. For several minutes, he drove in silence, only the hissing of passing cars in his ears. His anticipation was building.

For so long, he'd waited for this. To acknowledge and finally be acknowledged by his family. Now, everything was out in the open. He replayed the conversations from the past hour like a person might recall a first date. And then she said this, and I said that... His sisters were angry, even a little afraid, but in time they would understand how much he had been willing to sacrifice for them. And then he would never be lonely again.

After the highway, there was another thirty minutes of driving. His headlights shone on the cement road. Leafy trees and dirt piles sat on either side. Of course, it all looked black at this time of night. Each passing minute pulled him further away from civilization and closer to his grand finale.

Finally, his headlights shone on a metal mailbox with 'Martin' written on it, the paint chipped and dulled. He turned down the winding gravel driveway. This was the one place that never turned up during his preliminary research. He had no reason to suspect Henry Martin owned a second property— James hadn't grown up even close to that kind of wealth. The place wasn't much: one level, the walls honey-colored wood, the roof sheet metal. Still, it was a place that held great meaning to the Martin family. He learned about it from his sisters, each one telling him fond memories of the place. It should have been part his all along.

If they had already put together where he was, they wouldn't be far behind him, but he still had plenty of time to get ready.

When he reached the girl, she was still bound with zip ties, just as he'd left her. She was passed out. He'd given her a heavier dose than the others, enough to make sure she wouldn't wake up while he was gone. Even if she had, she wouldn't have gotten far. On the off chance she was able to free herself, she'd still be lost in the woods at night, another dangerous predicament to be in.

She wasn't in danger now. James wouldn't do anything to her until his sisters arrived. They needed to be here. They needed to see. They needed to witness just how far he was willing to go for their love.

SIXTY-FIVE

CARA

The police station was winding down. It was that small window between when most people called it a night and when the rowdier residents started making trouble.

Cara told the uniformed officer working the front desk that she had to speak with her husband, Detective Tate Gibson, immediately. With her phone gone, she had no way of knowing whether he was at the station or monitoring the crime scene of the latest victim. Or maybe he was at Elias' house, sifting through evidence. Staged evidence. When the receptionist told her Tate was on his way, she almost cried tears of relief.

Tate walked up to her, instinctively reaching for her shoulder. It was a tender touch, and she suddenly remembered that the last time she spoke with him—when she told him that James was her brother—had been the closest they'd come to intimacy in months. So much had happened since then, and even though Tate was warm because he thought she'd opened up, he still didn't know the worst of the secrets she'd been keeping.

"What's wrong?" Tate said. She must have looked a mess. "I didn't have any missed calls—"

"I don't have my phone." Her eyes cut across the room as

she pulled him closer to the door, away from lingering ears. "I'm in trouble and I need you to come with me."

His brow creased. "What kind of trouble?"

"I don't have time to explain everything. Not here, not now. But I don't have a phone or a car, and I need you—"

"Haven't you watched the news? We have another body, and we're dealing with the shitstorm Elias caused. I'm supposed to head back to his place tonight." His face changed, and he looked concerned. "Is that why you're upset? Because I told you Elias—"

"Elias isn't Gemini." Her voice was assured, serious.

"Cara, I told you what we found—"

"He's not the latest killer. I know who is, and he's taken Katelyn. Rachel's Katelyn. We think he's headed to our family's cabin, and I need you to tell all your units to meet us there as fast as they can."

Hearing the words aloud was so bizarre. It would have sounded like a dark joke, if every bit of it wasn't true. He stared at her, as though waiting for her to break into a laugh.

When she didn't, Tate said, "Are you serious? Who do you think is the killer?"

"James." Her throat and tongue were dry, but the words clawed their way out. "My brother." Something inside ached. James had given her hope that her family would one day rebuild. In an instant, that hope had been taken away, and there were more lives at stake.

He closed his eyes, opening his mouth slowly. "How could... did you..."

"There's a lot I've been keeping from you in the past year," she said, pulling his arm closer. "I'm sorry. Sorrier than you could know, because if I hadn't tried so hard to keep all this to myself, maybe none of it would have happened. But I need you to believe me when I say we're in danger. And I need your help. I'm scared."

Tate held eye contact for a second longer, then he nodded. He walked back to the receptionist's desk and she could hear him giving orders. Check the radio and send all available units. Her body, which had felt on the verge of buckling, stilled. There was much to fear. Fear of what James could do to Katelyn. Fear of what he could do to her sisters. To her. Fear of telling Tate the truth, all of it.

He walked beside her, again touching her shoulder. "I'll drive."

And just like that, she had the smallest, faintest feeling that everything might be okay.

SIXTY-SIX

RACHEL

Rachel's heart was beating so fast she thought it might break through her ribs, open her chest cavity for all to see. Even in the dark, sporadic lights passing, she knew where they were, and it was too far away. In movies, car chases were fast and pulse pounding, but in reality, they were slow and torturous.

"Go faster," she told Molly. "It's taking too long."

"I'm going as fast as I can. You know how these roads are at night."

Rachel looked in her lap to check the time on her phone, then she remembered she didn't have it. A phantom limb. She was used to having it with her at all times. She was used to help only being a phone call away. Now she had to wait, which was excruciating.

"What if he's not here? You said he mentioned going to a cabin, but what if you're wrong? He might have her somewhere else."

"Then we'll go somewhere else," Molly said. "We'll find her."

"I'm worried about finding her in time. It's not like him to keep victims alive. Why would he change his methods now?"

"I think he's more concerned with making a point. To us."
Molly paused. "I still can't believe Charlie, or James, is our
brother. And he's never said anything about living with you
or..." She stopped again, like she was intensely trying to think.
"I'm positive he said he lived alone. When did you get a
roommate?"

"Six months ago. Ryan moved in about a month before
Cindy."

"I've been working with Charlie at the shelter just as long.
We didn't know we were being targeted until bodies started
turning up. He's been playing us even longer than we realized."

Rachel looked out the window again, the passing trees like
dark phantoms in the night. Molly was alert, as if this made
sense to her, but Rachel considered it all madness. The crazy
theories James had put forth earlier about getting closer to them
and fulfilling Dad's legacy, his reasoning for killing the other
women... it was the speech of a psychopath. No part of her
trusted him. "If he hurts her, I'll kill him myself."

"There's the turn," Molly said, her eyes on the road ahead.

Rachel saw the rusted mailbox. She almost leaped in excitement, her hand on the door, ready to leap out of the car. As they
snaked down the driveway, she noticed a vehicle parked to the
left, two tires leaning on the leaves.

"You were right," she said, excitedly. "He's here."

"How do you know it's his car?"

"Who else could it be?"

As soon as Molly put the car in park, Rachel threw open the
door and started running toward the house.

"Wait. Maybe we should wait for Cara. She told the
police—"

"I'm not waiting for anyone." She was already climbing the
steps to the front deck. The house was locked, so she kicked
over the pot at the base of the door and searched for the extra
key. When she saw it was missing, she grabbed the pot and

rammed it through the glass. The shards sprinkled around her, and she hesitantly slid her hand between the jagged edges so she could unlock the door.

Inside, the place looked exactly as they'd left it. The way it appeared to her in memories and dreams. It was like no one had touched it in years, the place in limbo since she'd seen it last. The plaid quilt laid over the back of the sofa, the deer with nine-point antlers over the fireplace.

"Katelyn!" She screamed her name, but there wasn't a response.

She raced through the living room, her ankle throbbing, down the hallway, through each and every bedroom. She searched under beds, inside closets, hurried to the back deck. She looked everywhere and found nothing. Not even a sign that someone had been in the house.

Her hopes plummeted. Maybe they were at the wrong place after all. Maybe he'd only mentioned the cabin to Molly to throw them off his trail. Then, she thought of the car parked on the side of the road. Someone was on the property, even if they weren't in the house.

She thundered down the steps leading to the basement, flicking the light switch. Against the far wall, she saw Katelyn on the floor. Her arms were fastened together, and there was a rectangle of duct tape across her mouth. Her eyes were closed.

Rachel ran to her. She ripped the tape off her mouth, begging her to breathe.

"Are you alive? Are you okay?" she asked no one, her voice frantic.

Just then, Katelyn made a sound. A small whimper that almost overwhelmed Rachel with joy. She pulled her close, bending to kiss the top of her head.

She started to run outside for Molly when she saw something both foreign and familiar sitting on the kitchen counter. The old, blue landline complete with its spiral cord. She picked up the receiver and almost shrieked when she heard the dial tone.

Finally, a way to contact the outside world, a way to signal help. She trusted Cara had already sent the police their way, but they needed as many people as they could get.

She picked up the receiver and dialed 911.

SIXTY-SEVEN

MOLLY

Molly heard the sound of broken glass. She started running after Rachel, but something distracted her. A sound coming from the water, like something had been dropped in.

She looked back at the cabin. Lights were flicking on in various rooms as Rachel searched for Katelyn. Then she heard another sound, this time coming from the woods. A crisp, cold fear spread through her body. It was too dark out here. Too desolate. A person could hide anywhere and nowhere all at once.

The boathouse, Molly thought. Maybe she should go there. That was where the first sound had originated. She followed the beaten path leading to the water. It was dark and muggy, but she could hear the faint sound of water lapping against the shore. She wished she had her phone on her for myriad reasons, but right now it was to use the torch to guide her way.

Her foot landed on wooden planks instead of dirt, and she knew she'd arrived. She held her hands out in front of her, feeling along the coarse building, until she found the door handle and pushed her way inside.

Sure enough, the room was fully illuminated. All the tools

and equipment were there, just the way Dad left them. The only difference was Elias, who was sprawled out on the floor. His eyes were closed, and there was blood covering him, spreading from a wound on his arm.

"Elias," she whispered, moving toward him. Her hands were trembling when she went to touch him. When she pulled back her hands, she saw they were coated in blood, making her shake even more.

"Molly?" Elias' eyes were open.

"What happened to you?"

She could see the wound, a long slit between his wrist and forearm. Blood had spilled all around him, soaking his clothes. She was amazed he was still alive.

"That man from the diner," he said, his words weak. "He'll hurt you..."

"It's okay," she said, hushing him. "Don't waste your energy."

As she was scanning the scene, something shiny caught her eye. A piece of jewelry. Several pieces. A wedding ring. A watch. Two necklaces, one that said *Cindy*, and the other Molly recognized from earlier tonight. Fiona had been wearing it. James had left the jewelry here, next to Elias' dying body. Molly fought back tears; he was only here because of them.

"I'm going to get us out of here."

"Leave now. Don't worry about me."

Molly stood, her eyes roaming around the boathouse, trying to find something she could press against Elias' wound to stop the blood. She found a towel and marched toward him.

"Not so close."

Molly froze, the towel in her hand at her side.

James stepped inside from the opposite entrance, the door leading out to the landing dock. She wondered if he was prepping the boat to leave, but that thought retreated when she noticed the gun sticking out of his waistband.

"Where's Katelyn?" she demanded.

"She's safe. For now." James walked slowly around the room, peering down at Elias. "He was easy to get up here. I'd been calling him the past week, asking about the place. It took some pushing, but he finally agreed to meet me after the fundraiser. Katelyn was a little trickier. She can put up a fight, that one."

"Where is she?"

"We'll get to her soon enough. She probably hasn't woken up yet."

Molly had some hope. They were both alive, even if Elias was wounded. Maybe there was still a way out of this. Her eyes went from James' face to Elias on the floor to the gun.

"Whatever it is you're doing, you don't need to hurt anyone else."

"I don't plan on doing anything. I brought us all here because I wanted to do this together."

"Do what together?" Her eyes were still moving wildly between James and Elias. "You have to let them go. You can't keep—"

"Didn't you listen to anything I said earlier? Elias here is our new Gemini." He pointed the gun as though it were a baton. "We have to hold on to Katelyn because she's his last victim. Poor Elias, no longer able to live with what he's done, slits his wrists. Ta-da! The whole mystery is solved."

Elias had already lost so much blood he was barely moving. James' plan just might work, but she still couldn't understand why he insisted they meet him here.

"What is it you want? Why are you even doing this?"

"To help you. To help Rachel and Cara. We're bonded in a way few people have ever experienced, even normal brothers and sisters. We share this secret."

"I don't want to share any more secrets. Secrets have torn our family apart."

"Have they? Look at the three of you. You've been closer in the past week than in the past year. All this turmoil, the bloodshed... it's brought you back together again. And it's all because of me."

"This has to end, James. The police already think Elias is responsible. You could walk away from all of this, but not if you kill them."

She looked back at Elias. His eyes were fluttering. He was clearly weak from the loss of blood. He was still alive, but not for long.

"I don't want to kill him," James said, calmly. "I want one of you to do it."

"What?"

"Elias is still putting up a fight. You can help me finish him off. And then we'll take care of Katelyn."

Molly couldn't understand how he could rattle off his plan with no hint of remorse or shame. And he was just as casual when suggesting she might help him.

"We don't want either one of them to die," she said. "We're not going to help you."

"Nothing will make you feel more like yourself. Nothing will bring you closer to him."

And she knew the *him* he referenced wasn't Elias. It was their father. Molly imagined his face. She thought of the power of his presence.

"We're not killers, James. Just because Dad was doesn't mean we are."

"Henry? A killer?" Elias mumbled. There was a sadness in his voice that seemed to overpower the pain he was in. He must have been wondering what he did to deserve this. What all this was about. Now he knew.

James laughed. "Everything happened so fast, I didn't get to tell him the truth about his best friend. I didn't even get to tell him I'm his son."

Elias closed his eyes, and Molly couldn't tell if it was because of his weakened state or shock over what he just heard. "Just hold on, Elias. We'll find a way out of this."

"I wouldn't make promises you can't keep," James said.

"Shut up! This has to stop, James. You can't go on destroying lives."

"You could have come forward at any time. Put an end to the great Gemini mystery." He waved his hands around the room as though it were an exhibit. "You could have brought closure to all those families. But you didn't. You protected him."

"It's not because we were protecting him—"

"I've talked this through with each of you. You're all trying to make sense of this in your own way, trying to prove you're not like him. Maybe that's the problem. Because deep down, you *are* like him. We all are. And it's time to start embracing it."

Elias began to moan. The sound brought tears to Molly's eyes.

"And you're the most like him, aren't you?" James said. "You even told me. It feels good to inflict pain on others."

"Not like this. Not on innocent people. Not on Katelyn or Elias."

James walked over, gently placing his hands on Molly's shoulders. "There's no going back now. Elias has seen my face. He'll go to the police, and it'll all be over for me. But if he dies here, he'll take the fall for everything. Then nothing can tear us apart. Don't you want that? A family that's unbreakable."

"I have a family."

"And I'm part of it, aren't I? You said so yourself. I'm the closest thing you've had to a friend in a long time. I know I invented some stuff, gave you a different name, but our relationship with each other? That was all real. You're my baby sister, Molly. And I love you."

Molly looked away, felt a warm tear sliding down her cheek. "Cara contacted the police. They'll be here any minute."

"We still have time. I've got a car parked on the other side of the lake. We could be gone before they know where to start looking. Just the two of us, if you want."

"I can't do that. I'm not leaving Cara and Rachel. I can't—"

"You know, I always felt the closest to you. I knew the others would be harder to crack, but I still tried. Problem is, they have too much Margaret Grace in them. But us? We're all Dad."

She closed her eyes and sobbed. For the first time, she truly accepted what her father had done. Who he was. Gemini. A killer. The severity of his crimes flashed through her mind, as though she could almost feel the horror. She was experiencing it now, through James.

"I meant it when I said I did all this for you girls. We can get Elias and Katelyn out of the way. Have him take the fall for Dad and everything else. Then we can finally have the family we both deserve."

She thought about Rachel and Cara.

She thought about Elias on the floor.

She thought about James and all the missed opportunities she had with her brother, and how this was her only chance to make up for it.

SIXTY-EIGHT

CARA

Cara kept looking behind them, waiting for the brigade of red and blue flashing lights, but there was nothing.

"Why aren't they coming?" she asked Tate. "You told them—"

"They'll be here, but we're short staffed. Half of the department is at the crime scene downtown. The other half is at Elias' house." He paused. "I still can't believe this."

Cara scrunched her eyes closed, wishing she'd told him the truth about her father at a different time, a different place. Instead, she'd waited until they were on the hunt for Katelyn, and now she feared it was too late.

She knew he'd have questions in the days to come. Like her, his mind was focused on getting to the cabin, not processing the reality that his father-in-law was a notorious serial killer. That his son they'd only just learned about had picked up where their father left off.

"What are you going to tell the guys at the department?"

"The truth. That this James guy is the real killer. That he framed Elias for it, and is now holding a hostage up at the cabin."

"What are you going to tell them about Dad?"

There was a long pause. "I don't know yet. I don't know what to think myself."

She looked out the window, wondering why she'd felt it was so important to keep her father's secrets this past year. If she'd been honest from the beginning, she might have dirtied her family name, but a slew of innocent people wouldn't have died.

"Why didn't you tell me?"

She'd always known he would ask this question, but she still wasn't prepared to answer it. "I didn't want your feelings for me to change because of what my father did. I was afraid of losing you."

"You're nothing like him."

But she was like him. The way she was drawn to mysteries. The way she'd learned to protect herself by keeping secrets. Sure, she wasn't a murderer like her father, but her inability to act had resulted in too many lives being taken.

"If we'd come forward earlier, James never would have started killing. Rachel wanted to tell the truth, but I stopped her. Now Katelyn might die because of me."

"We're here."

Cara felt the car whip around the turn. She saw a car pulled over to the side of the road on the left, then another up ahead, on the right.

"That's Molly's car."

"I want you to stay here." Tate unbuckled himself, retrieving his service weapon from its holster. "I'll tell you when it's safe to leave."

"No way." She'd already pushed open the car door. "I'm coming with you."

They were both standing outside the car when they heard a voice.

"Help! This way. She needs help."

It was Rachel, stumbling down the flight of stairs that led to the top deck.

"You found Katelyn?" Cara shouted.

"She's in the basement," she said as she came closer. "I untied her. She's still unconscious, but she's alive."

"Thank God."

"I called the police. They said they're sending someone."

"I already gave them the address. It shouldn't be long." Tate looked around. "Where's Molly?"

Rachel appeared frightened. "I... I don't know. She didn't follow me into the house."

Tate exhaled, looking around at the dark surroundings. "I'm going to look for her."

"Check the boathouse. That's the only place I can think of," Rachel said. "She wouldn't go wandering into the woods at night."

"Unless someone was chasing her," Cara said.

"I'm going." He started to run, but then stopped. He glared at both of them. "Stay here. It's too dangerous. Backup will arrive soon." Tate disappeared, the dark forest swallowing him whole.

"Have you seen James? Is he here?" Cara asked.

"He's not in the house," Rachel told her.

"Do you think he's taken Molly?"

"I don't know." She looked back at the house. "I need to make sure Katelyn is okay."

"Where the hell are they—"

A gunshot. They both froze, looking around in opposite directions, trying to figure out where the sound originated.

"The boathouse!"

They started running, Cara leading the way. They all had the same objective now. Find James. Find Molly. Keep each other safe. A second shot rang out, making her jump. When they arrived at the water's edge, the boathouse door was pushed open.

Cara rushed inside. She had to see. Had to know. She covered her mouth and screamed when she saw the body on the floor, blood spreading from beneath it like a never-ending spring.

SIXTY-NINE

RACHEL

Cara was blocking Rachel's view. She pushed her sister out of the way, desperate to see what was inside. Who was inside.

On the floor, by the entrance, was James. He was face down, a pool of blood spreading from beneath his body. Molly was in the corner of the room, shaking. A gun sat on the floor a few feet in front of her. She was staring at it as though the weapon were a snake about to strike.

Across from her, Tate was hunched down attending to someone else. Elias, she realized.

"What happened in here?" Rachel asked.

Molly looked back at the body. "Tate showed up and shot him."

"He was armed. As soon as I saw the weapon, I shot," Tate said over his shoulder, before turning his attention back to Elias. "He's lost a lot of blood. I don't know if he's going to make it."

"Just hold on," Molly said, moving closer to Elias. "Help is on the way."

"I'm okay," Elias said. Each breath was staggered and his skin was pale, but Rachel thought she saw a smile forming on his face. "Protect yourselves."

"How did Elias get here?" Cara asked.

"James wanted it to look like Elias took his own life. And then he planned on killing Katelyn. She should be here somewhere," Molly said.

"I found her up at the cabin," Rachel said. "She's safe."

As the words left her lips, the tension in Rachel's body eased. Amidst all the confusion and bloodshed, at least she'd made it to Katelyn in time. The person she loved most wouldn't die because of her. She wanted to rush back to her, but Cara continued talking.

"How did you know James was here?"

"I heard a sound in the woods and I followed it. I found Elias. James wanted me to kill Elias and Katelyn." She locked eyes with Rachel. "He wanted us to all take part. To bring us closer together."

There was silence, no one wanting to push further. Rachel headed for the door, wanting to wait with Katelyn for the police to arrive.

A wet gurgling sound broke the quiet. Across the room, Rachel could see James beginning to move on the floor. He wasn't dead after all. She gasped.

"Stay down," Tate shouted, aiming his weapon, but James wasn't capable of doing much. Breathing, and nothing more.

Sirens broke through the silence, and it felt as though another weight had been lifted. Help was on the way.

SEVENTY

MOLLY

The bright, sterile environment of the hospital was the exact opposite of the old boathouse. Molly sat in the middle row of the waiting area. Tate was busy with his fellow officers, and Cara was with him. Rachel's ankle was being examined. Katelyn was being monitored as the doctors tried to determine what drug she'd been given. And James... he was in surgery. The doctors still didn't know if he would pull through.

Molly was alone, as usual.

She couldn't stop herself from replaying what had happened in the boathouse. James had complete confidence she would hurt Elias over him. He thought he could trust her. He believed that he'd converted Molly to his cause.

She'd been given a choice, and in the moments before Tate came rushing into the shed, she'd made it. She chose to do whatever it took to save Elias. She chose not to be influenced by James or their father. She wasn't like them. Sure, maybe in some ways, she was. She couldn't erase the memories she had of her father. She couldn't ignore the bond she had with James.

But she was her own self, and she had made a choice, even if she didn't get the chance to act.

"Hey."

Molly looked up. It was Cara. She was alone, holding two cups of coffee.

"Where's Tate?"

"He still has some work to sort through. I told him to drop me off here. I wanted to make sure you weren't alone."

"Thanks." Hadn't it always used to be this way? The sisters looking out for each other? Maybe she'd forgotten that in the past year, that she wasn't as isolated as she felt. She accepted the coffee Cara handed her. "Any word on Elias?"

Cara sighed. "Tate said he died before they made it to the hospital. He lost too much blood."

Molly slumped lower in her seat. She'd tried to talk sense to James, hoping both Elias and Katelyn could be saved. Now Elias was gone, another innocent victim, one the police were convinced was a serial murderer.

"Did Tate tell them everything?"

"If you're talking about Dad, no. They don't know about that."

"How did he explain James being involved? And the lake house? And us?"

"They're not going to sort everything out in one night."

"But they will eventually. We'll have to figure out what we're going to tell them about Dad and the shed and—"

"We'll have time to figure out what we're going to say. I think what matters now is making sure everyone is okay."

"Rachel is already on her feet. And Katelyn is improving, too."

"Not just them." She paused. "I want to make sure you're okay, too. It couldn't have been easy. What you saw in there."

Molly looked away, suddenly seeing her last moments with James. The trusting look in his eyes right before Tate shot him. It wasn't easy to remember. Anything but. And she feared the moment would haunt her the rest of her life, in a much more visceral way than her father's crimes ever had.

"I just wish he could have reached out to us a different way. All he wanted was a family, but we couldn't do what he—"

"I know." Cara leaned in closer, pulling Molly toward her. "Have you... heard about him?"

"He's touch and go. They aren't sure whether he'll make it."

The sisters sat in silence, and Molly realized she was unsure what the right outcome might be.

SEVENTY-ONE

The medicine pumping through James' system made it difficult to move, but eventually he regained control of his senses. First, smell. There was a sterile, sharp scent in the air. His nostrils stung with each inhale. Then, sight. The room was dark, a weak overhead light casting a yellow glow on a series of tubes connected to his body. He was in a hospital, not where he'd wanted to end up, but better than death he supposed.

He had a flash of regret. Maybe he was foolish to think his sisters would support him unconditionally. His actions were extreme. To most, they were evil. But he couldn't expect people that weren't like him to understand. When he killed those women, he was filling a hole inside, satisfying a need. It was an urge everyone had really, but most people simply stuffed themselves with drugs or lovers or money. James' craving was blood, different from the masses, but the same impulse.

Henry Martin would understand.

His father had tried to sever any connection between them, not knowing he'd passed down his most defining trait. His thrill for the hunt. His thirst for blood. They were bonded, and James wondered, if there was an afterlife, if his father was looking up at him now feeling a sense of pride.

He closed his eyes, the medication pumping through his veins pulling him back to sleep. Then there was a sound. When he opened his eyes again, he wasn't alone. It took a few seconds to recognize the face, but when he saw it was her, he smiled.

"You came?"

"I did."

He wanted to reach out his hands, but he didn't get very far. He was still too weak. Could barely move his fingers. When he tried, the tubes pinched his forearms.

"What do the doctors say?" Small talk. What else could you do in a situation like this? He was simply happy to not be alone.

"Touch and go. There's talk you won't make it through the night."

James smiled. "And yet here I am, beating the odds."

His sister smiled too. "The guard outside snuck off to use the bathroom. I needed to see you before he returns."

He was surprised, after everything, that she wanted to be near him. She stood in front of the bed. She bent down, and James thought she might kiss his cheek, but she was simply moving him, sliding out the pillow beneath his head.

"I think you understand why I have to do this," she said.

But James didn't understand. He was surprised she'd come at all, given what he'd put her and the other two through. As she moved closer, the pillow clutched tight between her fingers, he was simply happy. He didn't fully understand until he felt the fabric on his face.

Too much of his blood and strength had been forfeited earlier in the night. All he could do was thrash, like a beached fish. The pillow pressed harder against his mouth. Soft, and yet cruel. In those final moments, he thought of so many things. His mother and their apartment. His father and his rejection. His sisters, each one of them with a unique smile. Part him and part Henry. The cabin. The lake. The moon.

Then there was nothing.

The woman put the pillow back underneath James' head, and left as quietly as she had entered.

PART IV

SIX MONTHS LATER

SEVENTY-TWO

CARA

Cara leaned against the moving truck, staring up at the place where she had lived most of her life. It felt strange seeing it now, knowing it would soon belong to someone else. It would house a different set of memories, and she hoped they would be better than the ones she had.

"Are you ready?"

Tate came walking around the side. He was wearing basketball shorts and a hoodie. He loaded the last of the boxes into the back of the truck and slammed the door shut.

"Yeah. Let's go."

"I think we'll like a smaller place," he said. "Less upkeep. Closer to downtown."

It was like he was trying to convince her that they had made the right decision in selling. He feared she had second thoughts, but she didn't. She was as eager as he was to leave this place in the past.

A car pulled up to the curb. A young couple got out, staring up at the house with hope and excitement. The wife turned and saw them, and waved.

"Are you the sellers?" she asked.

"We are," Tate said. "Just loading up a few last-minute things."

"We know our move-in date isn't until next week, but we were both off for the holiday, and couldn't resist stopping by."

Cara nodded and smiled. "Congratulations on your new home."

"Hey, you're Cara Martin, right?" the young man asked.

"Yeah." It didn't happen often, but occasionally someone recognized her from one of her books.

"I thought this was your old place. Mr. Martin was my history teacher in high school." He smiled and nodded, the way people do when sharing a happy memory about someone who has passed. "He was a great man."

Cara smiled tightly. "Thank you."

"Enjoy the place. It's all yours now," Tate told them. He put a hand on Cara's shoulder, moving her toward the truck. Once inside, he asked her, "Are you okay?"

"I'm fine." She waited. "Sometimes I wonder if we did the right thing keeping Dad's secret. He didn't deserve it."

It's naïve to think you can go through life without regrets. Cara had many. If she could go back in time, to the night of her father's funeral, she would have listened to Rachel. She would have told the truth about what they found, instead of hiding behind her fear of how they'd be treated. If they'd simply told the truth, then four innocent women wouldn't have been taken. And Elias and James would be here, too.

"As far as the world knows, Elias was the Gemini killer and James was his accomplice," Tate said. "It may not be the whole truth, but it's enough."

"Not very fair to Elias."

Tate nodded in agreement. "But Elias didn't have anyone. No siblings, parents, kids. Besides, we're not keeping this secret for your dad. We're doing it for you and your sisters."

Tate sounded like she did at the beginning of all this. He

wanted to keep her safe, just as she'd wanted to look after her sisters. If the truth came out now, it would still be devastating. Strangers and the media would tear their characters apart. Sometimes she thought that's what they deserved. They were still protecting themselves, allowing others to pay the price. Then she remembered how much they'd already suffered. How much they'd already lost.

"Do we have time to swing by our place before dinner?" she asked.

"We have all the time in the world."

She squeezed his hand, watching in the car's side mirror as the Martin family home grew smaller and smaller, then disappeared.

SEVENTY-THREE

RACHEL

Rachel stepped out of the shower, tempted by the savory smells of garlic and rosemary. She pulled her robe tighter, walking into the kitchen to find Katelyn behind the stove. She liked seeing her there, at ease in this new space. She smiled.

Katelyn must have sensed eyes on her, because she turned around. "Finally. Hurry and get dressed. Tate and Cara will be here before we know it."

"Where's Molly?"

"I'm here," her sister said, walking in from the patio, carrying a black Labrador in her arms. "Potter needed to go outside."

"Do we have to let the dog around the table while we eat?" Rachel asked.

Molly pressed the puppy closer to her face, letting its wet snout graze her cheek. "Come on, Potter isn't bad."

Katelyn gave the dog a quick scratch behind the ear. "She's part of the family now. It wouldn't be Thanksgiving without her."

"Whatever." Rachel sighed. "I guess I'm overruled. As usual."

Rachel wasn't really a dog person, but she had to get over it. Having a pet was just one of the many compromises in her life in recent months. When they decided to get a place with Molly, Potter was part of the deal.

"I'm going to change clothes," Molly said, walking into her bedroom and closing the door.

Katelyn, having washed her hands, returned to the stove.

"Can I help you with anything?" Rachel asked.

"It's about finished."

"You've done too much."

"It's fine. Really. This is our first Thanksgiving in the new place. I want to play hostess." Katelyn gave her a soft peck on the cheek. It made her blush, that and the daily reminder that Katelyn was back. She'd come so close to losing her. First, as a partner, then, entirely.

After what happened at the cabin, two things became clear. First, that Rachel needed Katelyn in her life. Second, that she could no longer keep her in the dark. Katelyn had questions, and as soon as they left the hospital, Rachel answered them. She told her the truth about their father. How her guilt over keeping her father's secret had prompted her downward spiral, resulting in their breakup. She told her about James, the brother she learned she had and lost all at once. She expressed her shame that all the secrets she kept put Katelyn's life in jeopardy.

But Katelyn forgave her. Better, she understood the choices and mistakes she'd made. And knowing that the truth existed between them—even if they continued to keep it from the rest of the world—was enough for Rachel. She still grappled with the decision at times, even though Molly insisted Elias would approve of their choice, but Rachel recognized this season of her life as a second chance at happiness, and she wanted to take it.

Rachel wandered into their room, searching the closet for something festive and comfortable to wear. On the floor sat a stack of textbooks. She'd used last weekend's tips to buy supplies for next semester's classes. It was time to finish what she started.

Their bedroom was full of furniture from her old place, but gone were the empty liquor glasses and pill bottles that had served as her comfort in the past year. She didn't need them anymore, but still wanted them from time to time.

She often thought back to something Cara said, about each of them inheriting something from their father. Rachel had decided she inherited his need. She didn't yearn to inflict pain and suffering like her father did. But she often craved something to fill the void. It was something she had to battle, day by day, choice by choice. With Katelyn and Molly so close, she was regaining control.

She still had flashbacks to that night. Nightmares where she was rushing to the boathouse and didn't get there in time. But as soon as she woke, as soon as she felt Katelyn beside her in their new bed, she knew that it was all over. They had made it through the darkness, and the future ahead of them was bright.

SEVENTY-FOUR
MOLLY

Molly could hear laughter in the kitchen, and it made her smile. She was happy Katelyn and Rachel had decided to give it another shot. She was even happier when they suggested the three of them live together. After what happened in Rachel's old apartment, it made sense they'd want to relocate, and Molly didn't want to continue living alone. After the events of the last year, they needed togetherness. They'd found a great three-bedroom downtown, only a few blocks from Tate and Cara's new place.

It was nice being close to her sisters again. They were back to the dynamic they'd had before their parents died. Frequent dinners and phone conversations and movie nights. She'd grown particularly close to Rachel now that they were living together. Not only had their relationships with each other improved, but they seemed individually happier, too.

Molly sat on her bed, Potter pouncing on her lap. She rubbed her fur, appreciating the pet for making her feel happy even when she'd rather not be. She still had hard days, moments when she thought back to her memories of their father. All the while knowing he was a duplicitous cheater and murderer.

Moments when she thought about the boathouse, how she'd rejected James' love, watched as Tate put two bullets into his body.

She missed James. She missed Charlie. She regretted they never got to continue the relationship they'd started building. She liked to believe the bond she had with him was real, separate from the dangerous person he turned out to be. She viewed her father in the same way. The love she had for him was unbreakable, and she felt it, even now, while still hating him for the pain he caused.

On her bedside table was a frame with a picture of Elias at Fenway Park. She'd asked Tate to take it from the old shack, once police had finished searching the place. She stared at Elias' face, thinking back to those moments she had with him in the boathouse. He'd been adamant about protecting them, and he was doing that now, even in death. Those had been his last words. *Protect yourselves.* By taking the fall for her father's crimes, he'd given her family a chance to start over without the baggage they'd inherited. It gave them the opportunity to pursue a better life.

There was a commotion outside, and she heard voices. Potter started barking, sprinting between the door and bed to announce Cara's arrival.

"Give me a second, girl," Molly said, leaving the bedroom to join her family at the table.

SEVENTY-FIVE

The Martin family gathered for Thanksgiving dinner. There were new members to replace the ones they'd lost, which eased the grief without erasing it.

They shared a meal, each passing minute pulling them farther away from the heartache they'd experienced. There would be other trials to come, but their loyalties had been tested and proven, which made the future a little less scary. In more ways than one, sharing was at the very core of every family. Sharing histories and memories and secrets. Sharing the good times with the bad.

None of the sisters mentioned what could have been. How their brother could have been at the table with them had he taken a different path. It was the happy ending they deserved, but it wasn't destined to be. He'd chosen to follow in their father's footsteps, taking a path that pulled away from them forever. It was his choice.

It was impossible to think about James without thinking about their father and the imprint he'd left on all of them. He'd passed on his murderous streak to James, but what had he given the sisters? Cara had Henry's mind, a methodical and brilliant

maze. Rachel had his addictions. Molly had her father's intro-
version and anger, but she was better at controlling it.

What they had overlooked, and what was far more influential, was what they'd inherited from their mother. Margaret
Grace. Her truths were stronger than Henry's secrets, her goodness greater than his evil. And she had left parts of her spirit
with her daughters. They had her kindness, her compassion.
They had her eyes, in more than just the physical sense. They
chose to overlook the darkness in the world. They chose to see
the good.

Yes, Cara, Rachel and Molly had all taken something from
each of their parents. They were like both Henry and Margaret
Grace in different ways.

But one of the Martin girls was more like her father than
she'd ever admit. One of them was a killer.

The question was, which one?

A LETTER FROM MIRANDA

Dear Reader,

Thank you for taking the time to read *The Killer's Family*. If you liked it and want information about upcoming releases, sign up with the following link. Your email address will never be shared and you can unsubscribe at any time.

www.bookouture.com/miranda-smith

I'm always intrigued by stories that put an ordinary person in an extraordinary situation. The concept of uncovering a deep, dark secret about a family member isn't a new one, but it's one I wanted to explore. I was curious how a group of siblings would react to learning their father was a notorious serial killer. Once I started writing through the eyes of Cara, Rachel and Molly, the story took on a life of its own. Their internal struggles, as well as their relationships with each other, are what really drive this story.

If you'd like to discuss any of my books, I'd love to connect! You can find me on Facebook, Twitter and Instagram, or my website. If you enjoyed *The Killer's Family*, I'd appreciate it if you left a review.

It only takes a few minutes and does wonders in helping readers discover my books for the first time.

Thank you again for your support!

Sincerely,

Miranda Smith

www.mirandasmithwriter.com

 facebook.com/MirandaSmithAuthor

 twitter.com/msmithbooks

 instagram.com/mirandasmithwriter

ACKNOWLEDGMENTS

I'm always thankful to my brilliant editor, Ruth Tross. I'm thrilled to continue working on more books together! Huge thanks to everyone at Bookouture. Jane Eastgate and Liz Hurst, thank you for cleaning up the finished manuscript. Thank you to the book bloggers and reviewers that continue to shout about my books. Keep tagging me in your pictures and posts! Thank you to my many supporters in the Ball, Smith, Hester and Butler tribes. Mom and Dad, thanks for pushing me to follow my dreams. Chris, as always, thanks for the laughs, the hype and the love. Harrison, Lucy and Christopher—I love you.

Most importantly, thank you to my readers. If this is your first book of mine, thanks for giving it a try. If you've been with me since the beginning, your support means more than you will ever know.